BEAUTIFULLY
BROKEN

A BEFORE I BREAK NOVEL

AWARD WINNING AUTHOR
A. L. HARTWELL

COPYRIGHT

Editing by Pure Grammar Editing
www.puregrammar.com
Cover Design by KP Designs
- www.kpdesignshop.com
Published by Kingston Publishing Company
- www.kingstonpublishing.com

TABLE OF CONTENTS

TRIGGER WARNING

This book features some extremely heavy subjects that some readers may find difficult to read. And although I would love for you to read my book I do not want to upset/trigger anyone who is currently struggling with a theme in this book.

For a more precise overview of the triggers please check out the Goodreads page.

And for those happy to proceed, enjoy!

DEDICATION

I dedicate this final book to you, the reader that has stayed with me from the very first book *Bending to Break*. I will never forget your support. I hope you enjoy the last part of Olivia and Luca's story as much as I did bringing it to you.

And the final dedication is to the five-year-old little girl who never thought she could. Well look at you bloody go.

CHAPTER ONE

Theodore Belmont

Katrina's hand shot out and captured my knee, stilling me with a quick squeeze. "Relax. They'll be here soon." "Why do we have to wait so long? I thought the whole point of paying for a private service would mean, we wouldn't have to *wait*."

She didn't bother to hide the roll of her eyes as she stroked her small bump, choosing to subtly remind me that our unborn child would pick up on any frustration through the womb.

I wonder how mad she would be if her pregnancy books ended up in the bottom of our river.

"I pray that our son has more patience than his father," she mutters under her breath.

My smirk pleases her. My beautiful wife all but knows of my impatience and secretly loves it. It's kept her on her toes all these years and ensured that nobody would ever fuck with us.

Leaning in I run a hand over her stomach, loving her and our little boy that I pray will take after her. "Now, why would you pray for such a thing, mon amour?"

Katrina captures my hand and places a kiss across my palm. "Because I can."

Before I can kiss her the door finally opens, and the sonographer announces our pictures are ready. We're handed a light blue envelope with three tiny snapshots of our healthy baby.

I take them and help Katrina to her feet. "Let's go celebrate."

She grins wickedly, knowing exactly what I mean. "Only if we can get ice cream after."

Of course, more ice cream. Katrina, since finding out she was pregnant, has sampled every ice cream flavor in France and has yet to find the one that satisfied her cravings. Even our staff were hunting down new flavors in hopes of pleasing her.

"Of course." I kiss her cheek and grab her hand. We move quickly out of the pokey all-white room and into the waiting area where more couples await to find out the sex of their babies.

We're halfway out of the door when my phone buzzes violently against my chest. I try to ignore it, wanting only to focus on my wife and how many ways I can satisfy her before she tires.

Work can wait a few more hours.

It buzzes once more just as I open the car door for Katrina. Once she's safely inside, I pull out the irritating piece of metal and see that I have two missed calls from Chen.

I look into the car at Katrina who waits patiently for me and back to my phone.

Chen never rings. Ever. We've always communicated by email because nothing has ever been urgent enough to warrant a chat. Unless…

I stab roughly at the device, putting it to my ear. On the second ring, he picks up.

I wait to hear his terse voice, but nothing.

"Chen?" my demand echoes back into my ear.

"I've fucked up, Theodore."

On instinct alone, I move around the car and get in. As my phone connects to the speaker, I pass the pictures of our unborn child to Katrina.

"What's happened?"

"She's gone," the man that speaks to me doesn't sound like the man I've known nearly all my life. His hollow voice reeks of fear and a lack of discipline.

"What do you mean, she's gone, Chen?"

Katrina looks at me when she hears what I do, her eyes swimming with worry.

His fast exhale echoes into the car. "Olivia's gone," he clears his throat. "She's been taken and we're all fucking screwed."

Katrina flinches at my side, understanding who exactly Chen was talking about.

"Put Luca on the phone."

"I can't."

Fuck. I don't have time to baby him right now. "Why?"

"He's gone looking for her," Chen's voice drops to a whisper. "If he would have just listened to me, I could have prevented this. Protected them both."

"Who has taken her?"

"William Adler."

Katrina lurches forward to the sound of Chen's voice. "William Adler? Are you sure?"

"Yes."

Katrina looks to me, silently forgiving me for what I was about to do. "I'll be on the next flight out. Find Luca. Lock him the fuck up if you have to, but make sure he's there when I arrive."

We hear Chen's sharp intake of breath.

Grabbing Katrina's hand, I bring it over to my lap, holding her to me while I destroy one of my promises—hoping for her understanding.

"I'm bringing my own men and we do this my way, Chen. If you know of anyone on your team who won't deal, now is the time to get rid of the dead weight."

His voice comes in stronger, vibrating through the speakers. "They're all in."

"Good." I end the call.

Katrina is on me, bump and all before I have time to process my next steps. Falling into my lap, her haste lips meet mine with consent and love.

"I've already forgiven you," she whispers. "Just make sure you come home to us, okay? That's all I ask of you, Theodore. Just come home to us in one piece."

CHAPTER TWO

Olivia Heart

My skin burned with hatred, forming its own barrier against the man whose arms I was in. It sensed terror, forming a conclusion from the poison in my bloodstream.

It wouldn't be long until I felt the edges of my being fade.

It was a slow way to disappear. Meticulous and calculated. I knew this by the amount inserted into the morsel of chocolate that it was the exact amount for my weight.

Enough to keep me under, to fall into the unconscious, but not enough to become numb. I would still have to feel Will's arms around my waist, his mouth next to my ear, and his powerful muscles flexing under his suit as he held me to him.

While my conscious thoughts began to fade, my body took over, sensing a new threat, and tried to hold out. But it was no use. I was already losing.

How naive had I been to assume that I could have left safely with William on my own terms?

When did I become so pathetically weak that I gladly took the hand of a killer without putting up much of a fight?

My self-loathing would have to wait.

Suddenly, the sounds of blades slice the thick evening air above us, the violent noise a siren in my ear, warning me that time is running out.

Wake up. Olivia, open your eyes for me.

Luca's voice replaces the sound of my inner voice, warning me that I'm now a few steps away from being taken. I pull at my inner walls, trying to knock them down but they're too strong and my energy is fading.

Olivia, open your eyes for me.

We head closer towards the sound of blades slicing angrily through the air. We move far too quickly. The *thwap thwap* hums against my ears, growing louder, menacingly tearing its way into my eardrums. It peaks to painful levels and all I can do is absorb the pain.

Yes. I can use this.

Pain will have to be my anchor now that gravity isn't an option. A flare of survival bursts through my chest, enough to stave off sleep or a few moments if I'm lucky.

Before arriving to wherever we are, I was partially aware of travelling for well over two hours now. I'd been in an out of consciousness, hidden underneath Will's arm just trying to stay awake. But that was before the second lot of drugs that was shoved into my mouth before I could gain enough strength to fight.

We had switched to another car during the first hour of my kidnapping with Will whispering about safety precautions in my ear, but I knew the real reason. He wanted to slow Luca down enough that we could slip out of the country.

After that, I'd guessed we had travelled another hour, but I couldn't be sure. I'd spent most of the time struggling to stay in the darkened space behind my lids and not fall deeper into the abyss.

"Let's go." His voice blares into the mix of viciousness that surrounds us from all angles, scorching at my sensitive eardrums as we move forward,

Will dips me in his arms and my stomach rolls against him. *Let me go. Let me go. Let me go.*

"I'm going to put your headphones on, Olivia. I need to protect your ears. Stay still," he didn't wait for me to respond. Not that I could. My tongue is slack, my throat filled with more of the slow-melting gel that keeps me perfectly under his control.

His fingers brush against my skin, pushing away my damp hair as he covers my ears with soft pods. The roar dilutes to a soft consistent thrum instantly and I'd sigh if I could.

Now all I have inside this new cage is the hammering of my pulse as it creeps up from my neck and settles inside my brain — it's painful but I hold onto the lifeline, hoping it's enough to keep me awake.

As I'm shifted in his arms I'm pulled tight, cradled into his chest as we sway together. I'd lost my voice, sight, hearing, and now my sense of smell is clouded of him, suffocating me in his scent of wood, leather, and lemongrass.

I want to be sick.

In the past, I'd found his scent soothing and somewhat attractive. Now it burns the back of my throat and blocks my nose. It is overbearing and sickly.

We shift again and he squeezes me harder. He was choking me.

"It won't be long now, Liv. We have forty minutes left in the air until we're home," his voice crackled through my pods.

The pastel yellow door of my aunt's house appears in the darkness behind my lids and hope blooms. Home. In England with my Aunt Sarah. Where Alice would be and little Otto, her yappy Jack Russell. Where no danger, kidnappings, or guards could get to me, and a normal life waited.

I tried to swim through the fog, towards the door, but the darkness stretched, grew longer and wider until it disappeared.

I sunk into the floor before my fingertips even had the chance to grip the doorhandle.

"Everything's set up for us," his warm lips brush the top of my hair, and he whispers, "I'm going to change your life Olivia — I'm going to make it so the only person you'll ever need is me. By the time I'm done with you he won't be able to get to you anymore, none of them will."

My head doesn't move even when I will myself to pull away. I can't do this. Not again. Not when I was so close... *Move your god damn head, Olivia*

His fingers massage my shoulders, kneading my useless limbs thinking he's offering a small comfort, but he presses down on barely healed contusions. Pain erupts and burns. "We're going to fix this together. One day at a time until you see him for what he is," Will's nose glides across my cheek, smelling my damp skin. "It will hurt and somedays you'll hate me more than humanly possible, but I promise you that this is for the best."

While Will smothered me in his scent, I tried to find the yellow door again, desperate for something to hold on to, but it never reappeared.

Weightless and exhausted, I fall before I can help it, further into the abyss, letting the darkness swallow me up until there was nothing left of me, letting my brain find the protection it needed by switching off.

Where I was safe.

Where neither Luca nor Will could reach me with their lies.

****

My eyes opened unnaturally quick to dim yellow light. With my heart in my throat, I scramble up the bed until my back is pressed against the headboard—it squeaks behind me making me flinch.

I look up, the room sways before me, but I pull enough strength to take in my new surroundings.

This isn't my first time at this rodeo, and I won't be so foolish again.

I'm alone, sitting on a fourposter bed that has red suede curtains tied at each corner and a matching duvet. The heavy fabric feels damp below my thighs and hands. Dust clings onto the stale air and clogs my nose.

The furniture around me is sparse and aged, consisting of a single wardrobe and matching dressing table. They look as though they've fallen out of a museum with their deep oak wood slats and gold-crested handles.

Wrinkling my nose, I take in the floor. Even the carpet, a shade of royal deep green with tiny gold emblems every four inches, belongs in another time.

I look around, taking in as much as I can. The walls are sparse and without decoration—all except for a floor-length mirror next to a single door. I suspected it leads to a bathroom, but I'm too uneasy to check.

Pull it together, Olivia. Don't let it happen again.

Looking to the window, my new prison overlooks overgrown gardens, strewn with broken garden furniture and rotten wood. The lawn that once would have been beautiful stretches for miles with no road or dirt track in site. It's deadly quiet.

Shit. Once again, I'd been picked up and dropped in the middle of nowhere. But unlike Luca's prison, this was a hell hole.

"You're awake."

I wish I wasn't.

I jumped at the sound of his voice and paid for it. Will stood in the doorway of my garish cell, watching me with a tight fake smile — waiting for me to run. There would be no running. The pounding in my head hitting the top of my pain threshold would make sure of it. I'd fall in a few steps, and something warns me that Will would like the chase.

I cringe, cradling my skull, silently begging for the pounding to be stop.

"Ah shit," he laughs, his voice was close and too loud. I groan. "Take these, they'll help with the pain." He thrusts two pills and a glass of water in front of me. *Bastard.*

I slap Will's hand away, watching the two pills bounce off the duvet cover and the water tip into my lap.

Will snatches up the glass before I'm completely soaked. "Fuck sakes, Olivia. They're to help with the headache."

I finally look up, under my lashes to see him looming over me like the shadow he was quickly becoming, trying to attach himself to me. Just like the devil would.

Dressed in washed-out denim jeans and a sweater, he looks more like the man I knew from years ago.

A wolf in sheep's clothing. Never forget it.

In my time knocked out, he had shed his suit, ridding him of his hard businessman exterior so that he would be more… appeasing, but I know what's on the inside of him and clothing wouldn't distract me from it.

"You drugged me," I croak as I find my voice. "And brought me God knows where and you expect me to take more pills? Fuck you, Will. Seriously, fuck off back to hell if you think I'm that stupid."

He pushes a hand through his short hair, scraping his nails across his scalp before taking a seat next to me. His frustration eats at the space around us, trying desperately to sink into my skin. I shift away, hating the warmth he brings with him in this cold room.

He shrugs, "I had to get you out of Italy safely and you wouldn't have come otherwise."

"I wouldn't," I spat the words out. It feels good to be angry. It tastes sweet on my tongue. "I didn't want to leave, Will. You have no idea what mess you've caused by taking me. And if you think for one second Luca's just going to just let me go, then you are..." I suck in a shaky breath, anger disappearing with every painful thought of Luca. Damn it.

Luca... he appears like a ghost in front of me. I burn in pain, but I let it burn privately. Will cannot see how my heart has setup itself a punishing cycle of shatter and repeat.

He'll eat me alive if he senses my pain.

I won't swallow pills, but I'll swallow my self-pity. Luca will come find me and he'll make this right. I know it like the back of my hand. "He's going to do everything he can to get me back."

I almost sound convincing.

Will smirks as he leans his back against the post of the bed. "You think I'm naïve, don't you Liv?" his eyes light up, teasing me, trying to remind me of our younger years together. "Do you know what's also interesting about what you've just said?"

I didn't have the patience to play mind games, but right now it's the only thing stopping me from clawing at his eyes.

Ignoring the patch of my dress that sticks to my thigh, I move out of the wet spot and focus on getting air into my lungs.

21

Rage takes up a lot of energy — who knew? Whatever Will had given to me seems to still be running havoc in my bloodstream. Colors were far too bright; my skin was overly sensitive and putting sentences together took far much more energy than usual. Even still, with all that going on, vengeance was the one drug to drain me completely.

"I'm sure you're going to fill me in," I bite out, clutching at my chest. Even breathing is taking a toll.

"Luca's already let you go Liv. The minute you got in that car without him he'd picked Emilia over you. I mean come on; you saw the pictures of them kissing. Why didn't he stop you from leaving?" Before I can contemplate his question, he continues. "If that was me, I wouldn't have let you out of my sight." he chuckles, enjoying my misery. "Actually, I wouldn't have even dared kiss another woman if I had you waiting in my bed at night."

It took all the strength I had not to flinch. There was not a chance in hell I was giving Will the satisfaction of an 'I told you so'. Not when he was so adamant that his actions were reasonable.

And to be reminded of Luca when I felt so vulnerable was like an ice pick to the heart. Every part of me wanted to cry. My body ached for the release, and the unshed tears burned the back of my throat, but I swallowed them down. If I opened the floodgates while my walls were barely holding up, I knew I wouldn't be able to stop them.

I'd drown. And Will would gain an advantage.

He wanted me; I could see the devilish glint in his eye and a moment of weakness right now would be too much of a price to pay.

Will pushed off the bedpost and scootched closer but was careful to sit away with a little distance in case I decided clawing at him would be better. Smartest decision he's made in the past twenty-four hours.

"I'm sorry you got hurt, Olivia. I can't imagine how much it upset you seeing those pictures," his voice makes me want to peel away at my own skin. Condescension rolls off of him.

I twist the sleeves of Bones' jacket that swallows my frame, grateful for the armored cloth and my one anchor to the different life I lived yesterday. "We weren't together then," and I don't think we are now. We never got far enough to speak about titles or put an official stamp on what our relationship had evolved too.

But I loved him, and he loved me.

When he touched my body I understood his stamp of ownership, welcomed it because for the first time I felt something other than grief. It's fucked, I know, but his love and control combined was the wave of complete chaos that I *needed*. And most of the time I felt as though I was too close to drowning under his love, but at least I *felt* something.

Here, all I felt was numb.

Will shook his head with a gentle smile on his face that lit up his baby blues. "And you were after?"

"Yes," I lied, looking down at my splinted fingers.

"You weren't," he stands up and shoves his hands into his jeans pockets. "You were his victim, Olivia, not his lover. A relationship is based on trust and honesty. You're telling me that Luca gave you any of that?"

"Yes," I sneer. "I was getting more and more from him by the day, and you ruined that with your misplaced heroism. This isn't your life, Will, so stop pretending you understand. I want to go back."

Will either had the perfect poker face or he wasn't affected by my words, because he remained cool and relaxed without a sign of frustration across his handsome face. Not even a tic of his jaw.

A shiver worked its way down my spine. Something wasn't right.

The perfect poker face. Something was wrong with him; with the way he stared at me. Will's edges were hardening along with the muscles across the plane of his chest right up to the top of his shoulders.

"I don't believe you, Liv," he held out his hand to me, the same hand that had shoved drug filled chocolates into my mouth. "There's still so much you don't know. And I know how impatient you are and how much you hate to waste time so let's go to my office and I'll tell you everything once and for all."

Everything? Just like that?

My skin erupts into goosebumps and my instincts kick in, sending alarm bells ringing. As much as I hated Will right now, I knew that if I took his hand he would give me what I needed. It would be his version of the events that led me here, but I'd be able to see the truth through it all. I was certain of it.

Will had never denied me before.

"I need a shower first."

I need time to prepare for a war.

Will pulls his hand away and nods. "There's more painkillers in the bathroom and there's clean clothes in the wardrobe. I'll come and get you in fifteen minutes."

I watch him walk to the door, seeing the spread of his shoulders and the muscles that rippled beneath them. There was no chance I could fight him off if I needed too.

No chance at all.

CHAPTER THREE

Luca Caruso

Five hours and thirty-two minutes since Olivia had been stolen from me. Five hours and thirty-two minutes since she pushed me away. Five hours and thirty-two minutes since pain rippled in her watery eyes as she gave up on me.

And now as I closed in on the sixth hour, there was nothing I could do to get to her to fix this. She had disappeared into the night taking my heart and sanity with her. My beacon of hope had been snatched away before I'd gotten the chance to show her who I truly was, to try and prove that I was worthy of the love she had professed to me in the vineyard.

My plans were simple but required after she had finally given herself to me. I was to spend the rest of my life undoing all the mistakes I'd made in getting us here, and now had to prove to her that her heart was safe in my hands. Anything she needed to trust me would have been given to her without issue.

But nothing good ever lasts with us.

The moment Chen took off running towards the car, forgoing my demand to take Emilia away, I knew what had happened. The sharp twist in my gut and searing expulsion of oxygen told me it was too late.

Emilia was the distraction. I was the arrogant bastard trying to rein in control, and Olivia became the victim once again.

After Olivia left me in the distraction, she had been stolen by William Adler who had sent teams of armed guards after my men so he could swoop in like the vulture he was.

Everyone was hunted and it was all my fault for not seeing it.

The car following hers had been taken out with a single spike strip. By the time the car had come to a stop, they had been shot, left to bleed out in their seats.

Blood drenched my shoes and the stench of their decaying bodies in the evening heat coated the inside of my nostrils. I didn't mourn them or waste time thinking about their families. I left them at the side of the road.

We moved on to the team that was supposed to have Olivia in their possession. I'd jumped out the car just as it came to a stop. Bones turned to me, his mouth twisted into a painful grimace, and I knew straight away what had happened. Rum and Red tried their hardest to get to me, but it was too late, I was too fast and enraged with a thirst to place blame.

I'd lost it and punched Chen, hitting him so hard that his cheek split open. As his blood coated my knuckles, I hit him again in the stomach, forcing him to his knees in front of me. He had the good sense to take it and stay down. After all, he had failed me.

They all had.

I'd hit him once more, but when that failed to bring any satisfaction I left.

I'd left and found the first car she had been taken in and saw it burning on the shore of San Vito Lo Capo, parked between two palm trees. A young couple—tourists probably—after I'd aimed my gun at them confirmed two men and a young woman had swapped into another vehicle by the side of a small beach restaurant.

I'd got back into my car and drove aimlessly, hoping that the main road I took would lead me to my next clue.

My phone rang constantly but I shoved it into the glove box, refusing to deal with the people that had failed me. I ignored Dante too, who follows loyally behind, trying to run me off the road so he could talk to me. I didn't need to fucking talk.

I needed to fix this.

I refused to acknowledge that she was gone. Olivia had to still be in Italy where I could get to her. Where I could stab William Adler through the heart over and over again until he bled out. Until he paid for every single bruise and broken bone of Olivia's and this feeling of being gutted over and over again had stopped.

I should have realized his brief appearance in our lives wasn't a coincidence, heard the promise in his words when he told Olivia he would see her soon. Fuck, I'd been so far off my game that it was pathetic. I had all but welcomed him in to take her.

Theodore Belmont's name flashed up on the central screen.

I hit the call button, regretting it instantly. "You better not be in Italy."

His voice is even and cool and a complete fucking façade. "I am."

With the edge of my fist, I pound on the steering wheel. "I don't need you. Fuck off home to your pregnant wife, Theo."

Go home and don't let her go, you fool.

"No? While you've been driving aimlessly around Italy I've been setting up at your home. My team's here, Luca, and we're going to find her. Stop wasting your time and turn the car around."

Dante flashed me, his headlights catching my central mirror. "I can't. I have to find her. I have to bring her home."

"She's not in Italy anymore." My foot twitched for the break. I caught myself and gripped the wheel for support. "She left in a helicopter three hours ago. Stop wasting fucking time and turn the car around, Luca, or I'll have Dante run you off the road."

Three hours ago...

She could be in France, England, Portugal, Greece... For the first time in eight years I don't have eyes on her. I don't know if she's safe, if she's scared, if she even realizes what's happened.

My car veers to the left, wheels spinning stones across the grass banks.

"He drugged her Luca. The CCTV footage shows her out of it in his arms just before boarding the helicopter. Chen's men told me that she only went to protect you all. The reason she didn't fight him was because she was protecting you from being slaughtered in the press and their families from being harmed. Adler had them all boxed in—threatened Bones' kid. It's a fucking mess but you couldn't have done anything to prepare for this."

I could have. If I'd have kept my Pa's empire the way it had been, there wouldn't have been any space for people like William Adler to get to us. My life of trying to be a better man had proved fucking pointless after all.

"She was trying to protect you, Luca."

My heart expanded so quickly that it took too much space up in my chest. My throat burned and closed painfully as unruly grief mixed with rage. Olivia, my sweet Olivia, even after I'd hurt her had chosen me, chosen to protect me when I should have been the one to save her.

"I know this fucking hurts man, and right now it feels like you're dying the slowest of deaths but she needs you to pull it together. She needs you to find her before it's too late."

****

The shakes had started the moment I returned home without Olivia. My body stepped over the threshold, registering the void, and plummeted me into a soul-sucking abyss so quickly that I wasn't sure I'd ever recover.

I'd dealt with withdrawals before, felt them humming under my skin but Olivia had always been there to dose me back up before they'd gotten to this stage.

Swaying into the door frame, clutching at the solid wood, I try to keep myself up.

Shit.

"Here," a glass of amber liquid is shoved in front of me. It sloshes in the glass, wafting a potent smell under my nose. It was exactly what I need.

Snatching the glass from Dante, I threw the liquid back and swallowed while ignoring the judgment radiating from him. The burn of the whiskey took off the edge for the briefest of seconds until my stomach revolted. I bent over, my fingers digging into the frame as my throat opened and returned the whiskey onto the pristine floor.

I didn't deserve for the edge to be taken off.

I wiped at my mouth, hoarse, I asked, "Where's Theo?"

Dante sucked in a breath, stepping out of my vomit. "They're in the dining room. Come on, everyone's waiting."

I let him lead the way, choosing to focus on the way he moved instead of how good it would feel to slump to the floor.

He moved with his head held high, confident in his steps, but then I heard the sigh just as we entered the dining room.

The dining room was packed with men of all backgrounds and skill rushing around to secure the operation. When Theo said he'd brought a team, I thought he meant a few of his guys. No, he'd brought all of his key players. And if I wasn't such a mess, I would thank him and them for being here.

My presence was enough to demand their silence as everyone paused to look across at me, clutching the door frame for dear life. I didn't deserve their respect. I barely deserved to share the same air as them all.

Pathetic, that's what you are.

Jack Veen, my IT specialist, stood over a screen with Theo. Chen's men were huddled in the corner, surrounded by screens and phones trying to hide. And then there were five men I'd only met briefly, sitting with a map between them and several iPads that were running facial recognition.

Everyone waited for me to say something.

Olivia and I had spent a brief moment at this table during her first days in my home. I remembered the fire in her eyes as she glared hell my way. Fuck, she was so mad and accused me of lacing the wine I had shipped in for her.

I'd give anything to have her here now, screaming at me and calling me on my shit—anything was better than hearing the erratic thud of my heart that sensed its owner was missing.

"Someone give me something," I rasped, falling into the only empty seat in the middle of the table.

Anything—I need something to hold on to.

Theo was the only one brave enough to speak, regarding me with a pinch of pity in his eyes. "There were no men on their families," he cocked his chin towards Chen's men who couldn't meet my glare, "but there are plenty on Emilia who we suspect are being used to protect her in Olivia's... absence. We've let her go, Luca, in hopes she'll reach out to Adler. Once she does, we'll be able to track him and then we'll take care of her."

"We can't wait that long," I stood up on shaky legs, white knuckles to the wood. If Emilia thought a few men would protect her from me she never knew me at all. Her innocence is gone, long fucking gone. "Why can't we track him now?"

"He's off the grid, Mr. Caruso," Jack Veen said, as he pushed his Prada glasses up his nose. He wasn't what I expected. I'd expected corduroy jeans, mismatched socks, and a polo shirt. Instead, he sat at my table in a fitted suit with an expensive haircut and cologne. Clearly working for criminals like Theo and I was paying off. "All of his devices were simultaneously switched off nine hours ago, around the time that Miss Heart was taken."

I rubbed my chest, trying to soothe the ache.

"He can't just disappear," I snap, my eyes landing on Dante who slipped into the room with a bottle of water in his hands. Why the fuck isn't he doing anything?

Why is he so calm?

"He can't," Theo agreed. "We have all of his offices tagged and if he reaches out to any of his employees, we'll know about it. Will can't afford to disappear—he has to keep up appearances."

It wasn't enough. I didn't feel like the people around me were doing enough. My mouth opened, ready to curse the fuck out of them all, until Bones cut in.

"I gave Olivia my jacket," he blurted, his usually deep voice tight with remorse as he caught my eye. He's just lucky that Chen stood in when I'd pulled my fist back. So. Damn. Fucking. Lucky.

"Fucking brilliant. That'll tell us right where she is," I sneered his way, wanting nothing more than to reach over the table and carve the rest of his useless fucking face out until he was a single flap of flesh.

He'd let her go and I would never forgive him for it.

"No," he rubbed at his scar, sensing my threat. "My earbud was in the pocket. If she's still wearing it, we'll be able to track her."

Jack and Theodore congregated around Chen's chair as he pulled up the GPS on their earbuds. The flat screen that had been moved in and placed on the wall behind them lit up.

I held my breath as a small solar system of GPS trackers flickered across a map on the screen. Everyone was accounted for, all housed under my roof except for one.

And it was offline.

"Fuck," I swiped at the bottle of water in front of me. "Is there anything you haven't fucked up today?"

Bones' jaw hardened and I saw for a brief second, he contemplated whether to bite back. His respect for Chen was wearing thin, and right now I wanted to brawl.

"You were supposed to protect her," my voice seethed between us. "But instead you walked her right into his arms like the useless piece of shit you are."

"Me? What about you, Caruso?" he snapped his teeth, leaning over the table with his chest puffed out. "We wouldn't have had to leave the party if you had kept it in your fucking pants, or have you conveniently forgot that part, eh?"

Theo's head snapped up from his screen, his impatient glare landing on me "What is he talking about?"

Bones didn't bother to look at Theo as he addressed him. His eyes trained in on me, warning me that he was ready to go at any minute. Our boundaries of boss and employee were broken.

"Olivia wanted to leave after she found out that our *boss* here had fucked Emilia a few days after we took her. Emilia came prepared with photographs and Olivia was upset and wanted to leave. She wanted to get away from him when she saw the guilt written across his smug fucking face."

"I didn't fuck Emilia," I looked to Theo and saw the same look that Dante was currently wearing, he didn't believe me, and it fucking slammed me back into my seat. "I went to her, to tell her that Olivia was in Italy so she wouldn't be caught off guard if she saw her... Emilia was hurt and kissed me. It was one kiss. I pushed her away and told her that Olivia was all I wanted. That's the facts. Not this bullshit story Emilia has concocted with Adler as a distraction."

I looked to Dante who was taking his seat by Chen's men. He still refused to speak, refused to look me in the eye. Was he drawing sides?

"Why the fuck would I go back to Emilia when I finally had everything I wanted here? You knew how hard it would be on her if she found out Olivia was living close by."

C'mon. Think about this Dante. Use your damn brain.

Bones cut across the both of us. "Why didn't you just tell Olivia that instead of letting her be humiliated? Why didn't you take care of Emilia like you did the Russians? Emilia is partly responsible for putting Olivia in the hospital so why did she get away with hurting the one woman you're supposed to love!?"

"Because he couldn't reach Emilia," Dante's voice cut through the tension, "and we didn't know how deep her involvement went until today. We've all been blinded, assuming it was an enemy of Luca's, but we would have never known about Adler's true plans until the last minute."

Dante didn't look my way; he was too busy focusing on Bones. "Even Black didn't give him up."

And finally, I understood why my cousin had pulled away. He had overseen Black's plans and hadn't seen this coming. Too many lies had been told, that left us to sink in quicksand.

Theo shifted in my peripheral. "The facts are this: Adler has Olivia, and he hasn't tried to kill Luca yet. For someone who likes to tie up loose ends, we need to prepare ourselves for what's coming next."

CHAPTER FOUR

Olivia Heart

Will came for me just as I slipped on my sweatshirt. In the short time I was left alone, I had showered in the quaint bathroom with décor that reminded me of a bad motel and got dressed. I wasn't even sure this place had hot water, it looked too old to still be in use.

Hell, everything was crumbling around me, and so far away from the luxury of Luca's home. The sink, shower, and bath were all a salmon pink, a sure throwback to the eighties décor which didn't fit in with the bedroom. The floor was revolting, looking as though the last time it had been cleaned was a century again.

"I bought this place a few years ago," Will mumbled, slipping into the room with a glass of orange juice. "There's fifteen bedrooms and this was the best one. I haven't had time to strip it back to the bones and model it to my own tastes yet, so you'll have to excuse the décor."

"It's disgusting," I told him, pulling my sweater around my chest, missing the warmth of Italy already.

Will nodded in agreement before passing me the juice. "Drink this. It'll help with your sugar levels."

I took the glass but didn't sip. Clutching it in my hands I peered around him, looking into the hallway that was dark without much natural light.

"I must warn you before we leave this room Olivia that my men are all over the house and grounds. They're here for your protection so don't be alarmed when you see them."

I'd heard that before.

"Where are we?" I placed the glass down when I caught the acidic smell around the rim of the glass.

Will paused on the drink before letting his eyes scan my face, looking for something. "We're somewhere safe. Come on let's go to my office."

Slipping his cool hand to my elbow, he pulled me from the room and into the darkened hallway. Every foot was lit by a single candle on the wall, the flickering flames creating a menacing glow in the tight space. The décor reminded me of an old forgotten country mansion that had been left to ruin, and my earlier appraisal of this place seemed to be correct.

Through the landing window I saw countryside surrounding us.

We were either in England or Scotland. I could tell by the way the trees were starting to slowly turn brown and how the Autumn sun lit up the grass that speckled with morning dew.

It was an unmistakable view that brought me some comfort. At least I was closer to my family if I ever managed to escape this place.

We stepped onto the open landing before turning right down another corridor. We passed only one door before entering Will's office.

The smell of dust clogged my nose and stuck to the back of my throat as I took in the unlived space. It was bigger than my room with large furniture covered in dust sheets and gold-framed paintings on the walls that depicted a history of violence and war.

To my right was Will's desk that stood out like a sore thumb against the ancient wallpaper that was peeling from the top. The black marbled desk was arranged neatly with a computer, printer, phone, and a small round flat device that flashed constantly.

Behind the desk was a bank of monitors for the CCTV that covered the whole mansion.

Stepping forward to get a better look, I saw the men that he had mentioned walking around the large grounds with their arms full of large weaponry — their faces covered by balaclavas.

It made Luca's men look like a small football team rather than an army.

Will came up from behind and placed a hand on my shoulder. "When can I go home?" I whispered.

"You are home, Liv. Well, this is your home for now. Once we can confirm Luca won't be an issue and you get the treatment you need, we'll talk about—"

"Sorry?" I turned and stabbed my finger into his chest. "Who gave you the right to make those decisions for me, Will?"

He stood, his eyes scanning my face with that usual reserved look he used when he thought he was being evasive. Will was no master is disguise, not when I had known him so intimately.

He'd forgotten that when he pressed that chocolate into my mouth, he had revealed all, and he wanted me all for himself. He wanted to steal me from Luca like a child that prefers someone else's toy.

And I wasn't fucking stupid to it.

I saw right through the façade of pretending to give a shit about me. Protecting me from the bad guys, coming in on his white horse hoping that I'll falter and fall at his knees with gratitude.

But sadly, the truth was the only man's knees I would fall to was Luca Caruso's. Even if it meant feeling the wall of my heart quiver with regret when I thought about him. Or the unshed tears that burned in the back of my eyes when I thought about how worried he would be. But nothing hit me more than the fear I felt that I may never see him again.

"Nobody did, Liv. I'm sorry I got ahead of myself. I just want what's best for you." He pressed his warm hand to my arm and squeezed. "I went out of my mind worrying about you and now you're safe here with me... I'm just trying to figure the best way to help you."

Turning from him, I moved towards the covered sofa and tugged off the dust sheet. Underneath sat a tattered pink sofa that had seen better days. I took my seat, hoping he would take his at his desk so we could begin.

"Black came to you. When?"

Will sighed with annoyance as he took his seat at his obnoxiously modern desk. He was regal and a complete picture of calm, but I felt his agitation quivering under the surface. He wanted to control the narrative.

"Three days before your kidnapping. I was just coming out of a meeting when he attacked me with this tattered file like a mad man. I almost had security throw him out on sight alone, until he screamed your name."

Will's voice flowed like honey, offering sweet comfort and familiarity even when I knew the story was about to get much darker.

Pulling my legs up I rested my chin on my knees, providing cover to my sore torso. My bruises were starting to throb, and I knew being held in Will's arms for hours was to blame. Arnik would have a fit if he knew how bad they looked today.

"He rambled like a mad man about Olivia Heart who had been stalked and was about to be kidnapped and held hostage in Italy by his boss. Jesus—I had to drag him into an abandoned office before anyone else heard."

"Why didn't you go to the police if you knew three days before? You could have saved us all this trouble," I bit, feeling venomous towards my old friend.

All this pain that I had endured could have been stopped.

Will had the good sense to pretend to be embarrassed. "I needed to make sure what he was saying was true. It all sounded too farfetched."

"Well, it wasn't. While you were doing your little bit of research, I was being drugged in my kitchen and taken to be with a man that I'd only ever met the once."

I sucked in a deep breath trying to rid myself of the anger I felt but it spluttered into an inferno. Here I thought I was past this, that my love for Luca meant I'd forgiven him for all of the crazy shit he had done, but maybe not.

"It was difficult. Black came to me for my help because he was worried about what would happen to you. I took him on his word until he started demanding money when I asked for more information." Will pulls open his top drawer and out comes the usual file.

It takes everything in me not to roll my eyes.

"He wanted five million dollars from me, Liv," he shook his head, disgust painting his face, "to hand over all the information he had on you all. At first I agreed to pay him if he brought you back himself, but that obviously failed."

Yes, I was left with the consequences of such a failure.

He stood up and leaned over his desk, holding out the file, his shirt tightening around his biceps. "After Black failed to bring you to me, I had to change the plan. I only remained hidden, so Luca wouldn't know where you were when we got you back. It was all for you, Liv."

I didn't move. I locked my arms tighter, cutting off the blood to my legs preventing myself from getting up and ripping the file out of Will's hands.

There was no time to dwell. Files, photographs, and paperwork could be doctored. His facial expressions when he answered my questions could not. I didn't want to miss a thing.

"You had him killed."

Will didn't flinch nor did he show an ounce of remorse. He dropped the file onto his desk and moved towards me, taking the spot next to me on the dusty sofa.

"I did. I had to... I'm not proud of it but he wasn't going to stop until he got what he needed. He was going to cross both Caruso and me and then disappear. You would have been in the firing line."

I turned away from him, trying to ignore the ache in my heart that was breaching my ribcage, trying to find comfort. I didn't know this man. I only know the boy he used to be.

I needn't forget that.

"He wanted money. Both you and Luca have enough money to have fixed this. Nobody had to die, especially Black who had two young children." I returned my gaze, narrowing my eyes at his hands that had made the call to have Black assassinated.

Black was a greedy bastard and a pathological liar, but he didn't deserve to die for his sins. If that was the case, eighty percent of the population should be dead.

Luca and Will had done worse, and both were still alive. Where's the justice in that?

"He should have thought about them before he crossed me." Will leaned forward on his elbows and looked over his shoulder at me. He was far from the sweet boy I knew that had held my hand through the funeral of my parents; instead he'd become a man that saw death as a convenience.

He'd changed in the years we had been apart. His orbit blue eyes gleamed with greed and desire now, ready to take what he thought was owed to him. And I'd be damned if I gave it to him.

"He didn't cross you," I hissed hotly. "It was my life he was playing with, but nobody bothered to ask for my opinion. It was more important that I was kept in the god damn dark while you men played war."

"You're right," he agreed, flooring me in an instant, "but before you continue your little rant, I think it's time you understand more about the man that started all of this. Only then will you understand why it was so important for me to join this... war." Will's grin turns my stomach. I barely have the strength to swallow my disgust back down.

He stood up, exuding complete control as he picked up the file from earlier and returned to me. My eyes glazed the folder. No doubt this would be another side to the story, possibly full of fabricated lies, but there could also be small cuttings of truth.

Living this life without certainty was wearing me thin.

But being a victim was not a part of my new plan, so I took the folder without a word and opened it up.

My fingers twitched to cling the picture of Luca and I, and slam it against my chest, but I resisted. Because I needed to imprint this image into my memory of Luca holding me to his chest at the top of his private jet where I dangled precariously in his arms.

Even through the eyes of the camera I saw how much love he had for me as he stared down at my face. I felt it emit through the picture and warm the surface of my skin. I felt him loving and protecting me in our history and right now that was enough to see me through.

I have to get out of here.

I need to get back to him.

"That was the night he took you."

I was hoarse, "I know."

"We didn't know when it would happen, but we were always prepared. We gathered as much evidence against him so that when we got you free, we could bury him for good."

"I won't do that." I moved the picture to the side, always keeping it in my eyesight. Being anchored to Luca emotionally had happened so naturally that it took until Paris to realize what had happened. My anxiety had been to blame at first, but deep down I knew the real reason. And now a simple picture of us two, from my first kidnapping, assured me that I needed him.

Luca was everything I needed but he was also unforgiveable, cruel, and outrageously obsessive in his love for me — and that was a man I could trust with my heart. There was nothing and nobody that could stop him from getting what he wanted and that included me.

I'd pushed and locked myself in my tower of solitude, but he smashed every lock, kicked down every door, and made me open my eyes with force and determination. Nobody had ever seen me the way that he had or figured out what I truly needed.

Everyone else had given up on me except for him.

Will's hand grabbed my trembling fingers and squeezed gently before saying, "Right now you don't want to but once your head clears, you'll think differently about him, Liv."

I pulled away, hiding the disgust I felt from his clammy touch and began sifting through the file.

The next piece of paper was that of email transcripts between a lab and Luca. I was patient OH9 and urine samples that I had to provide for random drug tests at work had been used by the private lab to check my health. My sample had checked me for everything from kidney function to LH hormone which was described here as 'chances of fertility'.

The lab described my chances as 'low' due to the contraceptive injection I was taking.

"Liv, if this is too much we can stop."

No, no we can't. Not now I know Luca was having my fertility checked. Just when I thought he couldn't get any deeper into my personal space he outdoes himself with this. Damn, he was relentless in his pursuit to know everything about me.

Fuck. How can I explain this away?

"The next document is a blood test from your first day with him." Will slid the sheet across, "there's only so much a urine sample can tell you, but a blood test is more precise."

The blood test that Luca said was to check that I was okay after the drugs, was in fact checking to see if I was fertile. To see if I would be worthy in the long run? No, it can't be right. Luca had asked if I was protected the night we first slept together.

Or was he just asking to throw me off?

"What the hell?" I retreated behind the safety of my lids.

"Liv, look at me."

No.

I squeezed my eyes tighter, wishing that they would glue themselves shut so I wouldn't have to deal with this anymore. Ragged breaths filled the air.

Will's fingers clasped my chin, twisting my head until I faced him. His touch wasn't what I needed right now. If anything, I never wanted to be touched again.

Will sighed, "It took me a while to work out what his intentions were and then one night, after looking through this file a million times it clicked. He knew if all else failed and he couldn't make you stay…"

I looked at him and saw pity, and then I heard it vibrate through his rich voice. "He'd used the trauma you felt as a child as his last resort."

"W-what do you mean?"

"Liv, Luca knew that if you were pregnant, you would make it work. You wouldn't want an innocent child to suffer without the love of two parents. Not like you did."

Maybe he's telling the truth and Luca's obsession had hit a new low or just maybe this was one perception of general test results that Will was using to put space between Luca and me. Either way I can't let that space inside me grow, not when that space was reserved for Luca only.

"This shows I was tested for everything. You're looking too deeply into this, Will."

"Maybe," he bites out, but I'm too busy reading orders from Luca to the man that managed my old apartment building to care. Luca had demanded that no men were to be placed on the floor of my apartment, which at the time wasn't weird. There were only three of us to a floor. But now…

Jesus, Luca.

Just as I come to grips with his meddling, there were transcripts of text messages from Luca and Chen's team with strict instructions, dating a few years ago. The one that stood out the most took my breath away.

No men to interfere romantically with Miss Heart.

All this time I thought being closed off had acted as a natural deflection technique. But it had nothing to do with me and more to do with the man that pulled all the strings in my life.

A memory floats to the surface and the sting I feel in my chest burns. Luca had told me that if I found someone, he would have left me alone… he had lied.

I'd have only ever found someone if they were willing to go against Luca and nobody in their right mind would. Not when Luca had no qualms about dipping into forbidden territory to secure what he believes is rightfully his.

Lying to me, included.

CHAPTER FIVE

Luca Caruso

Twenty-four hours. A whole day had passed, and we had nothing — I had nothing. I'd spent half of the day pacing the dining room, barking orders at the team Theo had put together until I was kicked out and told to rest.

In other words I was told to fuck off.

I'd ignored Theo's advice and turned my pacing to the one place that would bring me closer to her — Olivia's room.

Standing in the same spot where she had embraced me only twenty-four hours ago helped me focus. Remembering her soothing touch and delicate smile was a tiny drop of pleasure swimming in a sea of pain. For a sweet five minutes I could pretend that not all was lost, and she was going to leave the bathroom, wrapped in a fluffy towel with a shy smile.

It was a dangerous game to play but I had no choice. It was the only thing keeping me on my feet and my hand away from a bottle of whiskey.

But I'm no fool and I know that she's not in there and that soon her scent in this room will disappear.

"Shit."

I'd failed her and the anguish I'd tried to prevent myself feeling returns tenfold. It cripples and the monster relishes in my self-destruction. I'm no longer Luca Caruso who has his shit under control. I'm weak and defenseless without a fucking clue on how I can fix this.

The irony almost brings me to my knees.

Would she even want me to fix this when she thought—no, I won't go there, not now.

My fears for her forgiveness would have to wait until she was safe, until my eyes were on her. I'd gotten through to her once and I would do it again.

I turn on my heel, ready to leave before I ruin my only sanctuary, to find Dante and my sister in the doorway.

Aida blazes over, mascara running down her flushed cheeks. "You fucking idiot," she slaps me so hard that she nearly turns my head. I flex my jaw against the welcome sting, glowering down at her. "You let her drive away knowing the threat that hung over her head! Are you really that stupid? Did her nearly dying not knock any sense into you?"

Aida's screams penetrate the surface of my skin until her barbs meet my nerves. I feel them hook in and sink. Unfortunately for her, her anger and hatred towards my idiocies are no match for my own, but they still hurt all the same.

"Don't talk about what you don't understand, Aida. I had no choice, she wouldn't stop and listen."

Aida lurches forward, closing the small gap until we're almost nose-to-nose. "It's you that doesn't understand, you selfish bastard. You snatched her away from her normal life, let her fall for you, and then you failed to protect her," she throws her bag down, ready to slap me again. "Do you understand what's in store for her now, Luca? He's going to torture you out of her system and put himself in your place."

Having heard enough, Dante ducks out of the room.

I try to protest, but she cut me off, placing her hand over my mouth.

"Don't tell yourself that he's only taken her because he thinks he's protecting her. Because we all know that's just wishful thinking." I see my fear mirrored in her glare. "Adler's gone to extreme lengths to get to her when he could have just gone to the police. Think about this, Luca. Why do you think he wanted her so badly?"

Pulling her hand away I ignore the irregular pounding of my heart. "I'll get to her before then. I'll find her."

"Good. Pull yourself together. You can fall apart when this is all over and she decides she doesn't want your stupid ass." She pulls her hand away and wipes at her mascara. A line of black smudges its way across her temple, ruining her perfect makeup.

She's right. This isn't about me or what I'm feeling. The last time I nearly broke was in her hospital room and Olivia hated me for not being strong enough when she needed me. I would be strong. I will get her back.

"Mr. Caruso, sir? Sorry to bother you but a package has just been delivered for you. It's from a William Adler." Marie hovers in the doorway, nervously holding out a large black package decorated with a blood-red bow.

Aida moves out of my way. In two strides I have the box in my hands and feel it's weight. Marie slinks off, back to the dark corner that the rest of the staff are hiding in.

Destruction decorates my conscience. Body parts, blood, and cuttings of Olivia's hair slide their way in before I can stop them. The room begins to sway until my sister's cool hand grips the back of my arm.

"After," she warns me, her voice only for my ears. "Come on, let's take it to Theo. There might be something in there that will lead us to her."

****

Theo stands at my side, ready to take over at any moment, but hell if I'm not strong enough to do this. If I can't face a simple fucking box, how am I supposed to face what's coming next?

I grit my teeth, shove my terror into the back of my mind and rip off the lid. Black tissue paper and the scent of Olivia's perfume steal away the air in my lungs.

It's her. I'd know her scent anywhere.

"Do you want me to do it?" Theo whispers, his hand hovering over the closest thing I have to Olivia right now. The thought of anyone else touching her stuff shreds me. It's too personal. She wouldn't want that either.

I shake my head. "No. Back off."

He does as I demand and pulls away to hover behind me. Opening the sheets of tissue was probably one of the hardest things I've ever had to do, or so I thought until I saw the contents. The dress that Olivia had worn to Aida's dinner was folded neatly alongside an open velvet box where the earrings I'd given her sat. The butterflies glistened in their diamond settings, blinking up at me with confusion.

"He's returning her things?" Aida whispered to Dante. "Why?"

"He's making a point," I hiss, picking up the black velvet draw string bag and yanking it open. "He doesn't want her to have any reminders of me—Ah, fucking bastard!" The velvet bag is crushed beneath my fingers.

The sick fuck.

Her underwear? He sent me her fucking *underwear*? Did he take them off? Did he force her —

FUCK.

Aida pries the bag from my fingers, peering in once before removing it from my sight. My heart pounds with revenge. I ache for it. Every muscle in my body prepares for it. My hand rises to destroy the box that taunts me, but Theo sweeps it to his side of the table.

"Wait!" he snaps. "There's more." He rips out an envelope, careful not to touch Olivia's things, and slams the contents down onto the table.

Newspaper and sleazy gossip magazine mockups of his final plan sit smugly on my dining room table. My name is plastered in black ink alongside a single word — KIDNAPPER.

Underneath my new title is a single picture of Olivia in my arms, her pale skin glistening from the lights of the runway as I stare down at her. Seeing that moment from the outside renders me speechless. The camera captures me just at the right moment. My eyes are wild with satisfaction and desire.

William Adler wants the world to see the monster, a reason to destroy me in the press, to reveal my obsession for Olivia by showing the world what an evil son of a bitch I am. He has enough to sink me forever. The article I skim over goes into great detail about my history of control, voyeurism, and infatuation. How I've been relentless, using my wealth and contacts in my pursuit to control all aspects of Olivia Heart's life.

Her time with me has been nothing but forced sex in public places, hospital stays, and painful submissive training — preparing her to be the perfect wife that will fuck at will and bare my children when I command it.

Acid forms in the back of my mouth for the second time in twenty-four hours. Not a single word holds an ounce of truth, but in the public eye that won't matter.

I'll be hung.

By the time I've finished reading, I realize what Adler wants me to see. I've all but felt the world shift from underneath my feet. If I come for her, he'll destroy me.

And he doesn't realize it, but he'll destroy Olivia in the process.

I'll slaughter him before he gets the chance. It's all I'm certain of, but it's enough for now. I won't let her be destroyed because of me.

"Shit," Theo whispers as he sinks back down into his chair. "This is his 'tying of loose ends'."

I can't speak.

Aida's hand reaches out and grips my elbow. "We've never bowed down before."

I look down at my sister, who for all this time has tried her best to be there for me, even when we haven't seen eye-to-eye. Especially when she found it impossible to understand why it was so important to me to keep Olivia in my life. But now her face holds the resilience I need to borrow.

"We haven't," I agree, finding my voice. "But I can't help Olivia if this gets out. I'll be locked up before that happens."

She shakes her head, refusing to acknowledge what's happening "You won't let it get to that. I know you, Luca. You'll find a way to bring her home." She takes a step towards the door. "And while you do that, I'll start greasing some palms. See if we can take his business down so there's no way to spread them."

Dante shifts into view, "I'll help."

"We all will," Theo agrees as he places the lid on the box of horrors. Between the three of us, we know enough people in enough countries to try and stop Adler. We can prevent the paper from landing on anyone's doorstep, but it comes at a high risk. The attention would be massive to our notoriously private family.

"We just have to be careful moving forward. We need to protect the element of surprise."

Chapter Six

Olivia Heart

I didn't buy a single thing I read. It was too convenient. Too perfectly put together. Don't get me wrong, there were part truths here and there, some that I already knew, but everything else was doctored to paint Luca as nothing but a psychotic stalker.

I saw how much Chen's team was paid for their service and it was a hell of a lot. No wonder they never stepped out of line. Alongside their vast salaries were bank transcripts that stretched to everyone who had been close to me. Dante had been the one to blackmail my boss into transferring me to Italy and he had closed all my bank accounts and made my move official in the eyes of the law.

Jessica, Jackson's assistant, had been paid $80,000 to turn a blind eye to my disappearance. No wonder she was so damn nervous all the time when she had that much money on the line.

The evidence was endless, but Will's patience wasn't as I reviewed it all carefully. He shifted at my side, pushed sheets in front of me, and pointed out the worst parts of Luca and I's story in hopes I would crack.

But I did what any sane person would do in that scenario and acted surprised. I did the sharp gasps and the hand to my throat. I pretended to be disgusted and shocked at the information he put before me.

Because being the perfect actress right now was my safety net.

Will needed to see my disgust. Needed to see that I thought of Luca as nothing but a monster. Because otherwise, he wouldn't be able to finish being my knight in shining armor and I would never be free.

I needed to be free to find Luca and anchor myself back to him.

Ached for it.

I craved to feel the serene calm only he could provide. There was safety in Luca's darkness, and I wouldn't be whole until I was back under it.

"This... is a lot." I push the file back into Will's hands. "I don't want to see anymore."

"I understand, Liv, but you need to know the whole truth. This isn't everything." He takes the file and saunters over towards the desk. "Do you remember what I told you about your Aunt Sarah?"

Of course, I remember, "Yes."

He shakes his head, irritated, I think. Maybe I'm not a very good actress after all. "I was telling you the truth. From what I could gather, Caruso was going to hurt your aunt if you ever told her the truth."

My Aunt Sarah's sweet face appears as I replay the moment when she and Luca had met the day of Alice's wedding. There was no threat to be sensed, no awkwardness, and Luca seemed okay with leaving me with my family. He trusted me.

I dropped my legs, stretching out my tight calves from sitting so tight. "Where's the proof?"

Will glares over at me, "Black told me."

That settles it. "Black would have said anything to get your money, Will."

Something snaps in Will and in seconds he's crossed the room and towers over me. Ripping me up from my seat, he forces me to meet his scalding sneer. "He had no reason to lie about that, Olivia. Nothing to gain from it. Why is this so hard for you to believe? Has Luca fucked with your head that much?"

One thing he wants is a reaction or reason to believe that he is the hero so I do what I'm good at and I counter. "It was hard for me to believe that you could kill and kidnap, but here we are." I pull my arm out of his grip, ignoring the pain receptors that hum from his harsh touch. "Don't try to manipulate me, Will, because it won't work. I'm far too aware of this situation we all find ourselves in and my rational thinking is very much still intact. I knew all of this, and I made a choice to stay with Luca and *not* because he's fucked with my head!"

"I saw how scared you were at the Belmont's Gala, Liv. You started to shake the moment he stepped into the goddamn room."

No.

Lies.

"I wasn't scared for me. It was you I was scared for. Luca would never, in a million years be able to hurt me—"

He cuts me off, taking a step back as though I've burned him. "Shit," his voice plummets to my feet, dripping with ice. "You can't even see the truth anymore, can you? He's got you right in the deep end, where he wants you."

I'm on the back foot. Spinning, trying to find my rebuttal under his sneer, and when I do find it, well, it's weak. "He doesn't. It's not like that! It's hard to explain right now but I understand him. I know what he *needs* from me."

"Fuck sakes, Liv," he snaps. "You sound like his submissive."

My nose scrunches with disgust, hating the word that floats between us. This was no Fifty Shades of fucked up. Luca and I had more than a perverse relationship. Yes, there was pain and a fuck-ton of toxicity, but he didn't get off causing me pain.

He wanted equal control of each other and struggled to communicate that in a normal way. But hurting me? He would never. He couldn't. It would kill him.

"Is that what got him off? You being at his mercy twenty-four-seven?" Will leans forward to capture my chin in his hand. Dark eyes pin me to my spot, taunting me. "Did he put you to work on your knees, Liv?"

Heat spread to my cheeks, lighting up my face. I don't squirm or try to hide. I'm stronger than he is. "No Will, he didn't," I hiss, "but he did get on *his* knees and worked me with his tongue over and — "

Will clamps a harsh hand over my mouth, pushing me back down onto the sofa until he's over me, crushing me into the cushions with his chest. I'm trapped by his thighs as he weighs down on me. A small whimper escapes when I realize just how much I've slipped.

Snarling, he leans down until his lips brush my ear. "I'll replace every memory of him, Liv," his finger tests the seam of my lips. I shrink away, trying to hide from him. "I'm going to fix you bit by bit. I've put you back together before and I'll do it again. And when I do, it won't be him that you crave, it will be me."

He presses the pad of his finger a touch harder. I felt and understood his warning loud and clear, but it didn't make a blind bit of difference. I was strong, stronger than I've ever been and there was nothing he could do to wipe Luca from my life.

Or so I thought.

CHAPTER SEVEN

Olivia Heart

He was beautiful. Incredibly, heart-expanding, steal your breath away beautiful, and he didn't even realize it. When he smiled, lifting those sharp cheekbones I loved so much, I felt the sun rise within my chest. The light touched all of the dark corners inside of me, banishing them until I had no darkness left to hide in.

He had the power to save me.

"You can't hide from me, Olivia."

I tried to touch him, but my fingers would slip through his ghost. "I'm not hiding from you, Luca. Not anymore."

His smile never falters. "You can't hide from me, Olivia."

Every time. The same sentence. The same smile. No matter what I do or how hard I try, I can't seem to get to him.

I snap awake, back into my body that's riddled with synthetic drugs that prevent my emotions from reaching the lowest low or the highest high. Sitting in the middle of purgatory I remain numb and slow. I have no control over my thoughts and desires.

Instead, I lull out into a sea of nothingness just waiting for the current to become strong enough to pull me under.

Five days have passed in a blur.

Will had dragged me back into my room after our heated discussion, where two men were waiting for me. The men pinned me down, placed thin sheets underneath my tongue and held my mouth closed until I was sedated.

I'd fought so hard, harder than I ever had before, but it didn't make a blind bit of difference. I was no match for them all.

This happened for the first three days until I gave in. I'd been here before, and it was useless fighting it. The more I fought the more energy I'd use. Energy is scarce and I need as much as possible if I'm to hold on.

In the evenings, when I was at my lowest under a blanket of pain, Will would slip into my room whispering his words of 'encouragement'. On the fourth day, as he brushed my hair, he decided it was time to break my heart.

"Here," he mumbled, passing me his phone. I took it, with my head still on his lap and let my eyes skim the far too bright device. "You need to see this."

My stomach tightened into knots but the rest of me felt frozen—stuck to Will's lap like the perfect lapdog.

An email chain between Luca Caruso and Emilia Vicolay burned its way into my retinas.

Will patted my head before smoothing down my hair. "They met up, Liv," he whispered. "My contact told me that they had dinner and she returned to his residence."

"It's not true."

There was too much hatred in Emilia's eyes for her forgiveness to be this quick. Or was it? How long have I really been out of it?

Will leaned over my shoulder to swipe at the screen. It was a slightly out of focus picture, but I saw Luca so clearly—I would be able to find him in a sea of faces. What I didn't want to see was Emilia on Luca's arm as they left the restaurant, together, smiling at one another.

Pain burst to life in a quick second until it fizzled away.

"You were too much trouble for him, Liv. Too complicated for him to fight for you, and certainly not worth going to prison for."

I feel his fingertips brush the top of my shoulders, but I don't shiver. I can't. I'm stuck between two feelings with neither of them strong enough to win.

I'm not worth it.

Of course, I'm not. Everything with me was complicated, painful, and came with far too much baggage. It all made sense now. I'd seen it the moment Luca didn't shake her off… I'd felt something deep in my gut.

Dropping Will's phone I pull my arms up and bury my face in my sleeves. I yearn for the darkness and know that sleep will be with me any second. This pain that's slowly uncoiling in my stomach won't be able to get me if I'm out.

"Don't cry, Olivia. C'mon now, he's not worth your tears. Your tears are for me only."

If there are tears, I can't feel them dripping from my eyes. All I feel is the poison swimming in my blood, diluting and watering down my feelings. A blessing in disguise.

Will moves me back onto my pillow before pulling up the blanket to cover us. I feel his hands snake across the sheets, searching for my hands until he brings them to rest between our chests.

I shut him out and close my eyes.

"Do you remember I held you like this on the day of your parent's funeral?" he whispered. "You were inconsolable, Liv, but you would only cry in front of me — you would only let me see your pain. It was beautiful."

I don't speak. This isn't a conversation that requires my participation. This is William Adler's moment to shine on his white horse.

"You trusted me to take care of you then," his lips touched my temple, leaving an invisible mark on my skin. "You needed me more than anybody else in the world. Just like you do now. It's funny how these things come full circle, isn't it, Liv?"

Full circle. He's right, of course. But funny? How is any of this *funny*? If I had the strength, I'd slap his filthy hands away. God, it would feel so good to hurt him, to feel him wince under my temper and control.

But I had neither.

I had drugs and him.

****

Somewhere, buried in the deepest part of my subconscious was the young girl that had been here before. I've sat in a room like this before, that's painted to soothe the mind, in front of a person trained to pick it apart and put it back together again.

The walls in this hell hole have been freshly painted a pale yellow that warms the mahogany furniture that had been pushed against the walls, allowing room for a single black, leather sofa and matching winged-back chair.

In between me and my new enemy was a small coffee table armed with a box of Kleenex. But even in my drug-fueled, barely conscious state, I knew that those tissues would remain untouched.

I physically had no tears left to cry. The tank was blinking red, warning me that I was completely empty. Dried out with dust settling at the bottom, but it was easier for me to deal this way, so I'd cope.

"You haven't said a word in twenty minutes," her voice that could pull you from hell sought me away from my self-pity.

I instantly disliked the woman who used a fake smile as a weapon to disarm me. It was too tight, with too much lipstick that sat in the smoking wrinkles around her mouth. I'd ignored her hand and looked her over, seeing the grey coming through her dull blonde hair and the awful structureless dress she wore.

I hated her.

"Do you want to discuss the condition further?"

I sank into my sweater, "No."

Her thoughtful nod and soft smile pissed me off. "I understand this is hard for you, Olivia. You've been through an awful lot, but it's important you talk about what happened. Bottling this up can be detrimental to your mental wellbeing moving forward."

There was that crinkled smile that made the hair on the back of my arms stand up. It couldn't be trusted. If she thought a soft voice and a smile would lure me out of my fortress, she would have to try harder.

"I'm fine," I snap.

She shifts in her chair, getting comfortable. I know from the way she watches me that we're going to be here for hours.

It's so obvious by her arrogance.

"Did you feel fine with your captor?" Her wrinkled fingers pluck a piece of thread from the chair. "Did you feel safe with him, Olivia?"

"Yes," I lie because lying is all I have left. Nobody can make me stop, nobody can take it away, and there's something satisfying about being the only one here who knows the truth.

Fuck you, Will.

"Even when you woke up in his home after being drugged and kidnapped?"

I turn to the window, focusing on the rain lashing down on the windows instead of the patronizing woman that sits across from me.

"Yes."

The weather outside is a perfect representation of how I feel on the inside. The rain that lashes against the glass is desperate to get in, to hide from the storm clouds threatening to thunder. I want to hide.

"What did he do to make you feel safe?"

"Everything," I tell her, wanting her to shut up. "He did everything to make me feel safe. A whole eight years' worth of it." A little bit of fog in my head clears.

She nods thoughtfully while tapping on her tablet. "You still felt safe with him after you found out he had been invading your privacy in those eight years?"

I bite my tongue, using the sharp sting and tase of blood to control my rising temper. This is what she wants, she needs me to snap and scream and fucking cry so she can tick a box and deem me crazy with a side of Stockholm syndrome.

But I won't give in.

"If you weren't trapped in his home when you found out this information, would you have felt the same?"

"I don't know how I would feel to a hypothetical situation," I hiss, turning to glare at her. "Let's not waste our time here, okay? I'm not going to share an ounce of information with a so-called psychiatrist that is being paid to treat and help keep me prisoner. So, give up."

Unfazed by me, she looks down and taps at her tablet, her fingernails clicking against the screen — grating on my nerves. "Did you hear me?"

Anger helps clear more of the fog and suddenly breathing doesn't seem so hard.

"I heard you, Olivia, but I disagree. You're not a prisoner here with me or Mr. Adler. We simply want to help you get past this awful situation."

I scoff, "Awful? What's awful is being pulled away from the one person that I truly need and lo—"

NO. Olivia, no. Oh god, not here with her. Those words are only meant for his ears and nobody else's.

The words stall in my throat. Heat seizes and commands my skin. Under her scrutiny, I'm suddenly a foot tall without an escape. I'd tried so hard to push his face out of my mind but the more I spoke the harder it became to control myself.

He was there, waiting.

"You love him?"

I stand far too quickly, stumbling over my feet as I move to the window.

"Where are we?" I deflect, squinting past the rain.

"Somewhere safe. Olivia, do you truly believe that what you feel towards Luca is love?"

Outside the wind picks up, forcing branches from the trees to bend towards the window. They twist and contort in a way that sends shivers across my cold skin.

"Everything I felt with Luca was real. I was under no illusions or a cloud of drugs." Tilting my head back I look up to the roof, noticing the paint that's crumbling away in the corners. Or was it? I can't trust my eyes at the minute. "I want to speak to him."

I need to hear his voice when he tells me that everything here is a lie. That I'm the only one that he needs and loves—not Emilia. Not her. Never her.

Those pictures could not be recent. I'd refuse to accept it until Luca told me himself. I'd shut him out too many times before and was always wrong. I wouldn't make that mistake again.

If you get the chance.

I turn back when her silence becomes too much to bare. "You think I'm crazy, don't you?"

"Not at all," her smile barely lifts the apples of her cheeks. God, she's such a dull woman that even her smile is boring. "I think you're an incredibly strong person actually. You've survived the death of your parents, a kidnapping, imprisonment, emotional abuse, a car accident, and a rescue. The fact that you're still defensive tells me that you very much have enough fight in you left, Olivia."

"If you don't think I'm crazy then why are you here?"

She puts her tablet on the coffee table in front of us, but the screen is blank. That's strange. "Because you're defensive over a man that put you through all of that. In usual circumstances you would be doing one of two things. You would either be ready to press charges, or you would be emotionally despondent."

"Well, I am neither, so your argument is invalid."

"Not quite," her condescending smile catches me off guard. "You fit right in the middle, Olivia. This is what usually happens to kidnapping victims that have been put in extreme situations. They seek to attach themselves to their captor for survival, whether that's by emotional or physical means."

Jesus.

Every part of my body itches to lurch forward so I can slap my hand over her mouth. Such filthy lies are being poured into this drab room and I won't hear anymore.

"It was never like that between us. I always had a choice with my mind," I take my seat on the sofa, right in front of her.

This so-called therapist tilts her neck, looking like a sparrow whose found a hidden gem. "But not your body?"

"He never did anything without my permission," I bit the words out.

She picks up her tablet and begins tapping. *Tip-tap. Tip-tap.* My fingers twitch to take the device and snap it in half.

"Did you feel pressured to have sex with him?"

"No," my breathless whisper clogs my throat. "I wanted him on my own accord. Every. Damn. Time." The words ground between my teeth.

Sex with Luca was nothing short of enlightening. I felt freedom in his body, under his control, under him. With every touch, every kiss, every claim I felt my heart thawing, ready to beat for him. She wasn't going to muddy those feelings.

Only Luca would have been able to bring me back to life.

"I've been here before," I tell her. "With someone like you, trying to dissect my inner thoughts and it didn't work then. And it won't work this time. I know who I am by Luca's side and it's not because of 'Stockholm Syndrome' or 'PTSD' or trauma from my childhood." I feel a smile tug at my lips. "It's because I own him. Every single part of him is mine. His desires, only I can deny. His cravings, only I can control and his heart, only I can crush. I own Luca Caruso body and soul and I made the choice to accept him."

"What does he get out of this ownership?"

I grin, "He gets to own me in return."

It's her turn to smile at me as if what I've said is the most amusing thing she's ever heard.

"Own you? Are you his dog? His little plaything?"

Plaything.

I feel a snap and cold air on the back of my thighs. Paint behind her begins to crumble, falling from the walls onto the green carpet. The rain lashing across the window suddenly stops.

My voice is too high as I try to stand. "What did you just say?"

"I asked if you're his little plaything."

That's when I see it. It's there in her high cheekbones and hair. Emilia, a much older and weathered version, sits across from me with glee — waiting for me to answer.

"It was never — he would never treat me like that. W-what are you doing here?"

Her cackle bursts into my ears just as cold hands wrap around the top of my throat, dragging me back into the corridor.

"Look at you, on your knees for me," his breath heats the back of my neck as he drags me from the floor. I swallow a cough, trying to focus on the ground before me.

It hits all at once. I had tried to run. I remember bursting out of my room, my feet pounding across the damp carpet until he caught me and slammed into my back. I'd fallen headfirst, knocking myself out and spent the past few minutes with an older Emilia.

"L-let go," I wheezed, dragging my hands up to his wrists. He was squeezing my throat so tightly that my eyes watered.

"Never," his dirty mouth pressed against my temple. "I'm having too much fun chasing you, Liv. You really know how to show a guy a good time."

By good time he means when I've not been drugged, he clears his schedule for the day so he can drag me around the house, torturing me with violence and threats to fuck me.

Everything changed the morning after he brought me here. I can't pinpoint the exact moment it happened, but all I know is that I woke up to the snarl of his face and his hands in my hair.

That was when Will told me that my new conditioning was starting and that by the time he was done with me, I would see the error in my ways.

The chase to ruin me is exciting for him, he practically salivates at seeing me crawl across the dirty floor until my knees give out or when he chokes me to the point of asphyxiation. I've cried and he's laughed. I've screamed and he's made me scream harder.

I've begged him to stop, and it only makes him want to hurt me more.

But soon he's going to grow tired of this game and he'll take what he wants.

And if he took me right now, I wouldn't be able to fight. Weak from lack of food and sleep, I can barely keep my head from falling off my shoulders, never mind fighting a man twice my size.

"Did he do this with you?" his arms loop around my waist and he pulls me back into the dining room. I'm shoved down onto a seat. "Did he get off seeing you crawl around that mansion of his?"

My mind flexes instinctively, protecting myself from the image of Luca. "No" is all I whisper.

"What a fool. There's nothing hotter on this planet than seeing you on your knees begging, Liv. Fuck, feel how hard I am for you." Will rips up my hand and forces me to touch his erection underneath his jeans.

He catches my gag and laughs wickedly. "You will gag when I slip my cock down your throat. Have no doubts about that," roughly shoving my hand down he begins to unzip.

This is it. This is where he takes what he wants.

I look at the disgusting creature before me, wishing for the taste of mint under my togue. For the drugs to lull me back into the open sea where I can disappear for good.

Will releases his veiny cock and grabs himself, keeping his greedy stare fixed on me. He begins to pump quickly from root to tip, getting off on what he sees in my eyes.

"You thought you could get away with taking my virginity and leaving," he grunts, pounding away at his disgusting flesh. "You thought you could just forget about me."

I fight the urge to look away knowing that's what he wants from me.

He grips himself so hard that his cock is bruising under his touch. "You and they are all the same, nothing but evil greedy sluts."

On the word slut he lurches forward, groaning into a spasm as he shoots his cum onto my thigh. The near see-through substance burns a mark onto my skin.

Before I realize what I'm doing, my head is bent over the side of the chair and I throw up.

CHAPTER EIGHT

Luca Caruso

The room fell into deathly silence, but I didn't care. I stepped back in and took my seat. Forgoing sleep, I cleaned myself up, put on my suit, and prepared for the day. Even if my chest was ready to crumble and cave in at any moment.

I'd drank myself into an oblivion last night after Theo had confirmed there was nothing new to report. I'd sunk into a bottle of whiskey with no care for what it would do to my mind.

I'd lost it after the tenth glass.

I'd destroyed everything in my wake. As my hands smashed at the interior of my house, I'd relished in the destruction. The monster and I were finally on the same page. Anger is where we escaped the pain and it felt safer here.

Glass littered the hallways Olivia had walked in. Plants and garden furniture sunk to the bottom of the pool that she swam in. The innards of my office met the window before they fell to their death and landed outside.

Everywhere she had been I destroyed, unable to face the memories until I made my way to my room—whiskey still drowning my grief.

I'd stepped over the threshold with the purpose of setting fire to the bed where Olivia had told my she loved me for the second time. I was so close, the lighter and whiskey in my hands, until Dante and Theo tackled me, forcing me to my knees in front of the painful shrine.

"Get the fuck off me," I hit out, sloshing whiskey at them both.

"Stop this, Lucie." Theo put me in a headlock while Dante wrestled the bottle from my hands. "Don't do this."

The monster inside me howled.

"Listen to him, for fuck sakes, Luca!" Dante snapped, lurching for the bottle before throwing it into the hallway where it clattered loudly. "Olivia needs a safe place to come back to."

I laughed, dropping to the carpet, my fingers clutching at the carpet. "She isn't coming back to me. She's gone." I shook my head. "Gone. Forever. I can't find her. I can't find her," a bubble popped in the center of my chest. "I'm dying," I gasped, clutching at my empty chest.

Theo sighed and dragged me up, his arms struggling to bring me up. I saw fury lurking in his eyes, and I deserved it. I was pathetic.

"I've tried to be patient, Lucie. You're going through a lot, and I like to think I've been as understanding as I can, but right now, I've reached my limit. Your weakness is revolting."

Deciding he was done with me, he brought his head forward lightening quick against mine, headbutting me into the darkness where I couldn't rein destruction on *our* home.

Theo's headbutting had saved me, not that I would ever admit it to him. As I sat across from him, I scowled, silently cursing him for the knot that sat in the middle of my forehead, but I was incredibly grateful. I'd been so close to giving up.

"No… way," Jack Veen, IT specialist mumbled, catching my attention. He poured over his laptop, his fingers furiously tapping the keyboard. "Sick bastard."

"Ah shit," Bones hissed from his corner.

Dante, Theo, and Chen lurched to stand behind him, but I didn't move. My legs had seized, and my stomach rolled, threatening to bring the whiskey I drank last night right back up.

"What is it?" Theo barked.

"It's a link. I found it in an encrypted email between Adler and his security outfit. The IP's bouncing like crazy. Hold on —" he hit a key and the screen behind him lit up. "I've been trying to steady the connection all morning and I think I've worked out how to do it."

Behind them all, the TV screen flickered a mix of green and red before it steadied. The clarity improved and before us was a live link into an empty bedroom. Nobody said a word as I stood up, leaning over the table, scrutinizing the footage but they watched me like the ticking time bomb I'd become.

A four-poster bed made of a deep oak stood proudly on the far left of the screen with blood red curtains. The carpets where puke green and the furnishings sparse. It looked like a cold, dank prison.

"Hold on," Jack whispered to nobody, "there's audio."

The white noise that came from the feed didn't last long. The bedroom door burst open, bouncing off the wall and a flash of brown blurred the screen. Olivia fell to her knees, hitting the carpet with such a thud that I felt her gasp in my stomach.

"Fuck you, asshole!" she hissed over her shoulder before scrambling back up.

I drank her in, quickly looking her over as if at any minute the feed would cut out and she would fail to exist. She looked so young with her hair flowing down her back, dressed in a cream sweater and jeans and her feet in converse. Olivia looked like the girl I'd seen in photographs, in her younger years.

Adler was trying to get her back, dressing her like the girl he knew before she grew up and realized what a toxic fuck he was.

"Thank god," Bones whispered as he fell into his seat. "She's alive."

Theo peeled his eyes away long enough to turn to Jack. "Where is this coming from?"

"No idea. I can't get a reading on the IP," he glared at his screen, despising it for failing to provide us with any more information.

Olivia moved to the bed, her long legs stretching out before her as she kicked off her sneakers. We watched as she carefully lifted up her sweater to inspect the bruises that were not only still there but worse.

There were many, many more.

"Great," she mumbled, "just what I need."

Oh, baby.

Not leaving her for a second, I opened my mouth. "Can we speak to her?"

Jack turned to me, shaking his head. "No the feed is only one way."

The burn of anger sliced through me, and impatience seethed, but I was back in control. Just seeing her again made it possible to find clarity. Olivia was alive and under my watch once again.

I'd find her.

We all would.

And we would all kneel at her feet.

Everyone, including Chen's team who very much despised me right now, watched the screen with a newfound hope. The atmosphere changed from soul-sucking desperation to solitude, and it was all for her.

"What did I tell you about giving them grief, Liv?" his voice, the fucking vulture's voice blared through the speakers.

Olivia didn't move or flinch under him as he stalked into the room to tower over her. She just watched and waited.

"I don't like being manhandled," she shrugged, "especially by cowards hiding behind masks."

Will ripped off his jacket and threw it down on her bed. "They wouldn't have to if you just did as you were told." Fuck, if he takes another item of clothing off in front of her, I swear on the grave of my mother I'll chop every single finger off.

"She's good," Theo nodded over the table at me. "She's still strong."

But for how long? She already looked exhausted and the bags under her eyes said she wasn't getting much sleep. I doubt she was eating anything either.

Olivia, my sweet Olivia, tilted her chin in defiance. A look I'd enjoyed many times before. "I don't have to do anything I don't want to."

Adler pushed a filthy hand through his disgusting hair. "You know what happens when you cause trouble, Liv. C'mon, you know I don't want to keep doing this."

She scuttled back up the bed, sensing the threat that loomed in his words. "You don't want to keep pinning me down and hurting me?" she snarled sarcastically, "here's me thinking you quite enjoyed making time to drag me around this place."

He was suddenly on her and I was on fire.

I couldn't breathe. My throat constricted in pain from the unused howl rattling in my chest cavity. The whole world underneath my feet stopped spinning as her words rattled round in my head. He was touching her — forcing her…

I bent over the table, but my eyes kept themselves glued to the screen. Adler had straddled her, covering her mouth with his hands. Motherfucking fuck. I'm going to peel away his skin and carve away at him until he's nothing but a pile of flesh.

"Don't act like you don't like it," he bit out by her ear. "I was just comforting you, Liv, or have you forgotten what it's like to be comforted?"

His slimy voice slipped from the speakers, coating my skin in grime.

"Get up," Bones barked at me from the other side of the room. "Be there for her."

I ignore him — I was too focused on Olivia as she slapped his hands away. The fire in her still burned brightly, she could do this. She could survive him.

"I don't need your *comfort,*" she growled, slamming her hands into his chest. "I don't need you, your drugs, or your fucking punishments! What I need from you is to get the hell off of me!" She rolled into the bed, trying to dislodge his hips with her own.

"Veen," Theo barked, "tell me you can get the IP on this motherfucker's place."

"You do need me — fuck!" Adler groaned from the connection of Olivia's sharp elbow to his groin. He grappled with her hands wildly, his face scrunched and red with pain. If only Olivia had hit harder. "You're not right in the head, Liv. You need to have a time out and think about what you've done today."

There was no time to prepare myself for what happened next. Adler was quick as he reached into his pocket and shoved whatever was in his fingers into her mouth. Olivia tried to fight him but his fingers digging into her jaw, prying open her lips, were too much.

She screamed, a sound that would haunt me for the rest of my life as he placed the tiny blue sheet on her tongue. Adler pinned her hands above her head with one of his and used the other to cover her mouth.

Wide eyes blinking up at him, fear pooling and spilling until I saw the tears track down Olivia's face. In seconds, she'd gone from wild fighter to submissive and subdued.

She sank under him. Her body limp and lifeless.

The table under my grip cracked.

"See this is what happens every time you fight me. But what choice do I have, Liv? You won't meet me halfway," he pulled his hand away, placing it at the side of her head to cage her in against the mattress.

"I-I never will," she choked out. Blue liquid dripped from the corner of her mouth, sliding across her porcelain skin until it hid within her hairline "I know w-who you *are*," she closed her eyes. "I saw it when we were kids."

Adler panted above, watching with wild lust as she fought against the drug he'd fed her. Panic and something else seized the control he had as he bent down, slapping her face, trying to keep her awake.

"What does that mean?"

She groaned, turning her head towards the window. "You prefer me like... this." her voice barely registered in the speakers, but I heard her. I always would. "In the back of my mind I knew what you were doing. Keeping me broken. Clipping my wings."

Butterflies swarmed my vision. Memories of Olivia smiling up at me as her favorite creature fluttered around our heads — bringing us together. I only ever wanted to see her happy.

76

Adler's shoulders tensed as her softly spoken truth tumbled from her blue stained lips. "That's not true. I just wanted you. Shit, I just wanted you to see me!"

A gargle cooled in her throat. "Liar. You want me this way, to be sad and hopeless because it gets you off. You like the control of knowing I can never leave again. You- you're so… stupid, you don't even realize I leave you every time you're in front of me."

"Shit." Dante dropped into his seat, his knees giving up on him. "This is fucked up."

"Be prepared," Theo warned, sensing something else was coming.

Something crunched below my hand, but I didn't look down. I couldn't leave her. She needed me to be strong.

I'm coming, baby.

Adler leaned down, tilting Olivia's head so she had to face him. With slow, carefully slimed fingers, he wiped away the blue that oozed from her lips, letting his fingers explore the curve of her neck — my lips. My neck. She was mine.

He was touching what was mine.

He was far too calm, far too relaxed, exploring the woman that didn't belong to him, and I knew my revenge would be slow and extremely painful. It was within my right to torture this fuck until his mind bent and shattered into a million pieces.

Her fight began to disappear with every passing second and I knew it wouldn't be long until she was completely helpless.

"Of course it will work. We have all the time in the world to make it work," he whispered, brushing her hair away from her head. "There is nothing and nobody in my way to stop me. Not him, not your family, and certainly not you."

She didn't reply but that didn't matter to him. All that mattered was her silence and being completely at his mercy as he placed a kiss on her lips. The fight in her was spent and she closed her eyes.

"Psycho," Theo muttered, turning away in disgust.

I didn't turn away. I watched every single fucking move Adler made and filed them away, so I'd remember which bones to break first. And when he was dead, I was going to replace every touch of her skin with my own. He would cease to exist by the time I was done.

We watched him for hours as he caressed her face. As he tucked her into her bed. Watched as he placed kisses on her forehead and brushed her long hair. Even though it hurt, I watched over Olivia as I had done for eight years, so at least she wasn't alone.

When he left and locked the door to her room, I had everything I needed to keep going. This time I had no plans on being gentle with those that tried to hurt what was mine.

It was time to let the monster do what he does best.

CHAPTER NINE

Luca Caruso

"White letter-hair hairstreak..." Olivia muttered to herself as she paced the bottom of her bed. "Could be... or," she turned to stare out of the window, her brow furrowed in concentration, "the weather is just right but it's too rare... could it be?"

"Is she losing it?" Dante asked as we watched her on the screen.

I swallowed past the razors that had settled in my throat since her kidnapping. "No," I bit out. She wasn't losing it. It was the opposite — she was trying to keep it together by a fine thread of her history, of her love of butterflies.

An hour ago, she had been rushed into the room by two thugs wearing black ski masks. Wearing a crimson red raincoat with her shoes caked in mud, she rushed to her desk, ripping out a pad and pen, ranting incoherent words.

While we watched her pace the room, Theo's guys were running a tracker on one of the thug's tattoos we had seen on his hand. It was a long shot but some prisons catalogue gang tattoos.

It was Bones who solved the mystery of Olivia's mysterious rant and I'd never been so mad at myself for missing it.

He turned his iPad to face me, pointing his finger at the screen. "This is what she's talking about."

I snatched it up, my eyes scanning over the article about the endangered species of Butterfly found only in Scotland.

My hands shook and I had to make a fist to hide it. "It's a long shot," but I needed this. Needed something to grasp onto.

Olivia and the butterflies that never seemed to leave her side could possibly be in Scotland.

"She's there," Bones nodded at me, his stare imploring me to believe him.

"He could be right," Veen jumped in. "We know one of the IP addresses is bouncing from Scotland."

Air inflated my chest for the first time in a week. I didn't want to believe in case we were all wrong, but I needed something to hold onto. Olivia was losing strength every day that passed. She was refusing to eat, choosing to throw the food out of her window and refusing to cooperate with Adler.

There were times he would lose control and she would disappear for hours, and most of the time she came back, traumatized and barely able to keep her eyes open.

One night she sat at the end of her bed, staring off into space—vacant and removed from real life. Her vibrancy had dulled along with the light in her eyes. And every second tore knives of pain into my heart. Over and over until she moved. Until she crawled up the bed and buried her head into the pillows.

But I didn't breathe a sigh of relief. And I wouldn't. I didn't deserve to.

Whatever Adler was doing to her in the time we couldn't see her was breaking her down, bit by bit. Stealing parts of her fight. Stealing her.

But it helped remove my self-pity and fill the hole up with black rage. It filled my body with adrenalin. Punched violence into my veins and hardened my skin until I was nothing but a savage who wanted to tear the pulse from Adler's neck with his teeth.

And right now, Olivia needed a savage.

Theo stood up and straightened his shirt that had crumpled from sitting for so long. "If she's there we need solid proof before we go in — let me finish, Luca," he ground out between his perfect teeth. He was missing Katrina but was too stupid to leave. "We need the element of surprise. There's a lot of fuckers to take out and we need to make sure Adler doesn't have the opportunity to alert the press. We need to avoid a cluster-fuck."

"Fuck that," I swiped the contents of the table. "Fuck the press. She can't wait much longer. She needs me now."

Rum moved quickly in my peripheral, stealing mine and everyone's attention. He was close to the screen, glaring at Olivia.

"What is she doing?" he asked.

I pinched the bridge of my nose. One thing hadn't changed about Olivia and that was her tendency to take her anger out on inanimate objects. She was tearing at the clothes in the wardrobe, throwing them into the corners of her room. She paused only briefly to rip the sleeves off a sweater before digging back in.

"Assholes. Dressing me like a fucking doll," she bites out at a black dress that glimmers under the warm light.

Dante raised an eyebrow my way, but I ignored him.

"Wear this, Olivia. Put a dress on, Olivia," she hissed as she wrenched out a pair of jeans and flung them across the room. "Do as your told, Olivia. Be a good fucking girl and shut up, Olivia — argh!" The jacket she tried to rip off the hanger didn't come loose on the first try. Leaning in with both hands she pulled it free with a frustrated scream, nearly tumbling.

"That's my jacket!" Bones joined Red at the TV. The one piece of clothing Adler had forgot to return.

She pauses only briefly before launching it towards her bathroom door with half a sob.

"We'll protect you, Olivia," she mimicked, her lips curling up with disgust down at the offending item. A sway to the side and she nearly falls. It's all I can do but watch her self-destruct.

We all watch as the jacket hits the floor and a soft ping echoes across the dingy bathroom tiles. Olivia huffs, pausing to peer at the bathroom entrance.

"What's she looking at?" Dante whispered.

We watch as she moved towards the bathroom. The ugly warm light from the bathroom hit her face, highlighting the weariness settling in her eyes and the dark bags from lack of sleep.

Olivia perched down, plucking something from the doorway that we couldn't see far into. Hidden by her hair that had fallen over her shoulders I waited for her to stand.

"Ah! Fuck," Rum hissed as he stood up, gripping his ear, yanking out his earpiece.

Veen lurched forward, hitting the keys on his laptop while Chen threw me his earpiece.

"I knew it," Bones' sigh of relief was so loud that I felt it vibrate in my chest. "I knew it was with her. I fucking knew it."

"Hello?" her breathy voice came out of the TV speakers, directly to us. My knees buckled at the sound of her beautiful whisper. I fell into the table using it for support.

I hit the button on my earpiece, placed it in my ear and spoke, "Olivia."

On the screen she froze. Her shoulders tensed defensively at the sound of my voice.

Relaxing my jaw, I softened my voice. "Olivia, it's me. Can you hear me?"

"Yes," her voice cracked with mistrust. "Yes, I can hear you. Is that really you?"

I had one shot. "Do you remember The Butterfly House? The Polyommatus. You told me I had one in my hair that day, do you remember that?"

She moved on the screen. Well, she crawled into the bathroom where we couldn't see her.

"Luca," her voice was so quiet, steeped in pain.

"We need five minutes to track her," Chen whispered. "Keep her talking."

I waved him off. Too focused on the sound of her sweet voice to focus on the ticking clock above my head.

"It's okay, I'm here."

She sucked in a breath, fighting a sob. "You have to stay away. I should go..."

"Not a chance, Bella. I'm coming to get you. Stay on the line for me, okay? We need a few minutes to track you."

"He has evidence—articles ready to destroy you, all of you," her tone lulls from breathy to panic, pitching a touch higher. "This is the only way to stop him from destroying you all. Luca, you have to stay way—*please.*"

"I've always found it extremely difficult to stay away from you, Olivia," I turned my back to the men trying to track the love of my life, urging them to move faster, "you should know this by now."

She sighs, dropping her voice to a whisper. "Are you okay?"

She stunned me and for a second, I forgot how to form a proper sentence.

My knuckles cracked from how tight I squeezed my fist when I realized she was worrying about me. "Don't worry about me. I'll be fine as soon as I have you back."

"I can't do this, Luca. I thought I was strong enough to fight him but it's getting harder. The drugs... the room with the... I'm so tired and everything is so hard."

She's never been so open with her feelings before. Usually guarding, keeping he emotional cards to her chest, but because of me she's lost those walls that protected her, and I've left her vulnerable to destruction. And now as the clock ticks there isn't anything I can do but listen.

"You can and you will. Hold on for a little longer, okay? Do you know where you are?" I ask her, moving back to the table where everyone was working.

"Maybe Scotland... maybe Wales. It's hard to tell. I've only been allowed outside twice."

I pull Bones' tablet forward. "The White letter-hair hairstreak is only found in Scotland, correct?"

"Yes. Wait, how do you know about that?"

"We can see you," *I can see you.* I hear the rustle of her hair against the mic. "Don't move, stay where you are, and I'll explain."

"What do you mean you can see me?" she whispers. Her voice drifting into my ear until it hit my chest. For the briefest of seconds I felt warmth touch my skin. I closed my eyes.

"Adler has a camera in your room. We found the connection but we can't get a trace on it. The earpiece you have is all we have to track you."

There was a brief pause. "Sick fucker."

Indeed.

"You've been with me this whole time?"

"Only for the past couple of days."

"You saw…"

I didn't answer. I couldn't.

The sound of her cry nearly buckled my knees for the second time.

"Bella, don't cry," I whispered soothingly while waiting for Chen to let me know how much longer. If Adler walked in right now, we were screwed. Chen held up two fingers.

"I can't go back in that room," she sniffed.

"What room? Your bedroom?" I began packing up my belongings, ready to leave as soon as they had a location. To my left, Theo was on the phone to his guys. To my right, Rum was on the phone speaking to my pilot. And Dante was on the phone, preparing Aida for a blow back.

We were without a solid plan for the first time in eight years, but I didn't care.

I knew I'd get her. I felt it in my bones.

"No," she whispered. "It's below the building. He puts me in there, in the box, when I refuse to…"

"To what?" the whole room freezes at the sound of her voice. Terror, fucking life-flashing before my eyes terror makes me pause. "To what, *Olivia*?"

She sucks in a shaky breath, "To cooperate"

"Has he touched you?"

There's a silence that stretches for far too long. My breathing is too loud. My heart is a second away from giving in… I'm close to falling apart.

"He's tried…"

Blood pumps so loudly in my ears. "You're going to watch me kill him, Olivia," I'm sharp and cold. "Do you hear me? This is that situation we spoke about in Paris. He lost all fucking innocence the moment he stepped into this… when he tried to touch you. I'm going to deliver his head at your feet."

"Yes. I hear you," she replies without missing a beat. She wants him dead as much as I do.

"He signed his life away to me the minute he hurt you," I tell her, turning back to Chen who nods my way. We had her. It was time to move.

"Scotland," he mouthed.

"Olivia?" Speak of the devil and he may enter. "What the fuck have you done now!?"

Adler's voice rings loudly through the flatscreen speakers and into my right ear. I've never wanted to destroy someone as much as the cretin that holds the love of my life in his filthy possession.

I hiss, "Take the earpiece out and hide it."

She does as she's told, quickly. I hear the muffle come from the speaker.

"What have you been doing in here, Liv?" his voice fills up both room and my skull. Her nickname is shards of glass against my fraying patience.

Another muffle. "I needed a minute," her voice bouncing off the bathroom tiles. She's breathless, timid and gentle as if she's sensing a battle heading her way.

She's preparing for him.

It guts me.

From the camera, all I see is his back and the way he towers in the doorway. She's trapped with nowhere to run to. He could step in there and take off her clothes, hurt her, mark her, and I'll have to listen to her screams…

A strangled moan echoes somewhere in the space.

"You've destroyed your room," he tells her as he bends in the doorway, his voice dripping with anger. "Why?"

There's no answer from Olivia.

Theo motions for me to move. The room has been packed up and we're ready to leave. I keep the earpiece in, holding my breath so I don't miss a moment.

"Answer me, Olivia, or you'll spend the night in the box. You really don't want to go in there do you? I know how much you hate it."

"I was upset. It was stupid but I—" she screams so loudly it makes my ears bleed. "Please, I don't want to go back in the box. I can't—"

The terror in her voice sets off alarm bells until they're screaming in my head. It takes everything in me to keep walking, to not pause.

"You need the time to reflect," he laughs, "maybe I'll leave you in there for longer. A few hours aren't clearing your head of all this mess."

I'm in the car, between Bones and Dante as Chen pulls away from the house with enough speed to disturb the drive. But every part of me wishes I was at her side, protecting her from the devil that she had once trusted, and not stuck in this fucking car that doesn't move *fast* enough.

"Please, no. I can't go back in there," she's begging. The woman that had put up so much fight against me was gone and had to resort to begging.

Adler has his bloodied hands in her chest, stealing her strength and tainting her, and for that alone I was going to make his death as slow as possible.

The sick fuck will regret ever laying eyes on Olivia again. He will regret the first moment he ever entertained the idea of taking her from me.

Theo in the passenger seat groans, "Sick, sick bastard," while tapping on his device, readying the team that's following us.

Adler's voice brings in a new wave of torture that I have to sit with—that I'll take to my grave. "What will you do to stay out of it?"

"Fight, Olivia," Bones whispers, clutching his new earpiece "C'mon now."

We're all listening. Willing her to survive a few more hours. Can they sense how close she is to leaving us all? I heard it in her voice, the contemplation of giving up and letting go. He's dug his way that deeply into her mind that she cannot see the future. It's disappeared into a blackhole.

My breathing accelerates. Everyone in the car tenses, sensing my blood thirst. Can they tell how I'm seconds away from clawing off my skin and letting the monster out? Can they feel him clawing his way out of my ribcage, hissing with the need to taste blood?

Retribution itches in the opening cracks across my skin. Hot flames lick at the back of my neck. I'm desperate to taste revenge but so fucking frustrated that it's too far away.

Adler's voice cuts over her reply but from the scream that tears its way from her throat and into my ear, I know it's not the one Adler wanted. There's a loud smash in the background, followed by Olivia's groan of pain.

"Just kill me already," she gasps. "I will never give you that, you sick fuck! Never! So fucking... kill... me!" she screams.

"We make it slow," Red hisses.

"We going dark?" Bones asks him.

"We are. I already have the needles," Chen nods at his team through the mirror. Their fury touches mine, steeping and feeding into the darkness and suddenly we become a cell of one. No longer fractured by our failures, we all step into each other's pain and put our differences aside.

A dark chuckle cuts through their conversation, laughing at their plans.

"Get on your knees," the sound of a zipper and snap of elastic, "and I'll show you how sick I can be."

The air dissipates through the car, and I know that's impossible, but I can't fucking breathe. My knuckles crack against my ribs. The fire in my chest blazes through my veins, weakening my hold across my chest, and I have no choice. No fucking choice.

I cave.

My ribcage cracks wide open.

The monster steps through, licking his teeth in anticipation for the first taste of revenge.

Three beeps.

"Will... wait!" her cry bounces off the edge of my conscious. "Don't do this. *Please*," she cries, raw fucking sobs that's glutton to the monster. "Put me in the box. Put me in the fucking box instead."

Two beeps.

"Shit," Chen's panic seers into me. "We're going to lose her."

"He hasn't taken your mouth yet Olivia, has he? Be a good girl and open those pretty lips for me. Show me you can come back, show me that he doesn't have you anymore and I might spare you. That's it—come on now."

One beep of the battery and our connection is severed.

CHAPTER TEN

Olivia Heart

I'm in God's waiting room.

I float above the surface of the earth, above the pink-tinged clouds until only the moon looms over me. I'm safe, bathed in its innocent bright light where no darkness awaits.

No boxes.

No dream therapists.

No guns.

No drugs to slip under my tongue and in my food.

I'm weightless with my own center of gravity. I'm strong here. I'm alone with no binds around my wrists. Nobody can force me onto my knees. Wicked hands can't hold me down here.

I'm safe here, having left my body with William Adler who looms over it, his face hidden within the shadows he's grown accustomed too.

A sharp sting tugs across my scalp. I shake my head, ignoring the sensation.

"Don't be fucking difficult," his voice hisses.

My hair is tugged over my shoulder in one quick sharp motion, but the pain seems softer, so much so that it almost doesn't register. I either haven't left my body completely or I'm getting used to his punishments.

"I should punish you for not taking better care of yourself," his voice, the voice that belongs to the devil, hisses against my neck and sends cold waves across my neck. "Look at your beautiful hair, Liv. It's all in knots. Hold still."

Another sharp tug and I'm pulled away from the clouds into the cold room of ancient green carpets and red suede interior. The damp coats my lungs, covering them in filth and grime. But I don't care, let the filth turn to mold where an infection can grow and kill me.

The girl that I find in the mirror is unrecognizable. Everything about her repulses me, even more than the man that stands behind my shoulders, brushing out my damp hair across my bruised shoulder blades.

She should be dead.

Look at you. Dull eyes. Wide blown-out pupils. Dead. Decimated inside, completely hollow like a corpse that's been plucked from its grave. *Just let me fucking go.*

A sloppy kiss to the side of the neck doesn't pull a shiver from my cold skin. It's like the nerves under my skin have died too. That's what Will is exceptional at, killing everything that he touches.

I've wilted.

On instinct, I swallow back my fear. My mouth tastes like mint. Under my tongue is sticky but I can't lift my hand to clear the strip that's melting there.

I'm too late.

"You look so beautiful," he takes me in. I watch him through the mirror admiring me, drinking me in until his eyes are full of lust.

To him, through hooded eyes, I'm a dream in the strappy blue gown that covers the whole floor of my bedroom with silk. But to me, I'm a starving creature with dead eyes and a failing heart.

I'm not beautiful.

I'm decaying inside this gown. It barely covers my chest. In another life this dress would have been on a lithe model's body as she took the stairs of some mansion, posing for the cameras that waited for her. But for me, it was the dress I would die in.

I can feel it. Feel the gown wrapping itself around me, mummifying me and preparing me for the afterlife. My sigh of relief fills the room. Will smirks, assuming my relief is because of his hands in my hair, and I let him have it.

Maybe, having the fight in me disappearing was a good thing because it'll make it easier to go. There will be nothing to keep me tied to this place.

Yes. I'll have more strength in the afterlife. I could come back, reborn with wings instead. I'll be strong and powerful and reinstated to the creature I was supposed to be.

Maybe the butterflies will carry me home to the family that I had lost. I picture my dad waiting for me on the other side, his large arms outstretched as he waits to comfort me.

"*Come on, sweet pea,*" *he would say, patting my back in loving circles.* "*Let's go to the park, shall we?*"

"*Daddy, what happens to the butterflies when they die?*"

"*They go to a safe place.*"

"*Where's that?*" *I look at my small hand in his and smile up at him.*

"*To heaven, sweat pea.*"

"*Will I get to see them in heaven daddy?*"

"*Eventually you will, yes, but not for a long time.*"

"Stop crying," Will warns me with a hand clutching the back of my neck. The pinch of my skin does nothing to alert me to danger.

I wipe at the eyes that still work. I clear the evidence and wait for the tears to dry on my useless hands.

"Good girl. Now come on. Our dinner will be ready, and we have much to discuss."

My lungs barely have room to expand inside the tiny space of my chest. They ache as I take the weight trailing behind me, until the silk is dancing down the steps to their final resting place.

I sit at the table a few minutes later, or it could have been an hour. But by the look of content on Will's face I think it's only been a few minutes.

A waiter slips into the room, keeping his eyes down as he pours the wine. If I had the energy, I would glare holes into his head for turning a blind eye to my suffering.

But instead, I focus on the monotony of his actions as he pours the wine. It's red, deeper than the shade of blood that slipped from my mouth only hours ago.

I see my breath before me and Will across the table with his back to the door. This place is always cold. Kept at freezing temperatures to offer no comfort while I'm dressed in skimpy clothes. Will prefers my nipples to be hard at all times and my lips blue. But his favorite is to run his hand down the goosebumps of my thighs as he teases himself. And when he isn't around, it's to ensure I never find an ounce of comfort in this forsaken place.

I'm only permitted to feel fear.

A trickle of more wine and my glass is filled, but I don't sip. Even now, after everything is colliding, preparing for a tornado, a small part of me rebels. I will not die with his wine in my mouth.

"Drink the wine," he warns me, leaning back into his chair as he rolls the cuffs of his white shirt.

"I can't," I whisper. "The drug under my tongue hasn't melted completely."

I don't know what I'm saying or maybe I do. I know the wine is laced with drugs like everything consumable in this place. Still coherent enough to know that any more and I think I'll overdose. My heart pounds against my chest in agreement.

He grins nastily. "Even after everything you're still denying me. I have to say, Olivia, you're a lot stronger than the others... the light is harder to snuff out in you."

The others.

The bodies in shallow graves below my feet howl into the night. Nobody but the two of us know of their existence, but soon it will be down to one. The injustice of it all would kill me if I was in any right state of mind to care.

They had been women who had wanted something from Will. They saw him as commodity to steal from. But instead of dismissing their advances he pursued them, tortured, and killed them. And it was all my fault.

I started this chain of events by hurting him. By making him into the weak man that couldn't handle rejection, and he made sure to tell me that one night when he stripped me bare and threw me outside, dragging me across the pebbled driveway.

I sip the wine, suddenly not wanting to remember the stories about women who were lured to this crumbling hotel.

My survival so far had been nothing but sheer luck. Will was taking his time to extract my pain—wanting to draw it out—until he was satisfied enough to let me go. Unlike the other women before me, he wanted me to bend to suit his fury until I broke into a million tiny pieces and then, only when I'm at my weakest, will he kill me.

But self-preservation is a hard thing to kill no matter how many times you drug it, how many times you force it into the darkness… no matter how many times you try to cut it out. She's always there.

It's engraved into the core of your DNA to keep you alive for as long as possible. It's torture in itself having her there because she just won't let me go.

"Or maybe I don't want to see your light go out," he muses, swirling his glass that he won't touch. "It has been… interesting seeing you this way. So weak and fragile for me instead of those dead parents of yours. It's been nice to have your full attention for once."

I open my mouth on instinct, to tell him to go straight to hell for even talking about them.

"No," he clicks his fingers, silencing me like he would a dog that's yapping too much. "You don't get to talk until I say you can, or have you forgot your manners?" He picks up the steak knife to his left and touches the tip with his finger. It's a subtle warning I've seen many times before—the cut across my ribcage attests to it.

I suck in a breath, wishing for the knife to be in my hand instead of his but I'm not to be trusted with sharp objects. That was made very clear the first time he threatened me with one.

"When you left that day, Liv, I had never felt so open, so exposed in my entire life. And you just walked away without so much as a glance back. And then you disappeared into the life that you always wanted, forgetting about the one person who got you there in the first place. I was raw because of you, an open festering wound."

He presses the tip of the knife deeper, drawing a bubble of blood. "And now it's you that's exposed, and you can't run away," he grins.

You can't run away.

Physically I can't leave this room but mentally I can leave whenever I want. I'll slip down the chair, through the creaky floorboards until I can rest safely in the dirt by the women he had killed.

I'm safer with the dead, I know that he knows that, but he isn't going to make my journey there easy.

I ignore my instincts raging at me to fight and focus on what will happen once I go. My dad will rush to hold me and even my mother will be pleased to see me, her smile softening when she sees me for the first time in years.

"Come on, sweat pea. Be strong now."

"There's no Luca to save you. No armed guards to watch over you. It's just you and me, Liv. Just like old times."

Luca's name pulls at something hidden within my ribs. It aches as it pulls through the wall of my chest at such an agonizingly slow pace.

Was he coming? Did I dream his beautiful promises into my ear? Maybe self-preservation had kicked in and saved me from Will's savagery by using the one man that could get to me, even a thousand miles away.

I'd laugh if I had it in me. He wasn't coming.

"I couldn't believe my luck when Black told me about your kidnapping. I was in fucking awe at first. Luca had done something that I had only dreamt of doing to you. I was furious at first, until I took the time to evaluate the situation, you know? To realize that if Luca could easily steal you away then I certainly could. I should thank him for showing me the way. What do you reckon?"

My gut twists so painfully that I fight to not clutch the table. I didn't want to hear Luca's name roll off his tongue.

"I wanted to be the first to steal you away, to hurt you, to make you cry real fucking tears with my cock inside your pussy—" he inhales a deep breath as if it's all too much, "but then I remembered I was your first and now I can be your last. He can never have that. I'm going to take you tonight, Olivia. No more games. I'm going to take what you owe me and then I'm going to kill you."

Air sent straight from the arctic blows down my back, freezing me to the back of my chair. A flicker of fight sparks inside but it blows out before I can establish the small connection.

Pathetic. I'm pathetic.

He's going to rape me and there's nothing I can do to stop it. Nobody to save me, but at least he's promised me death after. There are small mercies after all.

"What do you think?"

He sips his water, thinking himself as nothing but gracious while he allows me to answer for the first time this evening.

"You were never my first," it slips and falls from my mouth. My words crash through his façade, slicing through his arrogance in one fell swoop.

But that's self-preservation for you.

His eyes that I once thought of as beautiful are sharp and full of vicious threats. "What are you saying?"

With a shaky hand I place my hand on the table. Every cell in my body warns me about speaking, practically burns into my skull to keep my mouth shut, but it's too late—this is my last moment to hurt him back.

"You may have had my body first, but it was him that I *felt* first. It was him that my soul recognized and wanted. Not you. Not yours. He's my first and will always be my last."

So fucking kill me and be done with it.

I'll fall into my grave knowing that I had loved someone once. That miracles did happen and that I was strong enough to love without fear hanging over me.

It had been fleeting but it was enough.

My body is flung across the table. I crash onto the solid wood. My breasts and hips hit the cold surface but there's no sound from me.

I refuse it.

Red wine spills across the polished surface, pooling close by my left wrist. Harsh hands scramble through the fabric, trying to push it up and over my hips. My vision blurs for a few seconds before landing on the fingernails that dig into the wood with enough force to draw blood. It's my hand, my fingertips that I see.

And finally, I feel the pain.

Pain.

The fog clears a little, enough for me to understand what's coming next.

Will pants at the back of my neck, his hot breath doing nothing to stir a defense but his hard cock touching my entrance through my panties does. I go from frozen to frightened.

Energy whistles into my blood.

A glint of silver calls to me from my left as he palms me through my underwear.

Will grunts when he finds me dry. "You're going to feel this Liv, you're going to feel me burn him out of your soul. And rest assured, you pretty little thing, when I'm done with you, you'll only associate him with this pain." He pushes a palm down on my lower back, levelling me to the height he needs.

My underwear snaps between his fingers and flutters between my thighs.

I reach out to protect myself and hope he doesn't see.

He unzips for the second time today and begins to line himself, ready to hurt me with finality.

"Will wait!"

He pauses for a second, tightening his grip on my hips with frustration. I grab his hesitancy with my unsteady hands and turn to look over my shoulder at him. I'm slow, my mind and reactions are so slow, but I force myself to stare into his eyes — to see him through the fog.

It takes strength I don't have not to cry. I've given away too much already. I've had my power stolen numerous times. Too many men have taken from me.

Will is completely feral behind me with his fingers gripping at my naked hips. He's a second away from entering my body. From stealing what isn't his.

I flare.

It's enough to go from flame to fire.

I hide the disgust in my voice alongside my heart. "Kiss me. Kiss me before you kill me — *please.*"

A flicker of apprehension is quickly replaced with greedy lust as he pulls me up and brings me into his arms, all while smirking down at me. Disgust covers my skin as his hands slip into my hair, into the space saved for Luca.

I imagine Luca's fingers caressing me, standing by me as his sultry voice urges me forward, willing me to be strong.

Will tips my chin, his breath hot against my cheek. "Beg me again."

I sway in his arms. The drug under my tongue has completely melted now and in a few minutes I'll fall back into the void where time doesn't exist, and I won't be safe there. I'll still feel everything except the fury I need to survive.

No more. I have no more for him to take.

I look up at the man who had once been my refuge, who I had once thought of as my savior. "Will, kiss me. *Please.*"

"I love when they beg," he groans, leaning down into me, stealing my space as his eyes flutter closed.

I watch him as our lips touch. His are wet, warm, and disgustingly familiar as they slide over my mouth, but it doesn't matter. I've bought myself the time even if it's fleeting. As fleeting as the heartbeat that's supposed to stay in my chest that has now moved into my ears.

I pull him closer, urging my lips to move so they don't freeze and give me away.

"This won't save you," he chuckles darkly against my cold lips.

He tries to shove his tongue into my mouth, but I pull back. I watch his eyes widen before hardening into a glare.

I smile. "I know. But this will," the tip of the knife plunges into the bottom of his stomach. I thrust once with the palm of my hand and watch as the realization hits him. A gurgled cry of surprise falls around us as he begins to tumble slowly.

"You... you bitch!" he hisses.

A sharp laugh slips between my swollen lips as I watch him go, with his disgusting cock hanging between his fly. Delirious, I follow him, smacking his hands away that reach for the steak knife lodged in his flesh.

Blood pours and pours until it covers the both of us. It's the first warm thing I've felt in days, and it offers a soothing clarity to my frozen mind. I sigh into the heat before twisting the knife half an inch to the right.

Before we fall, I grab his elbow and with all the strength I have left I force him back into his chair. The knife is out by my hands, followed by a spurt of blood that splashes across my dress.

So warm.

Will screams as I slide the knife back into his skin, feeling the serrated edge tug across the layers of his flesh. I twist once more until I feel resistance and then dig deeper.

A strangled groan slips between his disgusting lips. More blood pools between us, sticking between my fingers. I twist again, just to feel the air return to my lungs. I can breathe fully for the first time in weeks.

I don't want to stop. I feel the desire blooming to prolong his pain for as long as possible, but my body is growing weak, and I have no choice but to stop. Taking my seat, I pull my glass of wine to my lips and reward myself by watching him struggle to contain his injuries.

Self-preservation tells him to pull the knife out and he does. It tells him to cover the wounds and he obliges. But it doesn't tell him that his injuries are too severe to fight. I've tore through his guts and shredded them and soon they'll fail to function and all that will be left of him is a puddle of congealed blood.

Self-preservation is a bitch like that.

CHAPTER ELEVEN

Luca Caruso

We're in the dark, under the solid cover of black as we stalk through the tree lines, following the muted light up ahead. There are five teams around the perimeter, quietly relaying information to each other as they don their gear and ski masks. I only see them through the one night-vision lens across my right eye.

We're monsters in the dark. Sizing up our prey.

"Twenty around the edge. Ten outside the house," Theo's voice pulls my eyes from the old hotel up ahead. "Heat signal in the house from the drone has another five but could be staff. Act with precaution."

I glower over at him and click my earpiece. "Everyone aside from Olivia Heart is to be killed. We burn this place down in the next hour. No exceptions. Anyone tries to escape, shoot them on sight."

"Damn right," Bones mutters, sliding on his gloves. "Smartest order you've given yet."

"Understood, sir," one of Theo's men mutters down into my ear.

Theo catches my eye. "There could be women in there."

I don't recognize my own voice now that it's slipped into the empty. "Women that haven't tried to help her."

Chen joins us, sliding a gun into my hand with a silencer. It's cool in my hands and heavy with purpose and filled with bullets ready for Adler's skull. I take a look at the man I've considered a friend and see the stitches across his face. If we get Olivia out of this unscathed, I'll apologize for my mistake.

"If you don't like it then stay here and go back to your wife," I say to Theo, taking off the safety.

"You know I'm not leaving you. Not now, you selfish son of a bitch," he's pissed as he dons his mask, pulling it over his pretty boy-face, and disappears into the shadows before he decides to headbutt me again.

"Sir," Chen steps forward with a bow, "Theo's teams will control the outside, clearing the path for us to get into the building. Once we get inside—"

I cut him off. "Only you and I are to go in, Chen."

"Not a fucking chance," Bones snaps, stepping over a fallen tree to join us. "We're all going in, Caruso. This is on all of us, at least give us the chance to make it right."

I'm in his face before he has the chance to blink. My hands wrap around the collar of his jacket as I yank him forward. "I'll give you this but as soon as she's safe I want you gone."

His scarred mouth breaks out into a sneer. "I'll leave when Olivia tells me to, and not a god damn second before."

Every rotten part of me itches to punch the teeth to the back of his throat, but I still hold enough respect for him to ignore the urges. He cares for Olivia; they all do. And even though they've fucked up, they're still willing to put their lives on the line for her. I'd be a hypocrite to not recognize it.

I had given them an out when she left but they refused. Their loyalty was still with her — I had to respect that whether I liked it or not.

"Do your fucking job and stay out of my way," I snap, pushing him away from me. Dante steps out of the shadows, resting a hand on my shoulder.

He squeezes once. "It's time to move."

So we do. We watch the power fade from every outside light surrounding the derelict hotel. Wait for the outside guards to call in for the power to be checked over their radios, and then we move.

We slip from the trees, ghosting through the hip length grass straight down the middle as Theo's team flanks our sides — aiming their night vision lenses and weapons at Olivia's jailors.

I breathe my first deep breath as they begin to fall, one by one in silence.

Other than the beating of my heart and the alarm of revenge ringing in my ears, we stay undetected.

We hang in the shadows, waiting for the two guards at the door to fall. They were hovering over a phone, laughing at the tiny screen, unaware of the carnage around them.

I watched, biding my time and pushing down my disgust for their jovial attitude. They didn't give a shit to the suffering in the building just behind them. They probably enjoyed hearing Olivia's screams, seeing the life in her eyes fade as their boss tortured her.

I blink into the rage. Feel it harden my skin and strengthen my desire for bloodshed. Nothing else matters but turning into the untouchable savage Olivia needs.

The guard holding the phone throws his head back and laughs. The first bullet in my gun pierces his throat, stopping the heinous act from going any further.

Chen took out the left guard who tried to scramble for his earpiece just in time.

"Clear." It was a simple word that echoed into all of us. I moved ahead, forgetting the team as I raced up the steps and kicked in the door.

It splintered away from the frame and fell onto the carpeted hallway. Silence and the subzero temperatures slide across my skin, but I barely register the place now that I *feel* the pulse of her in this hell.

I would feel Olivia anywhere and right now she was the heart of this old decrepit building—but it's beat was slowing, giving up.

"Left," Chen whispered. "Two heat sources. But one's fading."

I pause, turning to look at him—the man that had been by my side this whole time. His facial expression sets alarm bells ringing.

Dante and Chen step to me, holding out their hands as if to stop me from destroying every part of this hotel until I found her.

"Prepare yourself, Luca," Theo warns with a voice tight with pain.

"I have to find her."

My gun remained useless in my hand as I ran left into a dark hallway, kicking open doors every two feet. Anyone could be waiting for me, aiming their weapon to shoot me dead but I didn't care.

A. L. Hartwell

"Stop," Theo suddenly slammed me into the wall with his shoulder, throwing himself in front of the door I was just about to open "Let me go first, Luca. Let me make sure—"

With a snarl and my gun aimed at his head I motioned for him to move.

"Move out of my way."

My voice was loud enough to let Adler know that I was here and now I had ruined our element of surprise.

Fuck.

"I'll let this slide, Luca, but put a gun to my ahead again and I'm taking your kneecaps."

Theo shifts quickly and allows me through, but he aims his gun over my shoulder—protecting his asshole of a best friend even when he doesn't deserve it.

A trickle of nerves were my first warning that I wasn't prepared. My hand gripped the handle and I push it open. The room was only lit with candles, hundreds of them, glaring flames into my retinas.

This was hell.

I took one step, felt my shoes squash against the damp carpet before the stench of blood hit my nostrils.

By the window, bathed in moonlight, Olivia sits at the head of the table, staring through me—vacantly with a hollowness I had never felt before.

My heart stops. Time stops along with it. Even the men desperate to get into the room freeze behind me.

She blinks once and I feel the band around my lungs loosen a little.

She's alive.

Another tender step and I feel my throat closing. "Olivia…"

Blood coats her, clinging to her beautiful skin like war paint. I fight a hiss between my teeth at the blue gown hanging off her
106

body. I'm certain it's one of Katrina's signature creations, with a train that's wrapped around one side of the table. The gown acts as a vase, collecting her victim's blood as if she was preparing him for a sacrifice to the gods.

Her chest barely rises as I approach. There's no blush across her cheeks, no lick of her lips, no gentle sigh. There's nothing to tell me she knows I'm here and she's safe.

I call to her again. "Olivia."

A gurgle pulls me away from her. Her victim and soon to be mine, William Adler, slumps against his chair, his hands slowly gripping at wounds covering the bottom of his stomach. He barely has enough strength to turn to face me. but when he does, he knows it's over.

I see the fear flash in his eyes before he fills the room with his sick laugh.

The air is suddenly hot and dense, too thick to focus on anything but pulverizing him to a million pieces so he cannot make another noise.

"Welcome to the party," he grins, congealed blood spilling between his teeth.

CHAPTER TWELVE

Theodore Belmont

I'd watched my wife's hand lovingly hand-stitch the gown that clings to Olivia's body. I remember walking into her studio, desperate to see her, catching her humming a soft tune under her breathe as she stitched the low-cut neckline into place against the bodice with all the love in the world.

With a bright smile, she pulled the material to her chest and asked me, "What do you think?"

"I think it's beautiful."

She rolls her eyes before focusing back on the gown. "You always say that."

"Because it's the truth, mon amour. Everything you stitch is made stunning by your hands."

A smile tugs at the corner of her lips. My flattery is winning her over and she knows that, even as she tries to remain angry at me.

We had fought this morning for the first time in months over something as stupid as how much she was working while pregnant. But after much time wallowing in my office, I realized that it's not work to her. It's her passion and I never want to be the person to kill that.

Placing a kiss on her cheek, I take the stool next to her.

"Who's this for?" I ask her, eyeing up the sketch on the table.

She looks up at me, light dancing in her eyes. My wife loves when I ask about her work. "William Adler. He's requested it for his new lady friend," she wiggles her eyebrows suggestively.

Ah. The millionaire media tycoon who had been the first to support Katrina's career when she was so new to the fashion industry was now cashing in his favor.

"Why can't he pick a gown at your charity event?"

She frowns, worried about where I'm going with this. "He needed something more urgently and I had a little spare time."

She didn't. She barely has time to eat, never mind hand-stitching a gown, and that pisses me off more than anything in this world. Having her healthy is my top priority, but I bite my tongue. Now is not the time to piss off my hormonal wife — again.

"Olivia," Luca pulls me away from the memory of my wife to the room full of blood and secrets. "It's me... Luca. Please talk to me, tell me that you're okay."

She looks through him until she lands on Bones who's making his way over, holding out his jacket for her. It'll bury her. Even though we had access to her via a camera it didn't show us the true extent of her weight loss. Of the color that's disappeared from her cheeks.

It's far more severe up close.

Adler between us chokes out a cough, clutching to his guts that are seeping between the torn muscles in his stomach. Olivia turns at the sound, showing me a flash of red dripping steadily from her ear. Burst eardrum? Drugs? Shock?

"She doesn't want you," Adler gasps with a psychotic huff. "She doesn't want anyone. How do you still not get it?"

Luca takes a step back and grabs Adler by the back of the neck, dragging him up to his height. Walking him over to Olivia, he forces Adler to his knees.

I see the muscles in his shoulders tense. The tick in his jaw to unleash violence on anyone that dares enter his space. It's the Luca I knew before his father had died — the man that had no qualms about dishing out pain.

"Olivia. I'm going to make this last for as long as you need," he tells her, practically begging. "I'll hurt him in every way possible until he screams for your mercy and only you will have the power to end this. Do you understand?"

Olivia stands slowly, testing her body's strength before finally looking at Luca. The light catches her collarbone where the dress gapes open. Bruises cast across her skin, deep in shades of green and blue.

Adler falls in and out of consciousness between them, and my pulse thunders to speed this up. We don't have much time and I agree with Luca, Adler must pay for his sins.

I nod to Chen and Bones, silently telling them to prepare the next stage.

"Make it last," she whispers to him, finally. "Make him feel it all."

CHAPTER THIRTEEN

Olivia Heart

E yes full of shadows keep my feet on the ground. They stop me from floating above my body and back into the clouds that have offered me safety on many occasions.

I feel him watching me, forcing me to stay with him like a weighted blanket.

"I love you Olivia," he tells me, while pushing Adler back down into his seat. My heart thuds lazily in my chest, not responding to his declaration, not being able to work its way around the drugs. He doesn't see that I have no control.

Luca doesn't drop his gaze, sensing that once he does, I might slip away right in front of him. He's always been good at reading my face and knowing what I needed before I did, that hasn't changed. "I'm going to fix this. I'm going to fix you. I swear to it."

Fix us. That's what I hear.

A bubble settles in the middle of my chest, threatening to pop at the conviction in his voice. What if I'm unfixable? I sway on the spot, waiting for him to prove that what we have is salvageable even when my heart warns it's not.

Chen and Bones begin packing Adler's wounds with napkins from the table, sealing the material into his body with

111

duct tape. Red and Rum move forward together, injecting Adler repeatedly with needles full of black liquid, but he doesn't cry out or thrash, he simply glares at me.

"It's a mix of adrenaline and a nerve agent," Dante comes at me from the right side of the table. His voice travels over the sound of the duct tape. It's much louder than Luca's voice. "It will keep him alive for as long as you need."

"Fuck!" Adler groans while Chen tapes his hands to the chair, earning a backhand from Bones.

Luca moves away from me with fervor until he stands above Adler, towering over him with murderous intent. I had prayed for this moment over and over again, willed Luca to burst through the doors of my cell and make Adler pay for all that he's done. And I'd cried so many tears when he didn't come. And now that he's here, it doesn't feel real—it just hurts.

I'm still waiting for this version to pop and for Adler to be standing over me, ready to kill me. How many sheets did he slip under my tongue this time? Was this all just a safety mechanism my brain has concocted to protect me one last time?

The sound of revenge pulls me from my spiral. "What was the first thing he did to you, Olivia?"

Dante grips my hand and brings me to Luca. He side-eyes me, careful not to linger for too long, and I understand why. It's the monster standing at my side, not Luca Caruso, the man who made love to me surrounded by butterflies and told me in Paris that I own his heart.

"He- he slapped me."

I didn't get to tell him where before Luca backhanded Adler so hard that he spat a tooth across the dining room.

"Fuck you!" Adler snarls, spitting blood at me. "You deserved everything you got, you stuck up bitch."

The venom in Luca's voice protects me. "Second thing he did, Olivia?"

"Stripped me," I tell him, my hands shaking around Dante's.

Bones and Chen step forward, slashing at Adler's blood-sodden clothes with viciousness to rival Luca's tone. They don't care that they catch his skin, or that he screams for them to stop. All they care about is the deliverance of revenge.

Dante is next, using his hip to prop me up. "What was the third, Olivia?"

"He made me crawl... outside."

Luca's whole body hardens into stone.

Adler made me crawl naked across the pebbled driveway in front of his men, and if I stopped, he would grab me by the hair and drag me back to the start until I was breathless, sobbing for him to let me go.

Luca snaps, pulling a serrated knife from the inside of his jacket and plunging it quickly into Adler's right knee cap. Adler howls, his body bowing upwards while my guards hold him down into his seat.

"You're not so big now, are you?" Red hisses into his ear as he plunges another needle into the crook of his neck. "Don't go slipping out on us just yet."

I can't help myself. I lick my lips, tasting the blood in the air, wanting to devour the personalized karma Luca's creating just for me.

"More adrenalin," Luca growls. Theo comes up from behind Adler and jams another needle into the side of his neck. Our eyes catch and he nods once before standing back to let the men around me continue.

A spitfire laugh erupts from Adler. "Keep going, Olivia. Tell them everything that I did to you. Don't spare anyone's feelings. They're all dying to know what a fucking attention seeking slut you are!"

A shaky breath slips through my cold lips—he had said those words over and over when he dished out his punishments. I was an attention seeking slut, but he never quite realized even if that had been true, I would never have wanted his undivided attention.

I'd rather die.

I hold out my hand, stopping Luca from sticking the knife in his other knee cap. In only takes a second to feel his heat against my skin. Blood rushes through my veins towards the spot, rejoicing in the familiarity.

He feels it too. I see the strength it takes for him to look at me and not flinch. I'm not pretty being this gaunt or pale. My body isn't perfect anymore with its cuts, bruises, and welts. And I'm weaker than I have ever been.

And it hurts him to see me this way.

But it's the guilt hidden beneath the surface of his anger that starts to eat at me. I feel its teeth nibbling away at the frail tissue around my heart. Suddenly I worry that it might collapse in on itself—just when I have him back.

"He doesn't get to win," I breathlessly tell him, "he doesn't get any more of me. Or you. Finish this."

His face twists with pain—fighting his desire to serve me, or his, revenge. Those dark eyes that hold many more avenues to pain flicker from me to Adler until he makes a decision.

"Bones," his voice is tight. "Give me your knife."

"Thought you would never ask." Bones steps from the shadows of the room and hands Luca a knife made for gutting. Each edge holds four-inch teeth that curve at the tip, perfect for a relentless ending.

It glints viciously against the candlelight as Luca moves.

"Is that all you got?" Adler snarls, spitting at his feet. "A knife? Here's me thinking the great Luca Caruso would have a unique torture method."

The dark, closer to black smirk that takes over his face forces me to take a step back. I had dealt with Luca's rage firsthand before, even been at the mercy of it, but I had never seen this side of him.

He's all darkness. Dark eyes full of sin and retribution. His smirk is his own deadly weapon as he approaches his target.

My heart pounds to speed up the burning of the toxin in my blood. It wants me to be clear-headed to see this. But could I handle this on top of everything else? I can already feel the waning of my energy and soon my mind will follow.

What if I don't come back?

Luca, what if I don't come back? I want to scream at him.

Luca moves at my right, placing the knife into the flame of a candle that sits on the table, all while keeping his prey in his sight.

"It must hurt knowing that she could never love you," he says calmly.

"Love? You think someone like *her* is capable of love?" Adler spits at me, spraying my dress with blood. "I've never been stupid to think she could. The moment her parents died so did her capability to feel emotion." He laughs as his words sear into my chest. "She became nothing but a self-righteous, prick teasing bitch. Does that answer your question, Caruso?"

Luca nods thoughtfully, twisting the knife into the flame and into my heart. The silver glints blue under the light with every moment the heat licks across its surface. "You sound bitter."

"Bitter? You have no fucking idea," Adler chuckles, spitting up clots of blood that slide from the corner of his mouth and land on his naked thighs.

"I think I do." Luca moves the knife away from the flame. "I think you've always been obsessed with her, and having her made it worse. Didn't it?" he pauses to look at me once. A flicker of jealousy passes through his cold eyes. "Look, there's no judgment here—I'm not exactly innocent when it comes to wanting her either."

Bones grunts with disgust, glaring over at Luca.

"It feels like your blood is on fire and nothing will ever put it out; you're dying the slowest of deaths when you don't have her attention. It brutalizes you, hardens you to everything and everyone because they can't give you what she can. I know what it's like to feel bitter because I lived it for eight years."

I stumble forward, preparing to slap my hand around Luca's mouth when Dante holds me back. Chen joins Dante and takes my other elbow, giving me a light squeeze. But I can't focus on Chen's strange connection, or why it feels so right to have him by my side.

Luca moves so that he's behind Adler and places a hand on his shoulder. He doesn't see me anymore, he's too busy holding himself back enough that he doesn't kill Adler too quickly.

He wants this on his terms.

"She got so far under my skin that I'm certain if I carve away at myself now, I'll find her name etched into my bones," a dark chuckle fills the space. Even Adler has nothing to say to that declaration.

"Stop," I whisper. Scalding tears fall freely down my face. "Luca, please."

He ignores me. "I went to extreme lengths to get her. I stole her privacy, ended a life she was trying to build, and cut her away from the people she loved. So trust me when I tell you I know what it's like to be bitter."

He finally looks at me and I wish he hadn't. His eyes narrow, his pupils blow out as he tracks every single mark, bruise and injury across my face and body. I watch as he absorbs it all and places everything on his shoulders.

"Especially when she fought me, threw dirt on my intentions, when she tried to leave me..." he pulls in a breath before gritting his teeth and squaring his shoulders, "but I could never do what you did. Even I, a bastard who has a spot reserved in hell, couldn't stomach to do this to her. If she decided she didn't want me, I'd have sooner taken myself out of the equation than hurt her like this."

No.

Please stop.

"Luca," I fight forward, tripping in the heels that are too high. I need him to stop. I can't take the thought of my life without Luca. I can't. I won't.

Dante swoops down, catching me in his arms before I can fall to the ground. He's too strong and warm, with his mouth by my ear. "Watch Olivia, you need to see this to be able to let go."

And I do.

I snap my head back up to find Luca waiting for me, the scorching knife at Adler's neck, burning through his skin.

Adler's eyes widen, bulging out of his head, but he doesn't have the energy to scream. There's too much pain for his body to handle, and blood loss... well there's enough covering me to prove his time is short.

"If the last thing I do for you, Olivia, is honor a promise I made, then so be it." With a ruthless slice he cuts into Adler's neck, his eyes never leaving mine.

CHAPTER FOURTEEN

Luca Caruso

Like I had promised her hours ago, Adler's head was placed at her feet. It had been a jagged cut, not one that I would ever be proud of — the motherfucker didn't want to leave his body — but with a snap and another slice he became nothing but brutalized flesh. And at my hand he was gone.

Olivia didn't look to her feet for relief, nor did she try and remove Dante and Chen's grips from her arms. Her beautiful green eyes, with blown-out pupils, stayed on me, searching for something I couldn't see.

"Take a seat," her voice slipped into the silence, so delicate and fragile. I hear the tears in her throat and feel the shake in her hands even a foot away.

"All of you, take a seat," her voice is unusually high and breathy, like she cannot catch her breath.

A panic attack.

"Olivia," I call to her, willing the light to return to her eyes. "Take a deep breath for me, okay?"

She only manages to pull in air. "Take a god damn seat!" she hisses, baring her teeth.

Dante drops his voice as he lets her go, stepping over a puddle of blood. "Okay, Olivia, we'll take a seat." He looks at

118

her with fear, his eyes flickering from her frail mental state to us.

Move, he tells me. *Take a fucking seat, now.*

My feet move of their own accord, taking the seat next to the one Dante places her in. I stare at her, swallowing the painful changes under the glow of tiny flames. She's willowy in the gown that hangs from her shoulders and the dark blue silk highlights the greying of her skin. Her teeth chatter and her hands shake, but it's the lack of warmth around her that steals my breath for good. She looks an hour away from death.

I don't have time.

I need to get her out of here.

Everyone has taken their seats. Chen and Theo sit on either side of Adler who drains messily across the table, but neither of them is fazed by his death. If anything, they are put out that they didn't get to join in.

"Are they dead?" she looks straight ahead at Bones, of all people.

"Yes," I tell her before he can. I need to her to want my voice, to find strength in the control I have now that she's safe. "There's more of us outside, they're clearing away the bodies as we speak. You can leave here without fear."

Whatever has happened. I can fix it. I can fix you. I'll do whatever it takes. I just need to get you out of here.

"They can't hurt you anymore. He can't hurt you anymore." I swallow my pain "I made sure of that, Olivia."

She sucks in a shaky breath as her eyes dart to the man whose blood coats her precious skin, but she doesn't cry — she's past tears and rage. Olivia has helped take the life of another and nothing can prepare you for it. I've been where she is and it's nothing but a sinking pit of endless confusion for your first kill.

But I won't let her sink for what she needed to do to survive. And if she lets me, I'll remind her every single day that she did the world a fucking favor ridding it of him.

My thoughts are wild as I trace the blood covering her delicate fingers. Even though he's in the pits of hell he's still marking her skin with his violence. It sparks an animalistic urge to bathe her in my own blood, marking her with me instead of the piece of shit at my side.

I reach out to take her hand but pull back when she flinches. "Good, that's good," she shrinks away, wrapping her arms around her tiny waist where I can't get to them.

"Now listen, all of you. I only have a few minutes left before I fall," her hand slips up to her chest, hovering over her heart. She taps it twice with her index finger.

What's wrong with your heart, Olivia?

Tap, tap.

"We need to get you to a hospital," Theo offers kindly, stealing away my thoughts as he eyes up the dress on her body. He's noticed it too, the dress that was made by his wife's hands. I see the urgency to remove Olivia from the dress and to return to his pregnant wife who no doubt will be horrified that her gown had been used in this way.

"No," she rounds on him with eyes full of fire. "No hospitals. No doctors. No more pills. Do not take me to a hospital because they'll ask questions and right now, I don't trust myself to answer them."

Dante tries to soothe her. "But you're not well, Olivia, and we can answer them for you."

"I'll fall asleep. Like always," she mutters, waving him off. "I'll be fine when I wake up. I'm always fine, just don't take me to a hospital."

Tap, tap.

How many times had this happened? How many times had she been force-fed pills before she fell? How many fucking times!?

"Chen," she chokes out his name, as if it pains her. "Before I go, did-did he put a hit on my aunt when he first took me?"

I'm the *he*. And I'm in fucking trouble.

Chen doesn't look at me, but I sense his loyalty to me balancing on a fine edge between what's right and wrong. I feel the indecision radiating from under his suit. Fuck, we all feel it.

I nod at him, giving him the permission he needs to let go.

"Not a hit Olivia... it was a plan B in case things went south. It was only supposed to be used as a threat. We..." Chen's eyes cast to me in apology, "he wouldn't have done it."

"Ah fuck," Theo buries his head in his hands. "Fuck, fuck, fuck."

For the longest second, she doesn't move or make it known that she's heard him at all. I stare at her side profile, willing her to look at me. She blinks once before offering him a small nod.

Olivia rubs a bloodied hand against her chest, soothing the wound that's opening beneath her skin because of me.

"And the tests?" she groans, pinching her collarbone to stop herself from falling asleep.

"Tests?" it's my voice that cuts through the tension.

"*Chen,*" she bites out, ignoring me. "The tests... was it to check my fertility? Was that plan C, to trap me if I didn't give in?"

Theo glowers my way. "Jesus *Christ,* Luca. What the hell have you done!?"

Panic has me by the throat and balls, but it spurs me into action. I lurch forward, ready to grab her in my arms, but before I can, I feel the tip of a fork grazing my adams apple. She was prepared for me. Even while fighting to stay awake she knew my next move before I did.

A true fighter.

"Answer me, Chen," her eyes are on him when she presses it with enough pressure to draw a drop of blood. "Now."

"Olivia..." his eyes are as wide as saucers, much like the rest of the men who watch her steal back her power. And even with my life in her hands, I can't blame her. She can have it all, everything, even my death if it will make any of this better.

I deserve the fork to plunge into my throat. To die the same way Adler did, by her decision. Because what makes me any different from him? I've stolen her, forced her into captivity, threatened her and placed ultimatums over her head...

"It's fine," I snarl as the tip digs in further. "Tell her the truth."

Dante shakes his head quickly always trying to save me. "No, Chen. Not right now —"

He cuts Dante off, "Yes, it's true."

My lies bleed out finally. I am nothing but a lying, deceitful bastard who did everything and anything to get Olivia, and now she knows. Now she knows that I was never to be trusted and her instincts about me where always right.

Her hatred blooms as the tip digs further in. I feel the pinch and know with one single push up she could end me for good.

"So many lies," she whispers to herself, but I hear the meaning behind her softly spoken words. I hear the door slam on me for good. "Right to my face—like I was never strong enough to handle all of the truth."

"Olivia," I want to tell her I'm sorry, to get on my god damn knees and beg for forgiveness, but she keeps me pinned to my seat with a quick look of resentment.

"So many options for my future but none of that included what I wanted." She sighs, shaking her head. "I'm running out of time," with a dismissive shake of her head, she drops the fork into my lap—forgetting me as she speaks to the room next. "When I go, I need you to burn this place to the ground. Not an inch is to be left. Not a single file or brick can be salvageable. Do you understand?" she holds up a shaky hand as Chen opens his mouth, "and then you call the police about the bodies under it," her voice slows with every word. "Lead them to the shallow graves. You all need to get them out of there, do you understand? And then you point everything at that piece of shit there. You owe me the courtesy of following my request. All of you owe me the courtesy of getting those women home."

I can't think of the shallow graves underneath our feet. Can't think about how close she may have been to joining them. So I look to her.

"Olivia, we need to get you out of here first. You're barely breathing. Your lips are turning blue. We can talk about—" my voice is not the one she wants to hear. She stands and teeters away in her heels, towards the end of the table, dragging her bloodied dress across the carpet and over Adler's head.

She stumbles once as the train of her dress snags on Adler's chair. Red holds out his arm to protect her, but she slips by until she's before Bones.

I feel our connection fraying as she makes her choice.

"And one last thing," her hand goes to the table for support.

Bruises and welts across her back have me on my feet, closing the distance she's put before us. They're fresh. I know that much by how pink they are against her skin. I fight the urge to claw out my eyes and settle on getting her to look at me instead.

I need her to need me again. She must let me make this right.

123

"Anything," Bones nods his head as he assesses her with wild eyes. "Anything you need, Olivia. You have my word."

They are my words that fall from his lips.

"When I fall asleep don't let him touch me. Don't let him touch me…"

She looks over her shoulder and our eyes meet. There is no fire, no electricity, and no love left in her for me. She's an empty vessel running on drugs and survival.

My heart breaks into two ragged parts. Never to piece back together the same.

"Don't let Luca touch me."

And we all watch as she falls into a puddle of blue and red.

Chapter Fifteen

Luca Caruso

Don't let Luca touch me'

Don't. Let. Luca. Touch. Me.

Her hatred for me is all I hear as I watch Bones scoop her up from the floor, being careful to support her neck as he takes her away from this rotten place. I follow their every step, watching her, assessing her—becoming her guard instead of her lover.

My savagery had cracked wide open the moment I saw her and now I'm exposed to it all. I feel every mark on her skin, every welt across her back, and every shallow breath she struggles to make.

I feel the ache of her guards who help get her into the back of the car. They surround her with their heads low, wishing silently for her forgiveness for failing her so miserably.

Neither of us deserve her.

It's all too much.

Exhaustion adds its weights to my limbs, and I sink. "Where are you taking her?" my voice lifts over the silence, hovering like a rain cloud ready to burst.

Theo turns to me first. "They're going to a hotel a few miles away. We'll have her checked over there."

Bones shifts Olivia on his lap, cradling her in his arms, painfully reminding me of the first time he handed her over to me. I'd been so aggressive, so demanding to be the only person to touch her that I had snatched her from him like a petulant child.

He sweeps her hair from her face before accepting a blanket from Red. I had pictured this moment differently so many times, but it never ended with Bones being the one she needed.

"She's going to be okay," It's Dante's voice that seeps its way into my ears before his hand lands on my shoulder, "she'll come back from this. You'll see."

"I was supposed to be the one she needed. It was supposed to be me."

Nobody says a word until I move to get into the car. I won't touch her, but I'll be by her side. I won't let my eyes leave her until she's ready to talk to me.

Even now, I'm arrogant enough to still have hope. I could laugh, but the sound of my own mirth may just tip me over the edge into insanity, and I was no fucking good to her there.

Bones glares but doesn't deny me. Maybe the bastard feels sorry for me. Or the look of pure destruction is so obvious across my face it's enough to satisfy him. I take my seat by them, allowing a slip of air between my tight lips.

"Keep your hands to yourself," he warns me with a touch to the knife back in his belt, "or I'll cut them off."

"You don't need to remind me." I look down at her bloodied face that's cuddled into his chest. "I just need to be by her side."

The door behind me slams shut and I'm only half-aware of the teams moving around the property, preparing to remedy Olivia's wishes.

"Stop feeling sorry for yourself, Caruso," his gravelly voice fills the car as Red pulls us away. "You're not the fucking victim here."

Hatred swarms in my chest like a thousand wasps. "I'm aware of who the real victim is, Bones. I don't need you to remind me," I snap, leaning forward to bury my head in my hands. Fuck, I'm exhausted.

I hear him shift her so he can wrap the blanket around her. "Keep a hold of that awareness, Caruso. If she opens her eyes tomorrow and tells you to leave her alone, you'll do just that. If she tells you to plunge a knife into your fucking heart, then have the good grace to do it quick. But if by some miracle she needs you after all this, then you better be strong enough to fix it—to fix her—otherwise it'll be me that puts a knife through your chest."

I look up and catch Red's severe stare in the mirror before looking at Bones.

Bones continues now that he has my attention. "And trust me, the same goes for me, too. If she cannot forgive me for letting her get taken away, then I'll die by the same knife. Understand?"

The code. Their moral code that keeps them so tightly together had been tested many times by the woman that he holds so tightly to his body, but he loves her enough to forgo their rules. Not like I do. He loves her like a friend he's known his whole life. Like she's his family—I think. Shit, I hope.

"She's forgiven you," I tell him with distaste. It fills my mouth and I all but swallow it back. "She went straight to you."

"She hasn't forgiven me for shit," he laughs, probably enjoying my pain. "She just knows that I wouldn't dare refuse her demands... not after—" he doesn't finish.

He doesn't have to. He's right, of course he is.

****

They take us to a hotel, bypassing the check-in with a quick drop of my name, and several suites are opened for us. A female doctor called Lydia Evernight is brought in to assess Olivia, hooking her up to several machines and needles. She's an old friend of Katrina's, but it doesn't make it any easier watching a stranger disappear into the room Olivia's in and being refused entry.

I pace outside her door, listening to my earpiece as Theo's team begins dismantling Adler's operation. Veen has stepped in to destroy evidence, hard drives, and Dante is confident that there's nothing that can be traced back to us at all.

But there's still the threat of public exposure, so a team has been dispatched to Adler's head office to wipe away any remnants of the scandalous articles he had created.

Dante's voice echoes in my ear, "How is she?" I stop to glance at the door.

"Malnourished, exhausted, and withdrawing from high doses of antipsychotics, but still alive."

He sucks in a breath. "Her heart?"

Broken.

"I don't know," I tell him, even when it takes every bit of restraint to not walk into her room and demand the doctor tell me everything. "I'm waiting for the doctor to come out."

"Was she... you know, did that motherfucker...?"

Pain, excruciating pain drags its nails into my flesh at the one question I had been hiding from. I remember her screams, remember them like she's still screaming in my ear now.

"I don't know." It's all I can manage but every word is a knife to my chest, gouging its way deeper into my soul. "Dante, I don't fucking know."

Dr. Evernight steps out of the door, quietly closing it behind her, "Mr. Caruso."

I click off my earpiece, shutting Dante out before he can finish his sentence.

"Is she awake?"

"Yes, but just," she tells me as she snaps off her gloves "I've given her something to reverse the drugs, but it'll be a few hours before she's thinking a little clearer."

There's no sympathy in Dr. Evernight's eyes, just silent accusations, and I'm not sure if they're aimed at me. Does she think I did this? Tortured Olivia until I nearly broke her?

"And everything else?"

She sighs, "The welts on her back have been treated and should heal in a few days. Her left eardrum has been damaged so her hearing will be impaired a few weeks until it heals. As for the weight she's lost, it isn't as severe as it looks but she'll need to be put on a treatment plan to ensure a careful recovery. And for her other injuries..."

Vomit rises to my throat, threatening to ruin the plush carpet beneath our feet. Sensing I'm about to lose the contents of my stomach, Dr. Evernight steps forward and presses a reassuring hand to my arm.

"Whoever did this to her didn't get that far, Mr. Caruso. From what she told me–us, she stopped him just before he could. The injuries I was talking about was more of the mental capacity. I'm not an expert in that field, but I would say from her injuries that she's been through a lot and will need help processing her ordeal."

I rip my hand away from the doctor, needing to get away from her kindness, needing air... needing to see Olivia so that I can assess her injuries myself.

"I'm sorry," she tells me. "I can see this is hard on you."

Hard doesn't begin to cover it but I don't deserve her pity. I don't deserve to be in the same building as Olivia, mind some stranger's compassion.

"You look exhausted," her voice drops. "Maybe you should get some rest, Mr. Caruso. I'll be checking in on Mrs. Caruso throughout the night, so you don't need to worry. If it'll help, I can prescribe you with a sleeping aide?"

"No," I shake my head. "I need to wait here until she's ready."

I'll wait until she wants to see me.

"Wait, what about her heart?" I ask just as the doctor turns to be with Olivia and Bones. "She was muttering about her heart and tapping her chest."

Dr. Evernight softens a touch, the corner of her mouth turning up in a slight smile. "Her heart is surprisingly still healthy and strong. The... discomfort she was experiencing was from panic attacks. It would have been her body's way of trying to let the brain know that she was in danger."

I have no energy for anything else but a simple nod. Turning away from her, I sink into the chair I pulled up from the door and drop my head into my hands.

"Fuck."

CHAPTER SIXTEEN

Olivia Heart

She's sleeping."

"I know that. I just want to see her. Is she still covered in his blood?"

"No."

"Does she need anything?"

"Just for you to leave her alone, Caruso. It's that simple."

"Fuck you, Bones."

The conversation has been on repeat every hour on the hour, like a bad record playing over and over again. I've listened to them argue outside of the door, and every time, Bones wins. But I never say anything when he returns, nor do I thank him for keeping Luca out of the room. I just stare at the wall of my warm hotel room with the covers up to my chin, waiting for sleep to take me.

I'd barely managed a shower after Dr. Evernight had pumped me with an IV to begin clearing out the toxins in my system. Woozy on my feet, I had to cling to every surface until I was safe under the water. Bones stood outside, shouting every two minutes, threatening to come in if I didn't reply.

"You good?" Bones steps into the room, pulling off his belt full of numerous weaponries.

I sip the warm tea that was left at my bedside before answering. My swallow nudges a pain in my jaw, up to my ear. I wince, "I can't hear out of my left ear."

He nods "Burst eardrum. It'll come back in a few weeks."

"He punched me." I don't know why I tell him. He probably already knows, but I'm worried that if I keep this to myself, I'll internalize my pain.

Taking his seat on the edge of my bed, he's careful not to intrude in my space. He watched carefully while Dr. Evernight cleaned numerous wounds and wrapped them with bandages. One false move and I was certain he would have her out of my space and in a headlock before I could blink.

I'm pretty certain by the shake of her hand she felt it too.

"He can't hurt you anymore, Olivia. You made sure of it by getting us enough time to get to you. You stabbing him was the best thing you could have done in that situation."

I did stab him—my fingers still recognize the feeling of the deep slide penetrating the muscles of his stomach before it met with resistance. I remember the flash of warm blood dripping down the blade, tainting my hands, and the look of fear as Adler realized he was done for.

"It's not enough," a sob rips away from my throat with a fresh sting of tears. "It will never be enough."

Bones does the one thing his body tells him not to do. I see it in the way he hardens that he's not sure whether hugging me is the right thing to do. I make the decision and cling to him, burying my head of wet tangled hair in his chest.

"It's okay—crying's good, yeah? Let it all out," he soothes, patting my back in circles. "One day you'll look back and realize just how strong you truly are. And until then, I'll remind you every day of your survival until you believe it."

My cries shift to a whimper as I listen to the resilience in his voice.

"I fought him," I croak out. "Every step of the way, like you said, but it only made him crueler. He took... took pleasure in finding new ways to torment me."

He hardened under me, turning to stone. "What did he do?"

The undertone spoke of more questions that he was worried to ask. But I wasn't worried about answering them because the moment I stabbed my old friend through the gut I promised myself that nobody would hold that much power again.

In a way, stabbing William Adler was therapeutic and freeing, but I don't find it in me to care about that fucked up, life-altering realization.

"He wanted me to break so he could put the pieces back together to suit him, and every time I denied him... he would punish me. It came out of nowhere. One minute I demanded he let me leave and the next I was being pinned..."

Bone's hands stop over my spine just as my voice trails off. "Did he...?"

"No," I shake my head against his wet shirt, grateful, so bloody grateful. "No, that was his final move. Degradation and humiliation were more important than raping me."

His hand resumes the soothing pattern and I wonder if he's done this for his little girl, maybe when she had a nightmare? I sigh. "We could hear you on the earbuds until the battery died. We heard him unzipping his trousers..."

I pull my head back, looking up at Bones who was trying his hardest to smooth his expression to soothe me, "I bit him."

His eyes widened a fraction as he frowned down at me. "You bit him?"

"I had no choice. He wasn't going to do that to me, and I thought I was going to die so I thought I might as well go out fighting." Resting my head back on Bones' shirt, I relished in the warmth of his skin. "I think that's how I ended up with a burst eardrum. He punched me so hard it knocked me out and when I woke up it was as if nothing had happened, and he dressed me up for dinner."

"Fuck, Olivia," the patting stopped. Enveloping me into a hug he pulled me onto his lap, settling my head beneath his chin. "I'm so sorry. This was all my fault—I shouldn't... I lost my shit when he mentioned my little girl and—"

"I don't blame you, Bones," I sniffed. "I don't blame any of you."

"You should. If I would have just kept my head, you wouldn't have gone through any of this."

"Maybe so, but if it wasn't me, it would have been some other poor girl who didn't have a team of men looking out for her." I shift out of his arms, needing to rest on something softer than tense muscles. "That's what I'm choosing to focus on now because giving that psychopath any more of my pain is as bad as still being stuck in that hell hole. I can't let him torture me from beyond the grave."

Bones kept his eyes low, helping me back into the covers. "Has anyone ever told you how fucking strong you are?"

My heart squeezed painfully. "Yes, Luca did once."

His mask fell, uncovering his true feelings for Luca in record time. "Will you speak to him?"

"When I'm ready... maybe. I don't know."

"If you decide that you don't want to, you know that you're free, right? We aren't going to drag you back into his captivity. That's all done Olivia, whether Caruso likes it or not. If he so much as tries it, I'll put my blade in his chest. You have my word."

I rest my head against the world's softest pillow that doesn't smell of dampness, and let exhaustion finally win. Who would have thought that safety was with the men who had taken me away months ago?

Certainly not me.

"I know, Bones. I know."

****

The full rest I needed wasn't what I was going to receive. Two hours after falling asleep I was up, rushing to the bathroom to dry heave over the toilet. Bones ran in after me, pulling my hair back, reminding me of the first day we met. I almost laughed at the irony if it wasn't for my stomach revolting against itself.

"You good?"

"No," I groaned, wiping away sweat from my forehead. "I feel like my insides are on fire"

"She good?" Rum called from the bedroom.

"Fuck off, Rum, you're not supposed to be in here," Bones called back, looking down at me nervously with apology. "Go to bed."

"We want to see her," it was Red's voice next.

"Go away," I hiss. "I look like death."

"Nah, not possible," Red stepped in, pulling off his belt and took a seat on the floor. Rum was on his heels, following his lead, but he was more careful in hiding his shock.

I really had lost a lot of weight. Even a large white t-shirt couldn't hide the fact, if anything it made me look smaller.

"It's done, Olivia. We burned everything to the ground and the Police will get an anonymous email tomorrow regarding the bodies under the hotel. Once they complete their investigations, their families will get peace."

I turned to look at the toilet, feeling the urge to wretch again. "Th-thank you."

"Here," Red passes me a strip of gum. "It's ginger flavored. Should stop the retching for a little while."

My eyes hovered over his hand, looking at the innocent piece of gum. Two weeks ago, I would have taken it gladly, but now... now all I can do is question whether it's going to hurt me.

A piece of gum. Is that what my life's going to become? Nervously breaking out into a sweat around food and water?

Rot in hell, Will.

I choke out a laugh, taking it from his hand. "Thank you."

"It's okay," he smiled, showing me a set of perfectly white teeth that made me want to scrub my own. "Had a problem with drugs as a teenager and that gum was the only thing that helped with the withdrawals."

"It's a pain when you can hear it over the mic," Rum pushes Red into the wall of the bathroom.

Bones chuckles, eyeing them with warmth. "It's a constant yacking," he agrees. "Drives me up the bloody wall most of the time."

The gum tastes spicy and sweet, smothering the after taste of mint. I don't chew it, afraid that my jaw will seize, so I suck away the flavor, relishing in the warmth on my tongue.

I sigh and lean against the bath, watching them rib each other. The simplicity of the moment makes my heart swell two sizes too big.

They're distracting me from the inevitable and I've never appreciated them more. Especially now under the fluorescent light I see how worn they all are, probably running on minutes of sleep and coming down of an adrenalin high.

"Room for one more?"

I freeze at the sound of his deep authoritative voice. Bones senses my reaction and acts on instinct, sliding to sit in front of me, using his broad shoulders to block Chen from seeing me.

He holds up his hands to his team. "I just came to check on Olivia."

"Did *he* ask you to?" Red barks, leaning up on his knees, preparing to remove Chen if I so much as whimper.

The tension rolling off everyone suddenly has my undivided attention and I forget my fear. There's a large fraction between boss and employees and something tells me it's been left to fester since my disappearance.

"No, he hasn't," Chen looks to me. "I wanted to check on you myself."

"It's okay," I put my hand on Bones' shoulder, ignoring my bruised knuckles. "Let him sit with us."

With a huff, Bones returns to his spot and we all watch Chen take a seat by the door. His eyes linger briefly, trying not to offend me by openly staring at the state of my body and face. I know him enough — I think — to know that he's calculating my injuries and trying to work out how I sustained them.

He wasn't the only one who stared. "He do that to you?" I asked him, pointing at the stitches across his cheek.

Chen looks me in the eye without his usual mask of arrogance. "Yes, but I deserved it. I failed him and you. I got off lightly with only four stitches."

He truly believed that. It sat in his expression like a weight, pulling down at his thin lips.

"You didn't deserve that," I shook my head, hating that Luca's ugliness was sitting across from me.

"And you don't deserve any of this," he waves his hand up and down my body. "If I had been more careful—"

"Luca or I would have still ignored your warnings, Chen. It was always going to happen and I'm going to be okay with that one day. But right now, I'm going to focus on putting myself back together and so should all of you."

We stare at each other for the longest moment, testing each other, seeing if we could ever be anything other than soft enemies. He nods once to tell me that we can and that's enough for me.

A sniffle to my left pulls me away and it's Rum wiping away tears from his eyes. My six-foot guard, with scarred knuckles and tattoos covering the whole of his neck, cries so openly it squeezes at my heart.

"Don't look at me like that, Bones. You know I get all emotional when I don't sleep and—"

And I hug him because I know exactly how he feels.

CHAPTER SEVENTEEN

Luca Caruso

D r. Evernight was not one to be trusted. I realized as much when I woke up to the sun pouring into my room, spilling over my face on a comfortable bed and not the awfully uncomfortable chair outside of Olivia's door.

I had been waiting for an update when she slipped from her fourth check of the night, to jab me in the neck with a sedative. I don't know who ordered her to do it, but whoever did told her to make it as quick as possible. So quick that I didn't hear her coming.

"It was me," Theo muttered from the corner of my room.

With a groan, I roll to face him. The motherfucker looked well rested and recently showered with a steaming cup of coffee between his hands. I had never been more jealous in my life.

"I'd punch you if I had the energy. Right on your pretty-boy jaw."

"Save it for a special occasion," he looked me over. "You need to get in the shower and eat something. You look like shit warmed up."

"Yes, ma. I'll get right on that."

He put his coffee down to lean his elbows on his knees. "I'm not finished, prick. You need to fix that look of pity on your face too. Get shaved and get back out there to Olivia."

"She doesn't want to speak to me."

"No," he agreed with a glare. "She doesn't, but you need to wait until she's ready to, and while you do that, she needs to see you with your shit together."

"I would be there now — waiting — if you didn't have her doctor dose me, you motherfucker," I spat, rolling off the bed and heading towards the bathroom. I swayed, hitting the doorframe as I passed him.

"She doesn't need to see you looking like this, Luca!" he called. "You need to look like the man she remembered at Katrina's gala. The one who had his shit together. Making sure you had a few hours of sleep helps with that, so you're welcome, you ungrateful asshole."

He was right. I already looked somewhat human again, even under the florescent lighting.

"There's new suits in the wardrobe, courtesy of my lovely wife," he called, not finished being an asshole. "Speaking of, I'm going to fuck off back to her now before she gets on a plane to come here and kick your ass. Call me if you need me."

"I won't," I yelled when all I wanted to say was thank you.

****

Her team was resting in their rooms, all except for Bones who had taken permanent residence at Olivia's side like the loyal solider he was. That was until she sent him away, telling him to go shower and rest in a breathless voice that made my throat burn.

She sounded exhausted.

I hung in the shadows, waiting for him to disappear before knocking on her door. I waited, my hand hovering over the door handle, listening for her to call out. A minute of silence stretched between us. And nothing.

Dropping my hand I took my seat by her door, burying my head in my hands. Did she know I was out here? Did she know I was dying to see her? Or was this her way of punishing me for being the fucked-up son of a bitch that I am?

She had let them all in last night, except for me and Dante who stood outside like spare parts. Dante could have gone in, he knew it, I knew it, but he didn't want to leave me on my own. And I was grateful to him for sticking by me once again.

Chen didn't bother to fill me in on their private conversations when he emerged hours later, and I didn't ask — but he had the decency to tell me that she was okay and Adler's hooks didn't run as deep as I feared.

Before I settled into my spot for the day, the sound of whimpering through the door caught my attention. It was a fragile sound, one that came with tiny claws, sharp enough to sink into my chest.

My feet moved without permission and my hand pulled open her door without hesitation. Bathed in the darkness, Olivia thrashed across her bed in the throes of her nightmare, balling up the sheets in her hands so tightly I was afraid she would break more fingers.

"Stop," she cried, burying her head into her pillow.

"Olivia," my voice was merely a whisper as I hovered at the foot of her bed. I wanted to touch her, fuck I wanted her to feel safe in my arms again. "It's just a nightmare."

"It's cold. So-so cold. Stop, let me keep them on!"

The window. It had been opened and an autumn breeze had stilled the room, reminding her unconscious body of that hell hole. I stormed over, slamming it shut before ripping up the throw from the bottom of her bed and dropping it carefully over her.

She thrashed into the heavy material, pulling it closer to her chest as if it would guard her from the nightmares she wrestled with.

Bones should be here. He shouldn't have ever left the god damn window open, not when she was in this state.

She choked a sob, and the sound punched a hole in my chest. It took everything in me not to drop to my knees by her bed and pull her into my arms. Instead, I dug my knuckles into her mattress, restraining myself.

"It's okay," I whispered instead. "You're safe now. You're safe. I made sure of it," I told her. "I killed him, Olivia, you were there — you watched me tear his head from his body. I put him at your feet where the motherfucker belonged. Remember?"

My words, though dripping with revenge, soothed her enough that she sank back into the mattress, arming her body with her duvet. I watched her perfectly pink lips part slightly, releasing a shuttered breath of a pain.

Underneath the dim light from a crack in the bathroom door, I studied her face. Although the grey tinge of her skin had disappeared, the bruising around her jaw hadn't. It was last night, listening through the door, that I learnt of how she had survived Adler's sexual attack.

She had lashed out and bitten him, even under emotional distress, lack of energy and enough injuries to succumb to exhaustion — she fought tooth and nail like the fucking warrior she is.

I wanted to kiss her face and imprint my thanks against her lips for being so brave, so fucking strong against it all. Desperation bloomed under my skin to whisper my apologies in her ear until I was hoarse, but I wouldn't—biding by her request was more important than my pitiful needs.

I refused myself the courtesy.

I didn't deserve it.

"Get up," the sound of her voice made my head snap up. The muscles between my shoulder blades twitched in pain. "Don't kneel at my side," she told me, blinking her wide eyes at me.

"Olivia," I shifted from my knees to sit on the edge of her bed but with one look I froze in my spot. I wasn't welcome. "How are you feeling?"

What a stupid question to ask but it's all I had.

She pulled up quickly, grabbing the duvet and hiding herself from me. It struck a sensitive nerve, but I didn't allow myself to focus on the zinging pain.

"Please leave, Luca. I don't want you in here."

"I know—" I started, pausing to find the right words, "but you were upset and crying in your sleep. I didn't want you to be alone."

I didn't want to be alone.

Her eyes quickly glossed with tears while she settled against the cream sueded headboard. Sniffing them back she looked over my shoulder and towards the door that stood open a few inches.

"I don't want you in—"

"If this is about what I did to *him*—"

She bared her teeth with disgust. "It's not. That piece of shit deserved to die."

I panicked "Emilia?"

She winced but shook her head. "No. It's not about them. It's about you... the secrets you have kept from me and well, I don't want you to see me like this."

I took her hand without thinking, pulling it between mine and taking my seat by her side. "You will never be anything but beautiful to me, Olivia. You must know that. You must." *Please*, I silently begged her.

She all but flinched as she slipped her hand out of mine, hiding it away under her covers. Sensing my biggest battle yet, I composed my face before the hurt could settle into my skin and leaned back to give her space.

"I'm a lot of things to you, Luca," she started so softly, as if she was soothing a child, "but I was never enough for you to be open and honest with me. And though I don't blame you for Adler taking me, it was your secrets that put me in front of him."

My insides burned with grief but before I could remedy my pain she continued.

"He used your lies to hurt me. Drugged me and showed me pictures of you and Emilia together," she held up her hand to cut me off, "and because I had no trust in you, I couldn't discern between the truth and a lie. Do you see the pattern?"

My heart squeezed hard, sending a dizzying rush to my head. I couldn't deny her words and dirty them with more lies. No, her eyes and heart were attuned completely to me now and if I tried, I wouldn't stand a chance at gaining her trust again.

I wanted it more than anything in this world.

"I'm sorry," it wasn't enough. "I'm sorry that my lies came from the lips of a man who wanted to hurt you and I'll take that guilt with me to the grave." I stood up, giving her more space.

"I have no boundaries when it comes to control. And deep-rooted issues with trust and enough arrogance to have assumed you would deal with that and eventually bend to my will. Honestly, I wanted you to just give in and never cared for what that meant for you. Breaking you was my only goal when Black started this whole thing."

Olivia narrowed her eyes on my fists clenched at my side. It took every bit of strength to open my hands, to show her that I wasn't a threat.

"Like Adler, I saw an opportunity to finally get what I wanted. Black gave me a problem, but it also presented me with a perfect solution. I used it as a guise to steal you away and, yes, I would have always come for you, Olivia. One way or another I would have taken you — shit, the fact I managed eight years is a mystery to me."

"Why are you telling me this now?"

"Because I know that if there's any chance of you being able to look at me in the eye again it's going to be from me being honest. Right here. Right now. So let me finish and then I'll leave you to rest."

She nodded, although her eyes told me she wasn't ready. They swam with fresh tears and my fingers twitched in preparation to wipe them away.

"I had numerous plans to ensure you could never leave. I'd worked on them for eight years — using them to distract me when things got tough. The first plan was to push you into financial destitution, to blacklist you across New York so I could be there to present you with a job in my home country."

She gasped but it wouldn't stop me today. This was my karma and I deserved to burn for my sins.

I understood that now.

"The second was to put your family in harm's way. More specifically your Aunt Sarah. I knew how much you loved her and how protective you were of her. I was going to dangle the guise of kidnap over her head and force you to trade your life for hers."

"You sick motherfucker!" she snapped. In seconds she was up out of her bed, swamped in a large t-shirt with her fists against my chest. The hits were small, barely touching the surface of my pain level, but I felt the burn of her intent — she wanted to hurt me. I pulled her close, forcing her into my hold.

"The third was to move into the apartment next door and work my way into your life," I laughed, tasting acid on my tongue. "I vetoed that. You were never home enough for the plan to have worked and I wouldn't have been patient enough being that close to you."

"Stop," she cried, losing more energy standing up.

"I can't." I pulled her to me, flinching at her sharp hip bones digging into body. "The fourth was probably my favorite. It came to me one evening when I watched Mateo race around my childhood home. I was going to take you on your thirtieth birthday, keep you locked away until you were weak enough to want me. You would have fallen pregnant and by the time you realized what I had done you wouldn't be able to leave. Olivia, if a child is born with dual nationalities, by Italian law, my home country takes precedence. Our beautiful child would have superseded any of my threats. You wouldn't have been able to leave us."

She blinked, not quite believing the destitution I'd fallen into. "You asked me if I was using protection when we slept together..."

I shrugged. "It was a test to see if you would be honest."

Her panicked breath was hot against my chest. There were tears against my shirt, molding the material to my skin, but she was completely quiet. It made me feel raw, so fucking exposed that if she was to hit me now, I would crumble into a thousand pieces.

I would go from man to dust.

"These plans kept me sane, Olivia. And in a sick way they gave me the control I needed but..."

"But what?" she shook in my arms, gulping down sobs.

"The moment Bones placed you in my arms and I looked down at your face—God, you radiated an innocence that I didn't want to ruin. I couldn't. My plans fell away, and I refused to entertain them ever again. All I wanted was to earn my place by your side, the hard fucking way, and I messed it up because I couldn't tell you the truth."

Pulling her away from me I dropped her arms and took a step back. Olivia didn't look up, too focused in the throes of shock, and I knew I would have to get Bones in here soon.

The thought alone sent a wave of repulsion.

"I'm so sorry for being a disgusting monster. Truly, I am-"

"Are you done?" Bones steps into the room, placing his body between us. "She shouldn't be on her feet right now or listening to your shit, Caruso."

"I'm done," I bite out, watching Olivia shuffle back towards the bed with the weight of the world on her shoulders. "I'm sorry, Olivia, truly I am."

CHAPTER EIGHTEEN

Olivia Heart

I wanted to kiss Dante for two reasons. One for the comfortable, warm clothing he brought me and for my phone which he had kept all this time—keeping my Aunt updated. Dante had pretended to be me for two weeks, sending her pictures of Luca's pool alongside sweet messages and promises to call when I was less busy with work.

"You done?" he asked me after a small mouthful of porridge. It felt like thick, tasteless sludge in my mouth and the pain in my jaw smarted every time I chewed, but it was something.

"Yes," I felt sick. I hadn't eaten this much in such a long time that my stomach cramped, trying to remember how to work. Passing him the bowl, I suddenly felt grateful that he wasn't going to push me to eat more.

"Dr. Evernight said in a few days you can try something with a little more flavor," Dante smiled politely, ignoring the state of my wet hair that was on top of my head in a bird's nest of a bun.

"If you're ready that is," Bones interjected loudly from his window seat. He knew my burst eardrum was making it difficult to hear and I appreciated the intent, even if it made me flinch.

In the safety of my room, back with the men I trusted, I waited for the feeling of relief to arrive. But instead, I remained on the precipice of panic and dread — just waiting for the rug to be pulled from under me.

After my shower, I was suddenly grateful for the exhaustion that weighed down on my consciousness, preventing destructive thoughts to my recovery and having to deal with Luca's confessions.

There was a safety in hiding away, even for a little while. I have never been naïve when it came to my emotions. In time, when my body was strong enough to prop up, my mind I would have deal with what happened.

And I would survive it.

If only as a last *fuck you* to Adler.

"We have to go," Chen had come in at some point. "The police are crawling over Adler's hotel. I don't feel comfortable with us being this close."

"What are we supposed to do?" It was Bones who stood up from his seat, to stand by my side.

"We need to get out of the country," Dante stood up, sending me a small smile. "Nothing can point back to Olivia."

"It won't," Chen nodded, severe eyes cutting to me. "We made sure there wasn't a single trace of her in the building or Adler's personal things."

"It won't take a genius to work out he saw Olivia in Paris and then he had visited Italy," Bones said. "And now she's here in Scotland, the night after his hotel is burned down..."

"It's not enough to question her," Chen argued.

"It might be," Dante reasoned. "If anyone knew she was in the country it could—"

"Get me out of here," I threw off my covers. "Take me back to Italy." My knees swayed from underneath me. Black spots coated my vision, but Bones was there to prop me up. Jesus, the day my body was back under my control could not come soon enough.

"You sure?" Dante asked, not bothering to hide his relief.

"Nah, fuck that. You're not going back there with him."

That *him* was probably outside listening to Bones, and it made me wince.

"I'm not going back with him. I'm going back so the police don't put two and two together and make four. Like you said, I'm free, well let's make sure it stays that way. Get me out of the god damn country."

Nobody bothered to argue with me. What I said was what went whether they agreed or not—a new power I had stolen from Luca it seems.

****

Bones was unbearable with the wheelchair he had stolen from the small private airport. I had openly refused to get into the thing until he pushed me down, threw his jacket over me, and wheeled me so fast towards the runway that getting out would have been deadly.

Five 'are you goods?', a pillow and blanket later, I was on a reclining seat with Chen and Dante at my sides. My body felt fresh out of hell but for the first time in weeks I had enough energy to keep my head above my shoulders. I was all about the small wins recently.

Bones sat in front of us, hands on his knife as he glared at Luca who stood at the front talking to the pilot. To look at him,

Luca stood casually, with his hands in his trouser pockets and a polite smile on his face, but I knew differently.

His shoulders where too tense to be natural, creating this broad, straight line under his Armani Jacket that looked slightly too big for him. In two weeks, he had lost a little weight too, highlighting his already severe cheek bones. But luckily for him, he could pull it off.

My breath caught when the corner of his lips lifted. That smile was nothing but a nicety to distract his pilot from what this journey was. A retrieval of the woman he had originally kidnapped. But it still affected me in the most severe of ways.

I felt jealousy flare and my heart pound. I was ridiculous but so was our whole situation.

Was he relieved that we were returning to his home? Did he think I had forgiven him? Jesus. I shouldn't care but I did, and I hated myself for it. I needed his thoughts just as I needed a good night's sleep.

"When you're ready I would like to tell you what these last two weeks have been like for him." Dante whispered into my good ear.

"Why would I listen?" Luca sensed our attention and glared at his cousin. It was his signature glare that told whoever was on the end of it to shut up.

Dante wasn't fazed. "Because you're curious and there are no rules anymore.."

"Tell me now then."

He laughed heartily before pulling out his phone. "I would if Bones wasn't ready to pop a bullet in anyone that upsets you."

"It would upset me?"

"Yes."

A noise like a scoff mixed with a hmm slipped through my lips.

Ten minutes later, we were taxying the runway in silence. I watched everyone, suddenly so glad to be leaving the one place I would never visit again. Scotland was scarred land for me, and nothing would ever change that.

We pulled up, the nose of the plane above the wings when a sharp pain exploded in my ear, settling across my jaw and down my neck.

I bolted upright, holding my ear that felt as though it was being carved out by hot knives. Dr. Evernight warned me it could happen, but I didn't believe the pain could be this cutting.

"Olivia?" a cold hand touched the back of my neck and panic shot through me.

The rug was finally pulled from under me. No. I wasn't free. This has all been a cruel trick. I wasn't safe, no, I was back in my cold cell barely holding on to the thread of life with Adler hovering above me.

I screamed, ignoring the pain in my head, and jumped up. Green damp carpets and the cold glint of a knife sliced into my vision. I stumbled into something hard, groaning against the sharp pain that dug into my hip.

Another shot of cold touched my right wrist, long fingers preparing to lock me away. I wrenched it back from the claws of death with a sob, feeling my throat tighten back up.

"There you are," Adler grinned as he stalked towards me. "Thought you could get away that easily?"

"No! Don't touch me. Don't fucking touch me!"

"Miss, you need to take a seat!"

"Come on, Liv, we don't have time to play these games. I need to hurt you one last time."

My ear burst into a fire of pain, and I hit the carpet with a thud.

Another touch of cold pressed through my sweater. I cried into my hands, wanting to disappear before he took me again.

"Don't fucking touch her!" his voice, so faint in the background was nothing but a dirty trick—my mind's way of laughing at me. "You're too cold. It's triggering her."

A single bullet of warmth touched my cheek, pulling me out of my despair and into my eyes that were swimming with tears.

"Olivia, it's me. Look at me. Come on I need you to look at me."

I couldn't. He didn't belong here with me.

The heat of his touch spread up my jaw until his hand pressed against the pain of my ear, forcing it to recede a little. I looked up at Luca. "The pressure is going to even back out any minute now, okay? While that happens, I'm going to wrap you up, to keep you warm. Stay still for me and I promise it will all be over soon."

"Yes," I was breathless, struggling to feel his hands on my face and not the echo of terror waiting to take hold again.

Pulling a blanket around my shoulders, he tightened it around me. "Come on, let's get you back to your seat."

"I've got her."

"No, you don't. Bones. Take a step back and let me help her."

"I didn't know."

I didn't make it back to my seat, to be wedged between Dante and Chen who were probably freaked out. Luca pulled me up, I fell back into his arms and let him guide me to the seat next to his.

CHAPTER NINETEEN

Luca Caruso

My family couldn't swarm my house fast enough. Even though Dante and I had specifically told them not to, they forced their way through my gates, parking their vehicles in my drive and taking up residence in my home. They settled in my kitchen, baking traditional Italian desserts that Olivia couldn't eat when they realized they wouldn't see her.

But they still wanted to fill the house with warmth and the smell of baked goods instead of its usual silence, and for that I couldn't deny them.

Aida, armed with a glass of wine, was the first to find me, hidden away in my office where I could pretend to catch up on work.

"You look like shit," she tells me.

"Thanks."

"You should go rest," she tells me, like it's just that easy.

"I can't."

She sighed, taking up one of my seats. "How is she? Can I go see her?"

"I don't know and no." Damn it, I can't do this right now. "I think most of the time she's putting on a brave face, telling herself it's not as bad as it is, or she's still in survival mode. I just don't know."

"You're waiting for her to fall to pieces." Aida takes a hefty sip. "What if she doesn't?"

I scowl at my sister. "You think I'm underestimating the situation?" She wasn't there when a cold hand flipped Olivia from the land of the living right into a memory so dark it took five of us to get her to calm down.

"No. I think you're underestimating her."

I didn't have the patience for Aida's psychology bullshit. After one semester at a prestigious university, she thought she understood the intricacies of the mind and it often pissed people off — me included.

"She's going to be fragile for a while, Luca, but that doesn't mean she's going to fall to pieces. It's not in her DNA. The woman is a fighter right down to her toes. You know this — she fought her attraction to you for long enough."

"You have no idea what she went through, Aida. What he did to her. You don't just come out of that mentally unscathed."

"Ma?" Matteo called, hanging by the door with a football in his hand, saving his mother from the vicious words on my tongue.

"Non hai intenzione di salutare il tuo migliore zio?" You're not going to say hello to your best uncle?

Matteo grinned, flashing his gapped front teeth. "Dante's not here, zio."

For the first time in weeks I laughed, a full belly laugh that eased the tension within my office. God, how I missed his quick wit which he obviously got from me.

"I'm hurt, Matteo. You've wounded your poor zio with your lies," I told him with my hand over my heart. Aida rolled her eyes at me, turning in her chair to look at her son who stepped into the room.

"Where have you been?" she asked him, wiping a smudge of dirt from his chin as he grinned over at me

Scrunching his nose, he pushed her away. "Playing Titan 4 with Olivia," he babbled. "She wasn't very good, so I let her watch me play instead. Her favorite was Princess Petra because they had the same hair," he rolled his boyish eyes, reminding me of Dante when he was his age. "I wanted to show her more, but she fell asleep, right before I could show her the dragon cave. She would have loved that! You can pick your own egg and raise a dragon, Zio, your own dragon!"

Aida and I shared a quick look of confusion. Only Matteo could barge his way into Olivia's room and demand that she plays his favorite game, and of course she had the grace to do it.

"Matteo, you know you shouldn't be bothering Olivia. She's not well at the moment."

His bottom lip wobbled before he answered his Ma. "She told me it was okay, I swear it," he looked at me, imploring me to listen. "Zio, I didn't want her to be on her own. She looked so sad, and no pretty girl should ever be sad or alone."

"Matteo!" Aida scolded.

"No, he's right," I told her, my face tight with emotion. "No pretty girl should ever be sad or alone."

Matteo's sigh of relief filled the space as I got up and squeezed his shoulder. "You're going to become a good man, Matteo."

Nothing like his piece of shit Pa that had beat Aida so bad when she was six months pregnant that she had to stay in the hospital for two weeks. It was only by Aida's grace that Dante and I didn't put a bullet in his head.

Aida wanted Matteo to have a father, even if he was a piece of shit, so we settled on breaking both of his legs instead.

I was just leaving when Matteo's voice called to me. "Zio, um, are you a good man to Olivia?"

"Matteo!"

With a heavy sigh and a sinking heart, I left my nephew to be scolded by his mother. Not that he deserved it for asking such an honest question. I wasn't a good man, and I haven't been good to Olivia, but explaining that to him would ruin his innocent perception of his zio.

Olivia was in her room without Bones by her side. I knew as much from Chen who hovered outside of her door, checking his tablet as I approached. Like the rest of us, he looked exhausted, the bags under his eyes had gone from tan to black.

"Go rest, Chen," I told him, placing my hand on his shoulder. "I've got this."

"It's fine sir."

Ah.

"Chen, look, about what happened that day."

Chen held up his hands with a shake of his head. "It's forgotten."

"No. It isn't. I... shouldn't have reacted that way. You have been nothing but excellent since the day you took this job and well, what I'm trying to say is, I'm sorry. I was out of line."

He didn't expect it. Of course he hadn't. It was impossible for a man like me to apologize for his sins, but not anymore. I was going to purge every last one with frail hope that Olivia might understand.

Because it's all I had left.

"Sir," he accepted my apology with an efficient nod. "There are some things I would like to discuss with you when things have settled."

"Of course, and I'll be here to listen to them. Now, go rest. I'll stay here until the next switch."

"I won't, but I'll let you pass," he stepped aside. "You'll need someone on the lookout for when Bones wakes up."

With a grimace, I slipped by him and into her room. Even in complete darkness I found her balled under the covers, small and fragile but sleeping soundly in the bed that held some of my favorite memories.

She had whispered her love against my lips, wrapped around me and the silk sheets that now caress her skin. It felt like so long ago, a distant memory that I was already finding difficult to recall the finer details.

Her lips had been soft against mine while hands had slid across my chest, pressing down on my heart with possession that burned through my skin. I had died and gone to heaven.

"Ti Amo."

My heart had stopped.

"Now, go to sleep."

I laughed into her neck that night, enjoying her playfulness that she had very rarely shown.

Taking my seat by her bed was easy. Watching her sleep and knowing I couldn't hold her wasn't, but nothing hurt more than knowing one day she was going to wake up and throw me away.

Chapter Twenty

Luca Caruso

I've watched the sun rise around her for three hours, out of sight but close by in case she suddenly decided she needed me. I shouldn't be here—I should give her the space she needs but something, so deep down, tells me I need to be close by.

Olivia moves her hair over to one shoulder, looking out towards the vineyard, shaded by a single tree. She looks so small, so fragile beneath the large, twisted branches, but I know she's at peace.

I feel it in the way her chest rises and falls. I see the way she closes her eyes briefly to enjoy the gentle warm breeze against her face. It's freedom in a few brief moments and I want her to enjoy them.

She needs this more than she needs me. And even though that hurts, I deal with it the best I can.

I give her space and time. She spends her days with my Marie, healing while being kept occupied with small tasks Marie can think of to keep her busy. Some days my sister drops in, bringing flowers and cake which seems to tire her quickly.

The only time I ever get to hear her sweet voice is when she calls her aunt. I try not to listen in, to give her the privacy she deserves, but sometimes her voice is the only thing holding me together.

I'd give anything to have her speak to me. Even if it included giving up my fortune for a single word directed my way, I would do it in a heartbeat.

Anything. A single sound. A sigh. Just something. But not all sounds are good.

Especially last night. She had cried in her sleep, whimpering and thrashing against her pillow. I couldn't stand it anymore, I reached over and brought her into my arms. But she would wake at my gentle touch — panic hollowing out her eyes every time.

I had pulled away, sensing that my presence was causing her more harm, but she held onto my wrist. Silently telling me to 'stay' — so I did, but I didn't touch her. I moved back to the chair and kept watch — hoping I could keep her nightmares at bay.

"How's she doing?" Dante asked, coming up from behind me. A familiar scent of strawberries and vanilla drifted off his shirt. It had been on his clothes every time he visited, but he had yet to tell me he was seeing Laura, Aida's best friend.

I sigh, grateful for the interruption, "Better."

"Marie said she's eating more now and steadily regaining weight." He stood at my side, following my eyes. "She looks good."

"She does," I agree. But I still remember how she looked when we found her. The memory was burned inside my retinas. "He laced everything with that drug. Including the water in her shower," my jaw flexes at the memory of Olivia's body the night we found her. "She chose to starve herself to avoid... fuck, if I could drag him from hell to kill him all over again I would."

Dante tensed at my side, his shoulders lifting. "She's strong, Luca. Probably one of the strongest women you and I will ever meet. Someone like him, would never be able to get the better of her." For the first time in years, Dante places a hand on my bicep. "She may seem a little fragile now but underneath the surface she's tougher than a diamond."

Olivia shifts, looking up to Bones who makes his way over the grass. I feel his hesitancy as he slows, gauging her mood.

"Is she still only talking to him?"

I shift from the window, fighting my jealousy. "Mostly him, but she's speaking to Aida and Marie a little."

Dante moves to my desk and settles in his favorite spot, the right chair where I don't have the screen monitor to block his view of me.

"You know why that is, don't you?"

My chest tightens on instinct. My stomach knots but I don't let the pain show on my face. I can't tell my cousin that my new biggest fear is that Olivia is falling for her bodyguard and they're planning to leave soon.

It will kill me. And I don't want to give my theory life.

"Because she trusts him." *And not me.* I swipe up my glass, downing the whiskey that's been left to sit for too long. It's warm and bitter as it burns down my throat.

Dante shakes his head, long tendrils falling over his ears. He needs a haircut and some sleep. "Because he reminds her of her father."

"What are you talking about?"

Was all my family wannabe psychiatrists?

Shrugging, he leans back into his chair, rolling his shoulders. "Have you seen a picture of her father?"

"Yes..." I trace back to the first time her family tree was presented to me. He was a tall man, short blonde hair, bright blue eyes, and a kind face with deep wrinkles around the eyes. As kind as he looked, Olivia had taken after her mother in the looks department, severe in beauty with emerald green eyes.

"It's just an observation I made, but he's similar looking and he's the same age as her father when he died…"

"Maybe," I said. "She was furious with him on the plane. She singled him out and mentioned his little girl who lives with her mother in America."

Dante nods. "She feels safe with him, Luca. Not because she's in love with him," the pointed look that he throws my way makes me want to leave. I hate how much he sees, even if right now his keen eye has released an inch of agony from my chest.

I'm all fucking pressure these days like a god damn balloon waiting to pop.

"I only want her to feel safe."

"Good," he stands up, "because there's something you've let get away from you that might help her get there."

He pulls a folded piece of paper from within his jacket and hands it to me.

"They signed it over a few weeks ago," he told me. "I've only just caught up on my emails, but the place is pretty much yours. You just need to pick up the keys."

The piece of paper feels like lead in my hands, heavy with a future that I naively thought would be possible. There isn't a chance in hell that this would do anything but cause further pain.

I shove the piece of paper into my pocket, nod at Dante, and leave the confines of my office in search of whiskey that Marie has probably already hidden.

CHAPTER TWENTY-ONE

Olivia Heart

Olivia, he killed those poor women!" Alice screeched down the phone, her voice muffling the speaker for one second. "Mum's losing her mind right now. She can't believe that she let us play with him as kids—that she let him in the damn house!"

One breath.

I'm fine.

Two breaths.

I'm fine.

Three breaths.

"Four women. He killed four women and buried them in some abandoned building like a serial killing psycho! Can you believe this? Can you believe that William Adler killed those women?"

His name tears away at the Band-Aid holding my heart together.

"I—" I stumble into the hallway.

"Olivia, he used to sneak into your room at night to hold you. I can't believe this—*Christ*! How did we not see it?"

"He was a manipulator—"

She doesn't hear me over her rage. "Did he ever hurt you, you know back then? You two were always so close... God if he hurt you, I swear to God I'll dig up the bastard's charred body and burn him again."

I fall to my knees in a bruising heap, but the pain doesn't register. My chest, that's squeezed within an inch of its life has my full attention. I'm a heart attack waiting to happen. I just hope it's quick.

"No," it takes every part of me to cover my voice in steel so that Alice doesn't hear the fear, so she doesn't suspect that Adler had done more than hurt me.

If she knew the true extent of what our old friend did to me, she would never be able to look at me in the same way. I would become damaged goods to the one person who still saw me as capable and strong.

The thought alone made me sick.

"Thank God," she sniffs. "If he had hurt you and I didn't realize... I wouldn't be able to cope with that. Olivia, I feel like our childhood is being destroyed... the press is all over our school photos."

"Alice..." I fail to find the right words. My tongue moves inside of my mouth to tell her the truth, but I know I can't. How could I tell my innocent, law abiding cousin that I had been hurt, damaged by Adler and Luca had killed him for it?

Luckily, I didn't need to. Footsteps clicked against the polished tile, and I knew Bones would haul me up at any moment and take me back to my room.

"I'm sorry. I'm just in shock is all... this is so fucked up. He was our friend... you know? He hung around the house obsessing over you and it's... so awful what he did to those poor women."

Softly I reply, even when my stomach rolls with revulsion. "I know."

"Did you suspect anything at that Gala you went to? You said he spoke to you."

"Alice, I can't... I can't talk about this right now." I pause when knees bend in front of me, and I catch the scent that I would know anywhere. It's clean soap mixed with a hint of whiskey, and uniquely him.

Carefully, as if he's not sure how I'll react, Luca takes the phone from my ear and puts it to his own.

I look up and find him. Thick eyelashes frame the haze of alcohol in his eyes. I smell whiskey on him, no I can practically taste it on his breath. If I wasn't too focused on my own internal shut down, I may have said something about the time.

"Hello, Alice," his voice so deep and calm, for a second it soothes the ache in my chest. "Olivia, as you can imagine isn't feeling too well at the news and has gone to lie down. I'll make sure she calls you when she's ready to talk."

My initial, tattooed against his finger catches my attention as he talks. A man that loves me so much he had to mark his body to prove it, also wanted to hurt my family. How could that be?

"Don't worry..." he tells her. "Yes, of course."

I didn't realize my hand was reaching out for him until he grabbed my wrist, preventing me from touching him. I try to pull back, coming to my senses, but he holds me there. It burns and soothes at the same time, tightening my stomach in a way that almost feels wrong.

"I'll tell her. You too. Goodbye, Alice," he ends the call and pockets my phone.

Smoothly he pulls me up and waits until I'm steady on my feet.

"Can you walk?" he asks.

I nod even though I don't trust my feet.

"Are you drunk?" I ask breathily.

"Yes. Do you want to go back to your room?" he sighs while motioning for me to go ahead but I don't want to move. I don't want to do as I'm told especially by a man who's avoiding me like the plague.

"Did you know?"

He didn't venture a look at me. Instead, he peered down the hallway as if getting back to his office was more interesting right now. "I did. It's all over the news right now. Chen and his team are monitoring the British police's investigation, but they won't find anything concerning you."

"Unless they find Emilia through that offshore account."

Her name tastes like dirt on my tongue, and I hoped he would feel my hatred for the woman that he had let slip by. Maybe it was being free of the drugs, but every emotion I felt recently was amplified, almost excruciatingly too much to bear.

"They won't," he tightens his jaw. "We've erased all evidence of her connection with *him*."

My pulse threatens to explode. "You're protecting her?"

He finally looks at me, confused and exhausted. "No I'm not protecting her. I'm protecting them from forming a connection back to us — to you."

What he said made perfect sense to someone who was able to form rational arguments, but I was anything but rational. Full of anger, bursting with the need to lash out, I shoved at him.

He didn't move, even intoxicated he was like a brick wall. I hated him for it.

"You're so full of shit, Luca. Because if you were protecting me from a connection being made you would have found her by now and made her pay for what she did!"

I was screaming as I hit his chest, hoping one of my blows would hurt him as much as my chest hurt.

He didn't grab my wrists, nor did he push me away, which only infuriated me more.

"Why hasn't she paid Luca!?"

"Olivia, we haven't been able to track—"

I cut him off, kicking him hard in the shin. Still he didn't budge. "Why isn't she dead? Why does she get to walk around without fear!? Without the worry that a cold breeze will kill her, huh!?"

Footsteps fall in fast behind me, bouncing off the tiled floor and I knew who had grabbed me without needing to see him.

"Olivia," he whispered into my ear, imploring me to calm down but I couldn't. I don't think I'll ever be able to feel a sense of natural calm again. It had been stolen.

The sadness flickering in Luca's eyes wasn't enough to stop me either. "Dante, let her go," he demanded. "Let her get it out."

"You're nothing but a lying bastard!" I snarl, wild as I try to scratch him. "You stand there and dare to look at me with pity!? Dare to fucking touch me when you let her do this to me? To us?" I elbowed Dante, trying to dislodge his grip around my ribs but with a grunt he only tightens his hold.

Luca took a step forward, cautiously holding out his hands. "You're not mad about her, Olivia. Your anger is aimed at what I've done, about the lies I told to keep you. This about Emilia… well it's not true."

After everything, he had the nerve to tell me it wasn't true, that Emilia hadn't done this to me? That her actions to kiss Luca, to take Adler's money, and then lead me into a trap was not an evil part of this?

"Olivia, take a minute," Dante growled. "You're angry and not thinking straight. Let him explain what's happening and I promise you it will make sense."

The laugh that ripped from my throat said otherwise. "I'm thinking straight for the first time in ages! Isn't it weird how her name sounds so much like mine?" Another laugh and I was deep in my venom. "And how after all this he just let her go! The great Luca Caruso who burned a plane full of Russians for being involved in our accident, but he can't get to his ex-fiancé? A singular woman!? Fuck off!"

Dante's arms slackened enough for me to turn around and push him. He didn't stumble but he took a step back, knowing that the fight was lost. I was right and I had won.

I felt raw, bloodied in my quest to hurt Luca and I deserved such an opportunity. I turned back to sneer at him. "Maybe you were keeping her as a backup in case Adler had broken me too much. We know how off-putting it is for you, Luca, when I'm damaged, remember the hospital? You could barely look at me. Why the hell did you think I told Bones not to let you touch me!?"

He flinched, finally feeling something. "Stop this," he stepped towards me, warning me. "Stop this now."

"You can't even deny it, can you?" I spat, pushing him again.

He tried to grab my hands but Bone's voice, from the top of the stairs stopped him. "Don't you dare lay a finger on her, Caruso."

Knowing that this conversation was over I turned, shoved by Dante, and disappeared into the back of the house in search of a dark room where I could hide for a few hours.

Because if I didn't hide now, the rage pulsing solidly through my veins would never leave and I would hate Luca for the rest of my life.

CHAPTER TWENTY-TWO

Olivia Heart

I'm complexities, contradictions, and pieces that just don't match anymore. Every time I try to remember how this all works, I fail to find myself, to see the girl who once was brave enough to live alone in New York City.

Now I'm full of jealousy. Up to the brim of my glass and some of it had spilled, right into Luca's face.

I need Luca right now, desire him at the core of my being, but I also hate everything that he is. It goes against everything to want him this way, to need him to take my hand and soothe my aching heart.

Even with scalding tears and my screams he did nothing. He just stood there and took the brunt of my anger but did nothing to fix it.

Two weeks ago he would have forced me to listen, gripped my arm and given me no choice but to understand, and now... well now he's given up. I'm too damaged to be loved further.

When did I let myself become so weak as to let my heart do all of the talking? Did it happen when I told him I loved him? Or was it when he sliced open Adler's throat? Maybe it was when he told me all of his final truths and forced me to see the pain etched across his usually well-hidden expression.

No, I'm fooling myself, I know the exact moment I gave him my heart and I'm a fool for not seeing it before.

"Are you okay?" Dante's voice calls to me from the doorway of the library I find myself in. I wasn't okay and having Dante peer down at me wasn't making it any better.

I had hit my quota of pity four days ago.

"No," truly, it's impossible to feel okay. I'm marbleized pain, just waiting for the final hammer to my chest where I'll shatter to a billion pieces.

He takes a step in and shuts the door behind him.

"You were out of line, Olivia."

I balk, my wet eyes widen, following Dante as he takes the seat by the window. The sun shines from behind him, creating a halo around his silken hair. He looks like a Grecian god ready to strike me down.

"Excuse me?"

"You're excused," he bites with frustration. "I've tried to be kind to you both and give you the space you need to heal but that stops now. After what I witnessed out there..." he shakes his head, "this cannot go on. Nothing good can come from screaming matches."

"You have no idea how this feels."

"I don't," he agrees with a tight smile. "All I know is that you're killing him, bit by bit you're taking something from him whether you know it or not. Whether he deserves it or not."

I open my mouth to protest but Dante holds up a hand, kindly dismissing my effort.

"Luca is far from innocent, and I'll always be the first in line to remind you of that. He's psychotic, obsessive, borderline split personality sometimes..." he leans back, "but he loves you more than humanly possible. You heard him that night Olivia — you're etched into his bones, inscribed forever in the script of his being. That isn't a man who could hurt you, Olivia. Hurting you would only kill him."

"Dante, that's all well and — " ·

He carries on as though I haven't spoken. "I watched him destroy himself for two weeks out of guilt. Saw him throw up when he couldn't stomach the terror any longer. I stood by as he refused to sleep and eat until you were found. For hours he would pace the inside of your room, hoping to find the answers in your space, but really it was just to be close to you in some way."

Somewhere along the flow of his words I stopped breathing. This whole time I hadn't thought about how Luca had dealt with my kidnapping. I'd been too wrapped up in myself to notice his suffering.

"He failed and it killed him over and over again. I've never seen him lose control like that and I'll tell you this because you deserve to know, but when things got dark... well, he thought he was dying."

"Dying?" I stammer, wiping away my tears.

Bravely Dante looked me in the eye and delivered his next blow. "Yes. Dying. Without you Olivia he doesn't exist. The Luca without you is just a shell, automatically doing what he's supposed to but there's no life in him. He had you here and then he didn't. He slipped into withdrawal..."

Shame burned me from the inside. I'd heard those words before but from a different set of lips, but it felt so long ago. How could I get back to that place?

With a sigh, he leans over and so carefully pulls my hands away from my eyes "Olivia, look at me."

I do, I look right at him.

"Why did you come back here?"

"Because of the police."

Dante smiled, pushing a piece of my hair away. "You could have gone back to your family or New York. You're free—just like Bones told you the night we found you. Why did you come back *here*, Olivia?"

Because of... Luca. Because the place I once thought of as my prison had become the complete opposite. It had been the home I yearned for when Adler tortured me. It held the memories of Luca that I wanted to reminisce in until I had the chance to make more.

"Because... I wanted to come home."

Somewhere in the background a clock ticks impatiently, reminding me of how much time Luca and I had lost and here I was extending that.

"Exactly, Olivia." Dante pulled me into his arms, cautiously holding me against his chest. "He's written into your bones too. Just remember that when you next see him, and I promise you that you won't have to heal alone."

CHAPTER TWENTY-THREE

Luca Caruso

Sleep was avoiding me. I'd thought that with nearly three weeks without much sleep I would be able to close my eyes and disappear for a few hours, but no. Staring at my ceiling for hours at a time would have to do.

I could get up and stalk the halls for more hidden whiskey, but I'd run the risk of seeing Bones outside of Olivia's room and it wouldn't end well. Every time I saw his face, I wanted reach out and wrap my hands around his neck and squeeze until he disappeared.

He was there constantly, lurking, reminding me of how much I had lost, and I would never forgive him for it.

Especially not this afternoon when Olivia finally gave in and exploded, sending beautiful barbs of rage my way. It was more than a sigh, a whisper in the night, it was a declaration that she knew I still existed.

Her jealousy was a pure, white flame upon naked skin, and it was just for me. It was a simple message wrapped in pain and frustration, that somewhere deep inside her she still cared enough—to assume I wanted Emilia.

"Dare to fucking touch me when you let her do this to me? To us?" her savagery echoes into my head, but all I hear is, to us, to us.

There's an 'us' trapped in the recesses of her mind, but is it just wishful thinking to assume we have a future?

Before I can ponder my desperate thoughts, I hear the slight click of my door and soft footsteps pad across the carpet. They're slow and wary, hesitating in the middle of the room.

I close my eyes. I'm probably dreaming. There isn't a chance that she would come to me, not tonight.

There's the softest sigh before her steps resume until they reach the foot of my bed. There's a dip of the mattress and I know I'm not dreaming. Olivia crawls up my bed until she's by my side.

Our eyes meet in the darkness, drinking each other in as if this is our last chance.

My throat closes sharply at the thought. I try to sit up, but she pushes her palm against my chest. I look down and wonder if she's placed her hand over my heart on purpose.

Maybe she's giving me mine back. She's realized after all this time she doesn't want the fraudulent piece of flesh.

"I want to sleep by your side," and I swear I hear at the end of her sentence *'one last time'*.

I keep it together, holding open the covers enough so that she can slip in. I expect her to stay on one side, but she moves over and places her head on my chest. Just like the night before she was taken, except this time we're not exhausted from sex and declarations of love.

Just pain.

Olivia feels so small against my chest that suddenly I'm afraid of putting my arm around her—I could hurt her, crush her, smother her... fuck. How could something as simple as wanting to hold her to me become so complicated?

"Olivia?"

"Yes?"

"I'm sorry," carefully I place my arm around her. She doesn't flinch this time, but she also doesn't soften.

"I know you are," she whispers, lifting her head to look up at me. "But right now I don't want to talk about it or accept it. Or analyze everything you've done or worry over all of the answers you've finally given me."

My fingers trace from her temple to her lips, submitting the feel of her to memory. It won't be long now until she leaves me, and I need as much detail as possible if I'm to survive without her by my side.

"I want to remember who I was before everything. Before..."

Before I took her, that's what she cannot say because it'll wipe away our timeline together and maybe she knows that would kill me — to never have existed in her life.

"Before?" I sound cold, disjointed from how I really feel.

"Before—" she pushes up, surprising me by straddling my waist. The large t-shirt that she wears skims up her thighs and by instinct I slide my palms across her skin. It's so automatic to touch her, like taking in air, "before Aida's birthday," she looks down at my hands.

And my brain finally catches up with my body when Olivia pulls off her shirt and throws it to the side. I focus on her eyes, forcing my attention away from the beauty of her healing body.

I don't need to know that she's healing. I can feel it pulsing from her skin, calling me to admire her while she stares down at me. But her weight isn't where it needs, nor is her energy.

"I won't fuck you, Olivia."

"Yes, you will."

"I'll hurt you."

"You won't."

"Of course, I will. It's the only thing I'm consistent at."

"Look at me," she snaps, placing her palm in the center of my chest. I didn't realize I had looked away until my eyes where back on her, tracing the swell of her breasts right down to the dip of her waist.

Fuck, she was so beautiful it hurt to look at her.

I couldn't... no I shouldn't do this even though my body screamed for her attention. I wanted nothing more than to silence those screams by sinking into her and forgetting about everything, to live for one purpose of delivering only pleasure.

There had already been too much pain between us — maybe we could have this final moment. It's highly possible that she is giving me this as a final goodbye.

Her plea cut the cord to my hesitation. "Non lasciarmi" *Don't leave me.*

"Mai" *Never.*

Like a man dying of thirst, I pull her down to me, wrapping my hands around the back of her neck until my mouth took hers. Rolling over I pinned her underneath me, delivering kiss after kiss, trying to imprint my lips against her mouth and throat.

She's mine. Mine. Mine. Mine.

She's safe under me. I can shield her with my body, protect her from the outside world and wipe away every single one of *his* invisible marks. I'll replace them with memories of me if she'll let me. Fuck if she'll let me.

Olivia gasps, arching her back while I tease her nipple softly between my teeth.

"If it gets too much you have to say," I lick between her breasts, tasting her skin.

"It won't," she slips her hands down my back, dragging her nails into my skin. "Now," she pants, pulling down my boxers, "before I start thinking." I barely have time to move before she wraps her legs around me and pulls me to her body.

There's hardly any room between us, not enough to remove her panties so I push them to the side — tensing as the head of my cock skims her slit. She's wet — it's a relief but she's not ready. I see it in the pinch of her eyes while she holds her breath.

Her mind has already run away, pulling her back into the cold where she has no grasp of reality. I kiss her, warming her lips back up to me and silently reminding her that we can stop at any time.

"He didn't," she tells me.

"I know."

I don't want him in my bed with us but in this frail moment, she needs me to know that her body is still her own and it's her brain she's trying to fix.

I push, enough for her to gasp in surprise. "Look at me," I tell her, "watch what I'm going to do to you. Remember that this is what *you* asked for, Olivia, that you get to control everything tonight." I pull back a little, sliding my cock into her wetness. "Look at how you control me," I rasp.

She feels like home but I'm being held at the door, unsure whether I'm welcome or not.

"Luca," she cries, thrusting her hips in frustration.

I kiss her throat, feeling the hammer of her pulse against my lips. "Tell me what you want, and you can have it."

Gripping my arms, she looks down at our bodies so close to joining, treading a fine line between lust and pain.

Instead of telling me what she needs she reached between us, sliding her fingers delicately around my cock until I'm placed where she needs me. I fight off the groan of her heat, trying to hold myself steady enough to let her have this even when I feel the way her body calls to me.

"I want you to fuck me slowly," she breathes, tightening her grip as she pulls me in by an inch. My eyes shut for a second as a ripple of pleasure lights me up from the base of my spine to my skull. "Like the vineyard."

Her body under the moonlight as she writhed with pleasure fills my mind. Her teeth sinking into my flesh from her release... she controls another inch of me, pulling me in.

I dip my head hoping she needs to kiss me, and she does. Our lips connect just as her hands slide around my hips and pull me all the way in. A growl surfaced from my throat, vibrating into her mouth as her slick heat gripped me hard enough that spots covered the corner of my vision.

"Olivia," I rolled my hips on instinct trying to open her up. "I've told you so many lies but now I'm going to tell you all of my truths."

She met my gaze through half-lidded eyes, running her nails down my chest.

"You're the most beautiful woman I have ever met, and I'll never be worthy of you." I kiss the corner of her mouth, pushing in deeper in a lazy thrust. "You're kind and forgiving."

"Luca..." she holds me now, putting her arms around my neck where they belong.

"Fierce and brave," I sink my teeth gently into her neck, desperate to push away my need to take her harder and fill her. "So fucking strong that I'm envious of you."

Olivia gasps at my fingers rubbing small circles around her clit, teasing her enough to distract her but it's only pushing me closer to the edge. Sweat slides down my back and my skull pounds incessantly at my almost painfully slow thrusts.

She needs this, on her terms. Fuck, on her terms.

I'm not used to this speed. It's taunting, destroying, and completely breathtaking on every slide into her wet heat. My mouth twitches to lean into her, right against her ear and whisper dirty words of encouragement, but my mind keeps me back—locking me up tight, too afraid to push.

She senses my fear. "This... this isn't working." she's pissed, suddenly—pushing me away. "I can't..."

A brick drops into my stomach.

"Olivia, hold on a second," my fingers just miss her wrist.

She's out of my bed, snatching up her clothes before I even have the chance to collect my thoughts.

"I don't want you to be soft with me Luca and I know that makes me sound crazy. Hell, I feel crazy, but I can't do this!" She waves at the bed of rumpled silk. "I can't feel like a victim here too."

I'm walking towards her, my hands snatching the shirt from her grip.

"You will never be a victim in my bed, Bella," I growl.

My hand slips to the bottom of her back, she shakes in my hold until I tilt her chin. "Look at me."

She does, with eyes full of tears. For all the misery and pain she still holds her head high, refusing to feel the weight of it all

"You don't want to face what happened because nothing makes sense and right now you feel like your head is under water."

She nods.

I'm out on my ass, unsure of how to make this right. "And you want to go back to that night when it was just us?"

"Yes," she closes her eyes, as if admitting what she needs is painful.

"Then let's go back," I kiss her once before ripping the t-shirt from her hands and throwing it by the door.

"Watch," I snap.

Dropping to my knees in front of her I skin my palms up the side of her legs until my fingers are underneath in the band of her panties.

They come away in one glide. "You don't need these anymore." I kiss a bruise on the inside of her thigh.

Olivia gasps as I stand to meet her, pressing my lips against hers before pushing her against my bedroom wall.

"Wrap your legs around me," I demand. "That's it. Put your arms around my neck and don't let go until I tell you to."

The trust in her eyes is enough for me to thrust back into her without warning. She doesn't need it. She just needs to forget. And I need to help her.

She meets me on every roll of my hips, pushing down — closing the gaps. Every moan in my ear is a force upon my body, forcing me to pick up speed.

I feel ruthless as I fuck the cries of pleasure from her mouth. There are no doubts holding her muscles tight, no pain pinching at the corner of her eyes.

Just relief and freedom as her release nears. It reaches into my chest, filling me with strength for the first time in weeks.

"Let go. Come on my cock, Bella. That's it, come on," I demand, licking her throat as the first pulse takes her. "Take what you need from me."

"Oh, god!"

I bury myself deeper, succumbing to what can only be an explosion. It starts in the back of my head, sending shooting stars down every nerve ending until I'm on fire.

She cries out just as a fill her, squeezing around me so tightly that I almost buckle under the immense feeling. Olivia's head drops onto my shoulder as she comes down from her own orgasm, panting against my overly sensitized skin.

I place a kiss gently against her cheek, hoping I'd done enough.

CHAPTER TWENTY-FOUR

Olivia Heart

I would laugh if I remembered how to. An orgasm, as primal as it, had lightened the load just enough that when Luca set me back on my feet, I felt a little... freer.

It was wrong to use sex as a Band-Aid. I realized that the moment I straddled him, but I needed to feel the momentum of power in my body, desired to lose myself in pure silence if only for a few seconds and I knew he could give that to me.

And I wanted to laugh.

He was obsessed with me. And I still slipped into his bedroom in the middle of the night to lose myself on his psychotic cock, like the orgasms he gave me held the secrets to getting over my recent trauma. Oh and forgetting all of the shit he had done in between.

What's worse is that for a few seconds it did help.

It is confirmed when I look into his guarded eyes and my heart drops into my stomach. I was crazy for him, gone, so far off the deep end that the surface was nowhere in sight.

"Come on. Let's go to sleep," he took my hand, pulling me towards his bed.

I stopped halfway. "No. I need to go back to my room."

"No, Olivia. We've been apart for far too long. Don't argue with me right now." He tugged me once and I fell into step, letting my gaze flicker across his back where I'd painted his skin with desperation.

"This doesn't mean anything," he pauses just as he pulls the covers back. "Us, having sex doesn't mean I've forgiven you."

"What does it mean, then?"

I hover at the bottom of the bed, looking at his gloriously naked body. Stomach muscles ripple underneath his skin as he fights to keep his breathing steady. He stands, legs slightly parted with enough arrogance to strip the room of air.

Stripped out of his black suited armor, he's more man than beast right now and it makes it harder to keep my distance.

"It means I needed you for a moment," it's a rush of words, spilling untruthfully from my lips, but I don't know how to pull us back from this.

If he's hurt, he doesn't show it. The mask that he's perfected over the years slides gracefully over his face.

"You'll need me for more moments," he tells me, taking a calculated step towards me. "And I'll be here for you to hurt or use." His fingers push a piece of hair behind my ear, careful not to touch my skin.

Anger sizzles beneath the surface of my skin, despising his cool attitude. This isn't what I want from him, and he knows it. We work on push and pull and right now he's refusing to pull me. I'm still damaged, too fragile to stand toe to toe, and he wants me to know it.

"Where will this end?" I asked, fighting my emotions one breath at a time.

A sigh leaves his kiss-swollen lips and I step back. "Wherever you decide."

There's no fight in his eyes, only bone-weary exhaustion, and guilt. I pick up my t-shirt, dress quickly, and leave before I say or do something I'll regret.

****

I eat breakfast with Rum and Red, listening to them argue about the best basketball team in America. Red's all for The Lakers, listing their stats like he practiced the night before in his mirror.

Their argument, although frustrating to listen to with only one working ear, is a good distraction from the feel of a cool breeze against my skin. Clouds hang above us, trying to smother the sun that's helped me heal in relative peace.

But I'm done sitting back.

I spend time in rooms with the air conditioning on, taking deep breaths until the tears in my eyes recede. I compartmentalize my recovery, using my energy to focus on rewiring my brain to react in a non-threatened way.

Banishing myself from mirrors helped my body heal quicker. Now it's not so hard when I catch myself in a reflective surface and see the yellowing bruises still dusting across my skin.

I eat as much as I can, ignoring the urge to push my plate away in fear of it being laced, by always eating with someone. My guards have been good sports about it, distracting me with stories of their history together and encouraging me to eat without thinking about it.

"Good morning, Olivia."

I look up to see Chen hovering behind Red, his face composed and ready for business.

"Good morning," I greet him with a small smile, our relationship is easier after our compromise in the bathroom, but we're not friends yet and that's okay.

"What's up?" Red asks, eyeing his boss carefully.

Chen takes a seat by my side, pulling out his tablet. "Luca and Dante will be joining us soon and I wanted to speak to Olivia before they got here."

I sipped my juice, pretending my heart hadn't jumped up to my throat at the mention of Luca. "About?"

"It's information on the girls found underneath that hotel," he tells me. "I wanted to give you a heads up, so you weren't caught off guard when they arrived."

I eye him, looking at the sincerity shining in his dark eyes. "Where's Bones?"

"I'm here," he comes up behind me, placing a hand on my right shoulder before dropping into his seat. He passes me my sunglasses, his subtle way of telling me that my eyes are full of fear.

I put them on just as Dante and Luca step outside of the house, wrapped up in a tense conversation. They've returned to their roots, donning expensive black suits and perfectly shined shoes. But it's Luca who steals most of my attention, he's shaved down to a precise stubble and his hair has been expertly cut back to his trademark style to compliment his face.

He's an expert at hiding the monster in broad daylight.

Dante smiles my way before he takes a seat next to Bones, leaving the only empty spot at the end of the table for Luca.

"What do you have?" Bones asks, cutting through the awkward silence.

"The British police have identified the bodies underneath the hotel," Chen starts, sliding a finger across the screen. "There were five bodies in total."

I freeze.

Five women.

My throat constricts, "Adler said there was only four."

Chen grimaces. "Technically yes, but one of the women... was pregnant at the time of her death," he tries to show me the autopsy information, but I turn my head, ignoring everyone's eyes. Chen continues. "They identified Adler as the father."

"Of course he was," I bite through gritted teeth, while clenching my dress at my thighs. It takes everything in me not to grab his tablet and throw it to the bottom of the pool.

Cruelty is killing innocent women, but killing his own child is beyond... there are no words to describe the heinous act.

"Who are the other women?" Luca's voice at the top of the table pulls their attention away and I sink into my chair.

"Sarah Hunt, Petra Hemming, Sally Anderson and Lauren Turner."

"How did he pick them?" I ask.

Luca leans forward quickly, catching my attention. "Olivia, does it matter?"

I tilt my chin up in defiance. He thinks just because we slept together, he can start dictating the information I want. Well not today. "It does."

Chen turns to me. "They all have things in common. They come from small cities with little to no family and this..." he turns the tablet towards me. I take my sunglasses off to see past the glint of his screen.

This being that we all look alike. Long brown hair that cascades with a subtle wave towards the ends, bright green eyes that once sparkled, the same petite shaped body... but they're all younger than me, teenagers... a me from years ago.

"What is it?" Luca demands, snapping me away from the edge of a cliff.

Chen answers by turning the screen to face him. It's his face that I watch as he scans the device.

"Cazzo!" Dante stands, turning away from us to face the vineyard — too disgusted to look my way any longer.

Luca's frozen, his dark eyes refusing to leave the tablet until he can't hold it any longer. He looks across the table at me, fury and pain etched across his handsome face and the whole world falls beneath my seat.

They were teenagers. Hunted because they were the younger version of me...

"I did this," my voice betrays me. "Didn't I?" I ask him.

Bones touches my shoulder, but I shrug him off. I can't stand anyone to touch me right now. There are five lives missing off the plane of this earth because I once touched a man and left right after.

What a heinous vixen I was.

"No, you didn't do this, Olivia," Luca snaps.

I stand up on wobbly legs. I need to leave. There isn't enough oxygen out here and I know that's stupid, but I suddenly feel like we're all sharing air and there isn't enough to go round.

Death hovers so close as I look at them all, it clings to my shadow, and I'm suddenly scared they'll become my next victims.

"He was sick, Olivia, long before any of this. You are not what caused him to hurt these women," Luca says.

My hand slams down onto the table, knocking over my juice which pours into Bones' lap — he doesn't move, he's too busy watching me to care.

"I am what caused this. It was me that made him this way. I was the fucking catalyst and if I had just been a little kinder and less self-absorbed maybe he wouldn't have —"

Tears rush down my cheeks. I don't want to voice the worries that have dropped on me from a great height.

"He was evil the day his mother gave birth to him. That kind of desire, to hurt women, doesn't come from a single rejection as a teenager. It's ingrained in his DNA."

Luca doesn't get it, he wasn't there when Adler dragged me across the floors of his filthy hotel, sneering words of hate into my face. He blamed me for it all, for not being able to give my heart to him after we slept together.

"And you?" I ask, ignoring the way Dante turns to face us again with caution in his movements. "You said the night you killed Adler that this," I wave between us, "is because of me. That you are the way you are because—"

"Olivia," Red warns me.

I glare through my tears, relying upon rage to see me through. "—because of me. If I'm not the problem, not the common denominator, then what is it? Because from where I'm standing, I'm the reason you haven't been able to live a normal life for eight years and that there are five bodies waiting to be reburied."

"Are you comparing me to him, Olivia?" Luca sneers, rounding the table until he's at my side, towering over me.

Yes.

I shiver at his next words. "Do you think we're one of the same?"

"I think... that it's my fault you're the way you are, and he was the way he was."

Luca reaches out to grab my arm, but Bones yanks me back with force, forgetting that I'm human. I teeter in my wedges, hitting the arm of his chair before falling to the ground with an ungraceful thud.

"Don't fucking touch her," Bones sneers.

Luca looks down at me in a useless heap and loses it. The restraint snaps, allowing his fist to answer back, connecting squarely with Bones' jaw and then another to his left eye.

"You fucking idiot!" he growls, launching another punch. "Look. What. You. Did."

This is what my life has come to. Violence. Bloodshed and death.

I laugh as they go to war, trading blow after blow. Nobody intervenes. This has been building for a while now and there's a code to follow. Dante, Red, and Rum make their way over to me while Chen dances on the outside of the fight.

Luca knees Bones between the legs before slamming his elbows into the crook of his neck. Bones falls with a grunt, his knees cracking against the concrete.

"Smettila, smettila subito! branco di buffoni!" *Stop it, stop this right now! You bunch of buffoons!* Marie screams, thwacking at them both with a dishtowel.

Laurel rushes to my side, carefully lifting me up and away from the table as Luca pulls back, surprise across his face as Marie rains down on him.

"You will not do this! Not today! Not to Miss Heart," Marie bares her teeth, shoving at Luca with all her tiny might. "Not on my time, Mr. Caruso!"

"Marie," he smooths down his jacket, a slight blush creeping on his cheeks, "please stop hitting me with that damn towel — I've stopped!" he ducks another hit.

"Your ma! She be ashamed of you, Mr. Caruso."

"Hit him again," Bones grumbles, wiping at his bloody lip.

Marie doesn't take too kindly to him either, she turns with the agility of a cheetah and whacks him upside the head with her right hand.

"Stupidi uomini!" *Stupid men!* She hisses. Without missing a beat, she takes my spare arm and pulls me towards the house with Laurel, leaving the men to stare after us.

"They think with fists," she grumbles, her chin wobbling. "Not enough brain cells between them!"

"It was my fault," I tell her, huddling close to her motherly protection. I had misjudged Marie — the woman was nothing short of a fierce mamma bear when provoked. "All of this is my fault. They're dead because of me... those women didn't stand a chance against him because of what I did."

It's Laurel who takes me by surprise, her rough English cutting off my pity. "No. Not your fault. No," she shakes her head, loosening up the messy bun of auburn hair. "Some men are born without control. Yes?"

"Sì" *Yes.* Marie agrees, her mouth set in a grim line. "Most are born with the diavolo in them."

"And Luca, do you think he was born with the devil inside of him?" I ask, expecting a non-honest answer.

Marie stops to consider me, carefully wiping away my tears. I suck in a breath, fighting the overwhelming feeling to hug her — to relive a childhood I lost.

"Sì, but the difference between Mr. Caruso and that *man* is Mr. Caruso fights his every day — for you, always for you."

My brain had already consumed too much energy dealing with the aftermath of Adler's brutality and the fight moments ago had stolen more. So, I didn't ask Marie to elaborate on what she means, instead I let them take me to my room, help me slip of my shoes and into the bed where I could forget that everything was crumbling around me.

"Sleep now," Marie whispered as she kissed the top of my head.

CHAPTER TWENTY-FIVE

Olivia Heart

O livia," Bones starts while I make my way through the gardens, being careful to miss the sprinklers that are watering the lawn. I'd woken an hour ago to the complete darkness, having wasted a day in bed, and I needed to get out.

"Go away," I hiss, waving him away as I make my way to the garage. "I want to be alone."

"I want to apologize about earlier. Caruso got under my skin, and I acted like a complete ass."

"You did."

"And I'm sorry you got hurt in the middle of it."

"Apology accepted, now leave me alone."

The 3-inch touch sensitive lock glinted in the darkness, flashing red against my face.

Would it be programmed to my fingertip? Had Chen and Luca somehow miraculously lifted my fingerprint off a surface to give me access to my father's prized possession?

Turns out they had. On the third scan the garage door squeaked and began to lift up.

Bones panics behind me, "Are you leaving?"

Gritting my teeth, I waited for the doors to fully open before answering. The car hadn't been moved since Luca first revealed it to me. It sat underneath its protective cover just waiting to be admired.

"No, you know I can't. Right now, I just want to be alone." *Take the damn hint.*

"With a car?"

"With my *dad's* car."

Sucking in breath, I felt Bones shift behind me. This was not a subject to be taken lightly and he knew me well enough by now to not push. "I'll be in the house if you need anything."

"Okay," I mumbled, already forgetting about him as I turned the lights on and pulled back the cover. The Porsche Speedster was as stunning as I remembered. Cherry red paint beamed at me with a perfection my dad would have been in awe of. He always wanted to restore the paint to the original but worried that this particular red was end of the line, or that he would find rust in the steelwork underneath.

Lucky for me, keys sat on a hook by the garage door. With one twist of a key the doors popped open and filled the room with a scent of leather and... Luca.

I sat in the passenger seat, looking over at the driver's side. Had Luca driven this car before he kidnapped me? I can't imagine him taking this out of the garage, it was too old, too small, and not enough horsepower for the vehicles he loves to drive.

"It has to be taken out a few times to stop the battery from running down," Luca tells me as he steps in from the darkness and stands in the light. I hate him and how handsome he looks under the fluorescent lighting. It isn't fair to look that good in jeans and a plain black t-shirt.

"You don't have staff to do that?"

He pushes a hand through his hair, "I do for my other vehicles but not this one. This is yours so it's important that I take care of it." He points to the driver's side. "May I?"

I want to refuse him access, afraid that being this close to him may lead to another explosive row, but I stupidly nod instead. And when he invades the tight space with his scent of soap, whiskey, and aniseed — I regret not opening my mouth.

It's too much all at once.

"I was given the option to upgrade the car to an automatic," he points to the gearstick. "But I thought that would be beside the point of restoring a car to its original state."

"My dad would have hated it to be turned into an automatic," I blurt out. "He thought automatics were for lazy drivers."

"He's right — they are." He doesn't look at me, instead he leans back against the cream leathered seat and closes his eyes. I watch him for what feels like minutes, just breathing quietly until he opens his eyes. "Do you want to go out in it?"

I took a deep breath. "Where?"

He shrugs, "Anywhere you want."

"The beach?"

He raises an eyebrow, "It's dark. You won't be able to enjoy the sea."

"Darkness never stopped anybody." It's my turn to shrug as I hold out the keys to him. "It's either the beach or I go back inside."

He takes the keys from my hands, his light touch lingers for a little too long, burning the palm of my hand.

He clears his throat, feeling our fucked-up chemistry. "Shouldn't you tell Bones that you're leaving?"

"Yes." I lift up my phone, opening up a text message. "You should probably start driving before I hit send."

"I should have punched him harder," Luca growls, turning the key in the ignition.

The car roars to life, igniting a sense of Deja Vu in me which strangely offers comfort I didn't think possible from the little red car. It's only when we move, leaving the house and onto the open roads that I realize how much I needed to feel close to my dad.

****

I couldn't see a damn thing from where I stood other than the moon glinting off the water below me, but I refused to let that bother me. We stood near the cliff edge, held back by a metal barrier which overlooked the deserted beach. If I squinted hard enough, I could just make out the neatly stacked sun loungers and parasols littering the vast space.

I shivered against the tepid breeze pushing us away from the edge. It wasn't so cold that I felt the itch of fear, but it was close, under my skin just waiting to destroy my moment of peace.

"Why does this place feel familiar?" I ask out loud, not expecting an answer.

"He brought you here." Luca pointed towards two palm trees by a small beach bar. "Swapped cars right there before setting the first one on fire."

I paused, absorbing the information before I turned back towards the beach. "I was mainly out of it. I just remember hearing the blades of a helicopter."

Luca stepped forward, stiff, radiating a dangerous energy that I recognized. "I came after you as soon as I realized what had happened."

"I know." I did know. There wasn't a single doubt in my mind that he hadn't scoured his home country for me when I had gone missing.

Sighing, I made my way down the slope towards the beach, being careful not to trip in my wedges. Luca followed close behind, careful not to crowd me as I made it to the bottom where soft sand waited.

With my one good ear, I heard the sound of the water crashing against the bottom of the cliff, dampening the sounds of my own thoughts. And the pure light of the moon, glittering prettily off the water smothered the anxiety humming in my veins.

I loved this place already.

With a sigh, I kicked off my shoes and headed towards the water, letting my feet sink into the sand that was still warm underneath its top layer.

Luca followed, kicking of his shoes and socks until we stood side by side — our faces lit by natural light. We were complete opposites once again. Where I was lit up with natural light he stood back in the shadows, where he belonged.

"Do you really think I'm like him, Olivia?"

I focused on the water, scared to face him. One look at him right now and the pressure would cause an astronomical crack in my structure I was trying to rebuild.

"No, I don't think you're like him like that, you would never hurt me or... other innocent women. He was sick in a way that you could never be. I understand that now. But I do think... this, what you — " I suck in a breath of sea air, letting it cleanse my mouth of the harshness that lingers. " — have for me is just as dangerous."

"I don't understand," he steps forward, glaring out at the water. "You think me loving you is dangerous?"

"Yes," I bite out. "If Adler was right about one thing it was about me. Look what I've done to you, to your life, Luca! You could be happy with someone else, someone not so fucking damaged — who doesn't make you want to lie, plot, or murder. But instead you're here with me on this empty beach." I cut him off, taking a step back. I need to say this. "Hoping to fix something that's already broken."

"No!" he growls, grabbing me gently, cupping my face. "This is what he wanted, to come between your happiness as his last demented wish and I refuse to let you grant it. You are not to blame for his actions or mine."

I open my mouth to protest but he cuts me off, slamming his lips onto mine — pushing my anger back down until all I can think about is his tongue in my mouth and his fingers in my hair.

Against my lips he whispers, "He was sick. He wasn't in love with you. He didn't care about you, about your feelings, or your safety. Adler just wanted to destroy what he couldn't have because he was a coward scared of facing rejection."

He pulls back so quickly I sway. "Luca, wait."

His smile is soft and gentle. "I'm sick on you, I love you, I care about you, about your feelings and your safety, albeit a little too much." I grip his shirt, trying to stop myself from launching into his arms and burying my face in his neck. Instead, the tears fall, faster than they ever have before.

"Hate me, hurt me, fuck, put a knife through my chest right now for all the shit that I have done and failed to do. But don't ever tell me that I'll be happier with someone else." He kisses me again, desperately. "I can fix this, Olivia, even if I have to spend my whole life trying. I'll go to therapy for you, give up my millions, hell, you tell me what to do and I'll do it. Just don't walk away yet. Let me make this right."

Is it possible to feel someone else's soul ache by just being close to them? Like the guardian he is to Luca and me, suddenly Dante is all I can hear.

"All I know is that you're killing him, bit by bit you're taking something from him whether you know it or not. Whether he deserves it or not"

Luca and I's past four weeks have been very different, but without needing to know all of his side, I'm certain, as it is dark out here on this desolate beach that he has suffered. He's been dealt a galaxy of karma, forced into a loss of control, and had all his worst nightmares come true. But even when he could have left it at that he was finally honest with me, leaving nothing left unsaid when the repercussions were deadly.

I can't deny him any longer.

"Can we sit here for a while?"

CHAPTER TWENTY-SIX

Luca Caruso

I used to hate her silence. It was a weapon she often used to keep me out when she felt vulnerable, or when I was too close to seeing the real her, but right now she's silent because she's contemplating our future.

And there isn't any chance I'm going to ruin the small possibility with my impatience. I'm not a stupid man who doesn't learn from the important lessons in life. In that aspect I'm nothing like my Pa, and I have Olivia to thank for that.

So with her back to my chest, we sit in the sand watching the moon in the reflection of the choppy waters.

"I wanted to die," her voice is merely a whisper, catching in the wind until it howls into my ears.

On instinct I tighten my hold around her waist. She didn't have to say the words, I saw it the moment I found her in that dining hall. She had been stripped of all her strength until she was nothing but a vessel trying to survive.

"If I could kill him over and over I would, for even putting those thoughts into your head."

She sinks into me, softening just a touch. "I didn't welcome death because he was hurting me. I could... mostly deal with that and his sadistic lessons by tuning him out, disappearing into my head."

Just like she had after the death of her parents.

"But he knew how to get to me in there," her laugh is tight, wrapped in pain as she taps her temple. "When I was at my weakest and the drugs hit their peak, he would use you to pull me apart over and over, with the threat to expose you to the whole world."

"I know." A memory of his delivery presents itself. "He returned the clothes you were wearing with mockups of his plans," carefully I smooth her hair to one side, pushing it over her shoulders, "but they wouldn't have stopped me from finding you, Olivia."

Pain pinches at her beautiful face. "I understand you more and more now. You're the only person that can hurt me, Luca, and I you. Does that make us weaker together?"

"No. We're only weak apart."

"I'm afraid it isn't over," she turns to me and looks up into my eyes. "I trust that Chen and his team have done everything to wipe the threads of us all, but I can't shake this feeling that something else is coming — that there's still one attached."

The last thing I want to do is ruin our one moment of peace, but I made a silent promise to myself that I wouldn't keep Olivia in the dark anymore.

"Emilia?"

She turns back to face the sea, not before the hurt flashes across her face.

"Yes. I think… she's his insurance policy. Why else would he have let her live when everyone else died?"

Chen and Dante both had the same suspicions regarding my ex-fiancé, but until the words left Oliva's lips, I didn't think Adler would have had the foresight. But clearly, I had underestimated him once before and it ended up with Olivia getting hurt. Those days were over.

"We'll find her," I promised, kissing the shell of her ear. "And I know just how to do it."

****

Olivia and I didn't speak as we watched the sun rise, nor did we utter a word on the way home. Content in our individual silence, we left the beach with my jacket around Olivia's shoulders and my hand in hers.

When the gates swung open to our home, she was greeted by a sour looking Bones and escorted back to her room while I slipped into my office with a smirk on my face.

His words followed me into my space, "if by some miracle she needs you after all this then you better be strong enough to fix it—to fix her, otherwise it'll be me that puts a knife through your chest."

Not that his threat filled me with anything but annoyance, I still understand the severity of his message. I understood that tonight's thinly veiled white flag may be my last chance at redemption, so I did what didn't come naturally.

I swallowed my fucking ego, fed it to the parasitical monster clutching to my soul, and decided to throw everything into this. My promises could never be empty again and the prison doors keeping Olivia to me could never be locked.

It was easy to change when she was by my side. Her innocence and strength made me want to take a knife to my DNA, to cut out all of the parts covered in blood, and throw them down at her feet.

I just had to bridge the gap between Luca with Olivia by his side and Luca on his own, sitting in his office wondering if she was still planning on leaving him.

****

When I found her, she was walking bare foot through the gardens at the back of the house, running her hands over the heads of freshly bloomed roses. Her long hair was piled up messily on top of her head with long strands framing her face, exposing the top of her shoulders to the morning sun.

Olivia looked like the embodiment of mother nature, dressed in a slip of a green dress that made the green of her eyes pop with an innocence I hadn't seen in weeks.

If it wasn't for the pink tinged welts across her shoulder blades or the yellowing bruises at the back of her neck, I would have assumed she was completely free to enjoy the garden.

"Are you going to stand there and stare all day?" she calls to me, over her shoulder with a slight smirk.

"Would that make you uncomfortable?" my eyes caught sight of wings fluttering by the side of her right ear. The butterfly descended, sitting on the rose she had just been admiring.

"It doesn't make me feel uncomfortable," she smiled, she too noticing the creature close by. "Although the look Bones is giving you right now is."

"Fuck him," I pushed off the side of the house, ignoring the heat of her guard's glare who was sitting by the fountain, his arms across his chest. "He's just pissed that you haven't put a knife in my chest yet."

She frowns. "He's just looking out for me, Luca."

"I know," I tell her, hiding the bitterness I felt. "I've not come out here to talk about him, Bella, there's been an update on the last thread you're worried about."

The softness once captured across her face is gone and regret wrings its merciless hands across my lungs. But I swallow past the lump in my throat. She needs this, to be included in everything so she can see that I don't want to hurt her.

"You've found her?"

"Not quite. We've found her sister."

She takes a step to me, lifting her hand to shield her eyes from the sun. "I don't understand."

"Emilia is extremely protective over her sister, Everette, and we're going to use her to draw Emilia out."

"When you say *use her*, what does that mean?"

I turn my body, using my back to shield her from the sun so she can see my face. "Nothing extreme. We'll arrange a meeting to find out what she knows, and Emilia will no doubt jump to the worst conclusion and try to save her sister."

"And you think Emilia is still in the country?"

"I'm certain of it. She has enough money to leave, but she could never abandon her family, especially her only sibling."

Olivia crosses her arms, defensively. "When you say we..."

"Me and you. We're going to do this together—if that's what you want, of course."

Her eyes widen in surprise, and I want to kiss her. Did she think that my promises last night had been made in desperation only? Christ, the urge to touch her, to trace my fingers across her collarbone is as strong as my heartbeat when she looks at me like this—with hope—it's unbearably strong.

Why had I never seen the beauty in affording her freedom before?

"Luca..." she takes a tentative step, "are you sure?"

I shouldn't but I do. My addiction to her is harder to tamper down when she's so close. My fingers trace the strap of her dress wanting to push it over her shoulder, to see her naked by the roses.

"I am. You need the closure and I need to give it to you."

Her hands twitch at her sides, reminding me of the streets of Paris, when she had launched herself into my arms and kissed me with abandon. Instead of reminiscing, she locks down her muscles. "And what if my closure is the end of Emilia?"

She stares up at me, her eyes full of confidence and the fire of hell—Emilia's grip on Olivia started the moment those pictures were thrust into her hands at Aida's party, decimating her fragile trust in me. And to have that dragged into her torture for two weeks allowed her anger to fester into hatred. It was unforgiveable and I had to fix it.

"I will not stand in your way."

It wasn't enough for Olivia, she wanted more—needed to know if the doubt in her eyes had reason to be there. "Will it hurt you?"

"No, any remote feelings I had towards her disappeared the moment she teamed up with Adler. So, seek your revenge to fit her crimes, Olivia. All I ask is that you let me be there while you do it."

CHAPTER TWENTY-SEVEN

Olivia Heart

D ante had managed to set up a meeting with Everette Vicolay in two days' time under the guise that it would be him meeting her and not me. Our little trap was to be held in a small restaurant that wasn't owned by either the Carusos or Vicolays in the city. It was neutral ground that was more likely to pull Emilia out of her hiding spot.

Bones, Red, and Rum began preparations for securing the building, bringing me into the fold so that if anything went wrong, I would know who to run to.

Luca, Dante, and Chen had all questioned me separately about how I would deal with his ex-fiancé, but I chose not to share that information. My plan was fragile at best, teetering on the emotional side, and I truly didn't know what I wanted.

What could make me feel better?

Hurting her? Scarring her? Killing her? I doubted those methods would bring solace, but sometimes when I was alone and trying not to fall back into a pit of rage it was all I craved.

And when I couldn't sit in the dark for too long, I would search for the one man who would understand.

The first time it happened he was in his office, sitting at his desk on the phone—snapping at his accountant. Dressed impeccably in an Armani suit, I noted how he hadn't taken his jacket off, probably too preoccupied on the phone.

I didn't bother to wait for his conversation to end or for his near black eyes to settle on me when I slipped under his desk. There were memories to erase for the both of us and I couldn't risk Luca talking me out of it.

I nipped at his fingers when he tried to pull me up. He was hard as soon as my knees hit the carpet and a flare of satisfaction bloomed in my belly. The power was distracting, and I wanted it for as long as I could get it.

"Cosa hai detto?" *What did you say?* He barked into his phone as my fingers grasped at his belt and tugged open his fly. A low hiss slipped through the tight line of his mouth while he watched me remove the straps of my dress.

"Sì, sono qui. Vai avanti." Yes, I'm here. Get on with it.

I stifle my laugh; afraid it would tip him over the edge and ruin my fun. There was something so pleasing about seeing him lose control, watching the veins in his arms pop as he gripped his thigh, stopping himself from reaching me.

Dark eyes followed my every move, questioning my motives which sent me tipping into my own lust. The pulse of me began to ache, reawakening the dramatic thump of my heart and the slick heat between my thighs.

I wasn't damaged. Just hidden.

Leaning down I ran my tongue across Luca's knuckles, nipping at him to distract him from my hands in his boxers. I was quick at releasing him, sweeping across his cock with a delicate touch — feathering my lust against his skin.

No bad memories swept into my conscience. They remained bolted behind steel doors, guarded by knowledge that the man who had hurt me was dead and burnt to ash.

I survived.

And I would continue to survive, reaping the happiness that I deserved as long as I remembered who I was. That no chains strong enough, no matter how many in quantity or strength could bind me to hell again.

I almost smiled as I took Luca into my mouth for the first time. Under my lashes he had frozen, holding his breath as I tasted him. A moan settled in the back of my throat, surprising us both.

God, he was magnificent when he was lost in his desire.

My skin burned with lazy, slow to burn lust. It was the most natural emotion I had ever felt, so beautiful as it slithered through my veins until it reached my heart and the space between my thighs simultaneously.

I was in charge of my desire. I was in control of Luca, even with my knees digging into the carpet underneath his desk.

"Put the phone down," I mumbled, licking the tip of his cock lazily. "It can wait."

A threaded sigh left his lips before he put the phone down, slamming it onto his desk, not bothering to say goodbye to his accountant.

"Olivia—"

It was perfect time to take him into my mouth again, tasting the sweet saltiness, feeling the silky skin and every vein in his thick cock.

The overwhelming urge to take him deeper flared in my belly. Bright and bold. Opening my mouth, I took him deeper, lapping his girth with the warmth of my tongue. Around and around.

"Christ!" he choked out.

Fuck. I was so wet that it was dripping down my thighs, onto the lush carpet.

I moaned around him, laving my tongue in tighter circles around the head of his cock until his fingers threaded in my hair. His hold was possessive with a fine thread of restraint holding him back from me and what we both needed.

I hated it instantly.

Pulling away I glared up at him from under my lashes, while gripping the base of his cock. "Treat me like glass and I'll stop."

His eyes flashed, dark with frustration and I saw that he wanted to argue. He must have seen the fire building in my eyes because he simply huffed and settled tightening his hold in my hair, sending a pulse of pleasure to my clit.

"You won't stop," he pulled me forward, sliding his wet cock across the seam of my lips, "Not until I say you can, Bella."

I shivered into myself, consciously aware that I was wet and turned on beyond belief by the frustration flooding from him.

Sensing my need for more, Luca shifted forward as he pushed into my mouth, forcing his way into my throat without apology. I gagged, trying to accommodate him until he pulled back to let me gather myself. His patience lasted all of three seconds before he began to fuck my mouth.

Tears stung at the corner of my eyes on every thrust. My throat would be bruised tomorrow but these I could handle. I wanted a physical reminder of my decision, of my control over him.

"You dropped to your knees to *use* me, Olivia?" He grunted, thrusting harshly with a half-lidded gaze. "You need to replace your memories, don't you? Oh, Bella... I understand what you need from me."

Before I could prepare, he grabbed my jaw, sliding across my tongue to shoot thick, hot cum into the back of my throat.

Momentarily I drowned on the taste of him and the lust burning into my lungs.

God, this was too much. He was too much, but so was I. Before I could pull myself back into my body, Luca lifted me up onto his lap, yanking my head back by my hair and sinking his teeth into my neck.

I screamed, momentarily forgetting who I was or why I was here. The sensation of his teeth against my skin was nearly enough to set the fireworks off in my head. I would have come right there if he didn't pull away to look at me.

"Olivia, you don't understand what you've just done," he groaned, shaking his head. "Now I've had your mouth..."

The feel of his heart, thrashing against his chest was heady.

"...I'm suddenly glad you have a rabid dog protecting you," I groaned into the second bite. "Otherwise I'll never get a single thing done."

Suddenly I went from glass to steel.

CHAPTER TWENTY-EIGHT

Olivia Heart

Patience is a virtue. Unless you're the men in my life — who are dressed in black, all glaring over breakfast, trying their best to unnerve me enough so that I'll spill and include them in my plans. If I didn't know them as well as I did, it may have worked.

Dante is the first to break the silence. "The British police are putting a profile together," his eyes slide to me before resting on Luca. "Olivia is on the top of their list of people to talk to."

I didn't flinch, although my body wanted to. Instead, I sip my juice, focusing on the automation of my throat. "What do they have on me?"

"Not much," he shrugged. "But they're putting together the last time Adler was seen publicly, tracing back the people he spoke to. It's only a matter of time they notice the likeness of the women he murdered."

I tipped my face back, enjoying the warmth that I thought I would never feel again while my heart ached for those Adler murdered. "I'll speak to them if the time ever comes."

"You will not," Luca growls. "There is no reason to speak to them, Olivia. It's done. Let them close their investigation without your help."

"There will be a reason once they put it together," I grit my teeth, "and I'll be ahead of it, burying it deep enough that they'll never come looking again."

Standing up I dusted off the bottom of my black dress and slipped back into my matching heels. I was prepared for war, armed in the color Luca favored when he meant business.

Well, that's what he told me this morning as he watched me pick out my clothes. His dark eyes had followed me around the room, appraising my curves with unfinished desire.

After our tryst in his office, I had swept out of the room and disappeared before he could reciprocate. When he returned to me later on that evening, I had cut him off, pushing him out of the room in favor of my laptop and the project I was working on.

There was so much that I had to hide from him. We were treading a fine line, a whisper away from falling over it and I knew in my heart it would be me pulling us down if I wasn't careful.

Sometimes I felt hateful towards him, my rage bubbling like molten steel waiting to smother him and harden him for all that he had done. And other times I wanted to bury my face in his chest and listen to the one honest part of him, the heart that ticked for me.

It was too much to work through all at once. So instead of focusing on either of the extremities, I chose the safest option. His body.

"Not alone," he warns me, standing up and buttoning his suit jacket. He was perfectly put together, not a wrinkle in place, but something was different with him today. He seemed... dangerous, on edge. Like a single breeze may be his undoing.

"I dealt with these people before you, Luca. I'm capable of dealing with the police again."

Bones smirks at my side, enjoying this version of me a lot. He told me so last night when I told him I didn't require his security services at my bedroom door every night.

I sigh and pick up my purse. It's time to leave.

I step out, and they fall in line. My guards slot in their spaces at my sides, looking like men ready to slaughter. We're a line of black and fury, ready to fight for one another, and my heart swells two sizes too big.

We're an unlikely family, forced together by obsession, but we love each other nonetheless.

Luca steps at my side and Dante joins him.

"I know you're capable," Luca whispers, catching my elbow, "but I would rather you didn't have to deal with them."

I smile knowingly. "Unfortunately, we don't always get the easy way out."

****

Dante entered the restaurant with a saunter, hiding the purpose in his carefully calculated steps. Through my earpiece he's greeted stiffly, a soft female voice, that of Everette Vicolay, floats into my one working ear.

My eyes catch Luca's and the resignation I find forces me to pause, if only for a second. We didn't have time for this.

"You ready?" I ask.

"I'm not letting you out of my sight in there," he grabs my chin, tipping my eyes up to his. "You'll hear some things that will make you hate me more than you already do, but I won't leave you. You will be at my side until it's over."

"I know," I sigh. "Come on, we have some loose ends to tie up."

Red helps me out of the car, his tight smile following me as I cross the road with Luca at my side. Luca and I entered together, adjusting to the dark mood lighting of the small restaurant.

It was empty, red buffed chairs stood on top of tables, all except for a singular table in the middle of the room.

Everette stood in shock, her mouth gaping at the man by my side. I smile at her, the mirror image of her sister except Everette is shorter and graced with bigger breasts that make her look more vixen than model. But by the glint of revenge in her eyes, she was just as vicious as Emilia.

Good.

Luca is the first to greet her. "Everette. Please don't try to leave, you're surrounded, and I don't have the patience to watch you try to escape."

"I don't know where she is!" She hisses at Luca, not bothering to address me.

"We know," he agrees as he holds out a seat for me at the small table.

Dante nods at us both before leaving out the back, placing a wad of cash on the counter before he disappears.

Everette's body follows him, her hips turning slightly.

"Sit," I offer, my hand pointing towards the empty seat, "per favore" *Please.*

She hisses a curse in Italian under her breath while doing as she's asked. I'm pretty certain she called me a bitch, but I let it slide. I'm really not in the mood to waste my energy on her.

"What do you want?" She slams her hand passionately on the table, jolting the salt and pepper enough to make them rattle.

"We want nothing from you," Luca responds in a bored, dispassionate tone that comes naturally, but he watches her hand. If she stretches any closer, I'm certain he'll place the knife in his pocket between her fingers—pinning her to the cheap table.

Finally, after a beat of silence, Everette looks to me and visibly swallows. Sweat beads across her smooth forehead as we size one another up.

Like her sister, we are completely different women. They wear their emotions on their face while I keep mine hidden, like the perfect poker face.

"I'm sorry that you're caught in the middle of this, Everette," I tell her gently, "but it's the only way to put this to bed."

She scoffs, dismissing me with a wave. "You're sorry? After everything that he has done to her, because of you!? You disgust me. Both of you... disgusting, flaunting your sickness in front of her!"

I don't flinch as I slam my hand down on Luca's thigh, keeping him in place.

"Your disgust is misplaced. It should be held for your sister after everything she has done to get her revenge." My smile is tight when the cool air from the air conditioner kicks in. "If you want to hear the truth then stay. If you want to remain blissfully unaware, then leave. Either way, I don't care for your opinions."

"Incoming," Bones' deep voice rumbles in my right ear.

My eyes slide to Luca. He searches my face, looking for a sign that I cannot handle this. He nods when he doesn't find it and grasps my hand under the table.

"You have a few seconds before your sister arrives," Everette looks to the door, her eyes widening with fear. "Stay or go."

"She'll stay," Emilia steps in from the back, bathed in darkness before stepping into the restaurant. Unlike the first time I saw her, she doesn't look her usual self. There are bags under her eyes, her hair is a mess piled on top of her head and her clothes look rumpled.

"Smart. A witness," I smile, motioning for the woman who set me up to take a seat across from me. By the way I'm acting, anyone would think we were two girlfriends meeting up for lunch.

Emilia takes her seat, blushing profusely under the heated gaze of Luca. Under my touch he vibrates with rage, barely tethered to his restraint, and right now I need him to relax.

"I could kill you right here," he snaps at her. "Slit your fucking throat for what you've done."

Everette jumps in, "You won't touch her."

"No he won't," I agree. "But I might." I turn to Emilia, coaxing a slight smile upon my lips. "And you would deserve it wouldn't you, Emilia?"

Emilia sniffs, lifting her chin as she tries to gather her composure. Unfortunately for her, she left it at the door when she decided to save her sister at the last minute.

"I didn't know what he was going to do," she lies, easily. "He told me he was going to get you help. To keep you away from him," she scowls over at Luca, her hatred covering her lack of confidence.

"We both know that's a lie," I sigh, slipping my hand from Luca's thigh. "You took pleasure in knowing what type of man Adler was and you knew what he would do to me. It's why you were so confident the night I was taken — you knew how much it would kill Luca once Adler raped and murdered me."

From the corner of my eye Luca freezes.

"You thought that once the dust settled and Luca got over my death you could come back, didn't you?"

"No," she snaps furiously. "I just wanted him to know how it felt."

"How what felt?" I ask softly.

Everette shook her head but we both ignored her.

"To be destroyed," her bottom lip wobbles and I feel the pain she's held for years begin to taint the air. She looks to Luca, trying to summon her hatred for him but it's too late. She knows it's over for her.

"Adler wanted to destroy me, Emilia. He stripped me, drugged me, walked me like a dog, beat me, tried to rape me..." My lungs barely fill with air and I feel dizzy, but I refuse to falter, "all because I had refused him once, years ago. I refused to give him all of me and the evil I endured was because of that. Do you understand why I'm telling you this?"

Everette grabs her sister's hand, looking at me with horror, but it's not me that's the villain in this room.

"I don't—"

I can't look at Luca when I speak, just knowing that he's at my side is hard enough. "Because you are just like Adler. Luca rejected you over and over again and instead of leaving him, cutting your losses, you chose to wait and destroy him. You and Adler are one of the same."

"No!" she cries. "I am not like that beast... yes, I gave him information and yes, I got you out of that house, but I didn't want this—I just wanted..."

Shaking my head I lean forward. "You were hurt. I can't imagine what it felt like being with someone so completely devoted to another."

Her big blue eyes fill with water. "You can't," there's a bite to her tone I don't appreciate. "It was always you, hanging over

216

us like a dark cloud, and he would never admit to it," she wipes furiously at her eyes. "Imagine the man you love in love with someone else."

"I told you from the start I didn't want anything serious," he tells her calmly. "You could have left at any time. You were not trapped to me, Emilia."

She scoffs. "Of course you would say that, Luca, but I loved you and it wasn't as simple as walking away. I had hope..."

As she glares over at him, wanting so desperately for him to feel her pain and hurt from it, I thought about what it would be like to walk away from Luca. It would hurt, no, it would feel like razors wedged between my ribcage with every breath slicing into me. It would be slow torture brought on by my own decisions.

"You were always so absent, but I had hope that one day you would realize she wasn't right for you—that I would be enough. You wouldn't have had to change for me... I always accepted you the way you were." Emilia's voice pulled me from my pain. "Even when you would stand me up or forget my birthday, I stupidly thought that once your obsession burnt out with her you would be mine—completely."

"Never," Luca shrugged, owing her no further explanation.

Fire suddenly burned in her eyes, swallowing up her pity party for one. "You always were a selfish bastard," she hissed. "In bed and out—"

Everette snaps. "That's enough."

Emilia turns to me, eager to lash out. "The last time we fucked it was your name that he moaned. Did you know that?"

Luca tenses and I'm certain without looking at him that he's embarrassed. Emilia's out to hurt him—still it's what I expected, but I had to be sure.

The corner of my mouth turns up. "Are you sure? Our names are pretty similar after all..."

"I'm sure," she bites with a glower. "As sure as I am that the only reason he was with me was because of how similar our names are."

"More fool of you for staying," I sigh. "Sounds to me like you're a glutton for punishment. It's such a shame Adler didn't take to you instead."

That gets her, the rise that I need to end this once and for all. She lurches out of her chair, ready to slap me but I stand, catch her hand, and shove her back into her sister. I'll never allow another person to hurt me.

I click my earpiece while Luca grips my hip, bringing me over to his side. "Red, there's a document under your seat. Bring it to me now."

"Olivia, what are you doing?" he whispers into my ear.

I turn to look at him, softening just a touch. "Fixing this."

It's all I'll give him and luckily, he doesn't have time to push when Red saunters in with the black file I prepared last night. I take it gratefully before stopping him with a hand on his arm.

"Can you escort Luca out please?"

CHAPTER TWENTY-NINE

Olivia Heart

N o," he tells me. "I'm not leaving."
"You're not," I agree, gently pushing him towards the door. "You're just going to wait outside for me."

Red holds open the door, letting the sunlight in, and right now I'd give anything to go out there and hold my face up to the sky. But instead I have to finish this.

"Five minutes," he stops just at the threshold. "And I'm coming in to get you."

"Ten," I argue, crossing my arms over my chest. He won't deny me the extra time, not when he knows he owes me my freedom and the option to make my own decisions.

He doesn't like it though. His hands twitch to grab me and pull me out of restaurant while his eyes glare at me to submit.

"Ten," he finally agrees, leaning into me. "Keep your line open or I'll come in and shut this down."

I nod, momentarily stunned by the proximity. I don't understand the reaction — it's not like we haven't been this close before. Unsure of my strange reaction, he kisses my cheek once before stepping out into the sunlight.

"Say the word, Olivia, and we'll be in there." Bones' voice floats into my ear from his spot at the side of the restaurant, shaded by palm trees.

Taking my seat, I ignore the glare of Emilia and the worry of her sister. Their feelings are not important to me, and I want them to know that.

"Right, shall we get this messed cleaned up?"

"Cleaned up?" Emilia raised a perfectly shaped brow. "Like it can? After everything?"

"After everything," I agree, opening up my surprise. "All you need to do is sign every single one of these and it will be over. Nobody else will get hurt."

Everette is much smarter than her sister, she at least has the audacity to look suspicious while Emilia simply stares at the lifeline — making me feel sick with pity.

"You sure?" Bones hisses. "I have a clear shot. Say the word and I can take both out."

I pinch the bridge of my nose, fighting the urge to say yes. It would be so easy to watch Emilia get what she deserves, and surely I would be doing the world justice by extinguishing her evil?

I shake my head, remembering that she is a product of Luca's obsession for me, and I have to allow some concessions.

Keeping a hold of my humanity is still important, even when the darkness seems to have a louder voice.

"The first document is a statement that you will sign. It includes everything that you have done, participated in, and accepted alongside Adler. Which includes but not limited to Blackmail, fraud, tax evasion, and aiding in a kidnapping."

Emilia splutters, narrowing her eyes in on me. "I'll go to prison!"

"Only if you cross me, and I don't think you want to do that anymore," I tell her. "Think of this as my insurance plan. If anything is to happen to me, Luca, or my guards this will end up in the police's hands."

She looks to her sister who has buried her head in her hands — too stunned to argue.

"The second is a refund request from your bank account to mine. You will be refunding the amount of two million euros that Adler sent you through his offshore accounts — "

"Holy fuck," Red whispers into my ear.

"Dante," Luca growls after.

Dante, last night, had been kind enough to give me the information I needed with a promise that he wouldn't say a word to Luca until I had everything. And he kept his word.

"And you will agree that no further payments of five hundred thousand euros a month are required from Luca Caruso in the upkeep of your livelihood."

I keep my tone cool, professional, easily slipping into the lawyer I could have been, but deep inside a fire burning too bright to abide by the law. I want this to hurt.

"No!" she snaps. "You can't do this to me."

"I can," I smile, "I will, and you will sign this document, or I'll destroy you. And trust me, Emilia, I have enough on you to make sure you never see the light of day again."

She pales across from me. "You would implicate them... they would know that Adler was killed by Luca and his men."

I shrug, "I'll admit to killing him in self-defense and with the report from my doctor after, they'll see I suffered enough that nobody will question it. Nobody will know about Luca and my men by the time I'm done spinning the story. I'll protect them from you, Emilia, rest assured."

"You think you have this all worked out, don't you?" she sneers, finally resulting back into her anger.

"I do, and because I'm doing this you will walk away with only an empty bank balance. Isn't that nice of me?" My eyes find those of her sister's who looks worried. The anger has dissipated and the realization that it's either this or death settles on her face.

"Just sign them," Everette hisses, grabbing my pen and pulling the folder to their side of the table. "Be done with this, with him, and —" she looks at me like the devil when she has no fucking clue who the real devil is, "and *her.*"

"How do I know that after I sign this you won't kill me?"

I grin, flashing her my teeth. "You don't. Just like I didn't know what was going to happen to me when Adler drugged me. What I would suggest is you sign these documents and get the fuck out of Sicily." I hold up my hand, cutting her off. "It's for the best."

"Fuck you," she snatches the pen from her sister's shaking hands, "And him."

Sweetly I reply. "I intend to."

Someone chokes in my ear but if I had to guess I would say it was Bones.

I pay no more attention to my earpiece and focus on the large girly scrawl that graces the documents I spent days writing. I had poured myself over them, looking for loopholes until there was none.

Once the documents are signed, I pull them to my side, leaving the pen that she's touched and stand up. Grabbing my bag I head towards the door, feeling lighter than I did twenty minutes ago.

This is enough revenge for me.

"How can you love him?" she calls. "How can you love a man that has taken so much from you?"

I look over my shoulder at the woman who dares sneer down her pretty button nose, who has the audacity to question my love when hers sent her to the pits of hell.

Clicking my earpiece, I pull it from my ear and drop it into my bag.

"Because he's shown me that love isn't perfect and it's the most honest thing he's ever done for me." I owe no further explanation and I show her by shoving open the door and stepping back into the light.

My guards, Chen, Dante, and Luca stand waiting for me — all with the same look, full of pride and love. I soften under Luca's heated gaze. He wants me, right here, against the wall of the restaurant I just destroyed his ex-fiancé in. I see it in his pulse that hammers in his neck. I feel it as he licks his lips in warning. He sees me for who I was before I was taken, as the strong woman that could handle him at his worst.

I smile, letting him know he has to wait a few more hours.

"Anyone fancy getting some ice cream?"

CHAPTER THIRTY

Luca Caruso

I wait and it kills me. Every single minute that Olivia is on the phone to her aunt I feel my patience cracking. It's been a long day and I've barely had time to talk to her since she assassinated Emilia with a well-executed takedown.

We were a sight for sore eyes after she forced us all to the small café I had taken her to for ice cream months ago. We sat around a large circular table, dressed like assassins or funeral goers, being force-fed ice cream by Olivia who was trying to find our favorites.

It took me a few minutes to realize what she was doing. She was forcing us into a close proximity, trying to mend the many broken fences I had smashed my way through during her disappearance.

Everyone had tried and indulged Olivia in her one request. Even Chen who at first seemed perturbed by her need for ice cream, found one he liked and offered her a small smile when he realized her intentions.

Dante knew what he liked and settled into conversation with Red and Rum, going over the latest sports results from some American basketball team.

All that was left was Bones and I once Olivia left for the restroom to wash her hands of all the sticky ice cream she had force-fed her guards.

"Has she forgiven you?" he asked me quietly while pushing away his lemon gelato.

"No."

He scraped a hand over his scar, rubbing it in a way that made me think he was uncomfortable. "I'm not so sure... she seemed protective of you in there."

"As she did with you all."

I don't want to let the possibility of earning Olivia's forgiveness sink into my skin. I haven't earned it and I needed to earn it. If she gave it to me so soon it would feel forced.

"What are you doing?" her voice, soft and full of exhaustion pulls me from the memory of Bones smirking at me.

"I was waiting for you," I tell her as she joins me on the bottom of her bed. In a silky black camisole and matching shorts, she's a vision of beauty.

"You were thinking," her small hands push up my suit jacket and begin working to free my cufflinks. "You get this look when you're deep in thought. You look so serious and cold."

"I'm sorry." Apologizing seems like the next best thing, even if I'm not sure that's what she wants.

"Don't be," she smiles. "It's hot when you do it. So, tell me, what were you thinking about?"

Oh, how the tables have turned, Miss Heart.

"Today. You." *Always you.*

She pauses, wary. "Are you angry with me, you know, for what I did by pushing you out?"

"I was," I tell her, slipping out of my jacket, "but then I realized that you needed to do it on your own. You didn't need me to make the choice for you."

She moves behind me on the bed, placing her legs on either side of my torso. Carefully I massage her legs as she runs her hands up and down my back, pushing away every knot that was created from her pushing me out of that restaurant.

"I need to tell you something," her voice is light but there's worry in the undertone.

"Okay?"

Olivia sucks in a sharp breath, only adding to my worry. "My Aunt Sarah has been speaking to the police."

"About?" her hand pushed under the muscle of my right shoulder blade. I almost groan from the relief.

"Me."

I turn and grab her hands, needing to look into her forest green eyes. "They're coming, aren't they?"

She nods. "Yes, in the next few days I believe. My aunt gave them my number, so I assume they'll be in contact."

The panic I thought that had disappeared when we found Olivia returns full throttle. I stand, needing to move, to prevent it from settling into my limbs.

"You don't have to speak to them."

She watches me calmly. "I do. They need to close off their investigation and I'm the last person on their list."

Through gritted teeth I reply. "He's fucking dead. He killed those women and he's dead — I sliced his throat for you, Olivia. What else do they need? Cazzo!" *Fuck!*

Olivia stares at me, waiting for me to pause enough to see the look on her face, and when I do my chest tightens.

"Because they need to be thorough." She gracefully steps off the bed until she stands before me, smelling of her vanilla moisturizer. "And so they can see we have nothing to hide."

"But we do," I bite out. "They'll see what I've done, who I am, and then they'll take you away before I can fucking fix this." I turn, refusing to let her see me break.

Her hand touches my shoulder, tipping me from rage to grief. I fall to my knees, wanting the floorboards to break beneath me and take me to hell where Olivia will finally be free of me, and I can repent for all of the shit I've done.

Instead of hell, heaven finds me and wraps her arms around shoulders — anchoring me.

"Nobody is taking me away." She presses a kiss to the center of my back, burning me through my shirt. "You'll be by my side the whole time and once this is all over, we can talk… about us."

All I hear is she'll want to talk about the moment she finally leaves, when she realizes that she cannot trust me and I'm too much for her. It's inevitable.

"Luca look at me, please."

I don't move. Olivia lets go, crawling on the floor until she settles on my lap and forces me to look at her.

"Do you remember the moment in the bathroom, in Paris?" she whispers against my lips, while kneading my shoulders.

"Yes." I bite her bottom lip, remembering how simple that time had seemed.

"Do you remember what you did?"

Of course, I did. I had jumped on her the moment the door opened, smothering her mouth with my hand while asking if she could be quiet for me.

"Yes."

"I want you to do that again. I want you to remember who you were after. That's the Luca that I want, the one who knows what he wants and takes it."

"I don't understand," my head hurts, a throb settling at the back of my skull. "I'm trying to pull back, to give you the space you need after everything, but you... don't want it?"

She grazes her lips over mine. "I'm fighting my way back to the person who wasn't afraid of the cold, food, or her own dreams, and you giving me space... well it just isn't you. It's not the man that I fell in —" she sighs, looking down at the buttons on my shirt. "It's wrong and messed up, I know, but I need you to fight back to the person you were before he took me. Of course, there are things we need to talk about and change but that can wait for another day." She places her hands on either side of my face. "What I need is for you to take me here on this floor, several times until neither of us are coherent enough to think about anything else but sleep."

Fuck. Me.

"I'm starting to feel used, Olivia," I hiss against her lips as I my hands slip up to the nape of her neck, pinning her close enough to my mouth.

She smirks. "Mi dispiace per quello" *I'm sorry about that.*

Oh, she wants to go there, to use my own native tongue against me knowing that it's become a weakness of mine. Well, it's another to add to her list.

"You will be sorry. Get on your knees." I push her off, sliding my hands under her stomach until she's settled on all fours in front of me. If she wants the Luca that demands complete control, then she'll have him. "Put your head down and ass up."

She slowly responds, letting out a soft sigh as her face touches the carpet.

"So beautiful," I whisper, while tugging down her silk shorts, pleased to see that she isn't wearing any underwear. I leave her shorts around her knees, wanting to restrict her from moving. "Put your hands behind your back and hold your wrists."

"Luca…"

"Now. Olivia. Now." She does as she's told, her face and shoulders flushing a perfect shade of pink.

Oh, my dirty Bella wants to use my body and has no qualms about it until she's ass up in the air, pussy on display, and now she feels shy.

I chuckle as she shivers into my hands, whimpering softly as I massage the back of her thighs. With every moan I feel the ache in my chest soften until it's manageable, but most importantly admiration for the strength Olivia still has, to have it in her heart to pull me away from my own deserved darkness.

Leaning down I taste her, licking and sucking on her clit. She gyrates against my face, greedily searching for her release while I fuck her slowly, so slowly with my tongue. I apply the lightest pressure, only enough that she feels me between her thighs.

Damn, I could do this all day.

"Don't tease me, Luca," she begs breathlessly.

"But this is what I do, Olivia. This is what you wanted." She groans as I push one finger inside her pussy. It's not enough but it's all she's getting for now.

"I want…"

"You want?" I blow against her clit. "What do you want, Olivia?" Another finger and she cries into the carpet. These are the tears I love, from frustration and need, not from pain. Never pain. "I'm all ears."

"I-I can't think," her walls tighten around my fingers as they lazily fuck her, enjoying the filthy sounds they make.

"That's a shame," I control my voice, trying to quieten the rush of euphoria threatening to tip me into desperate need to be inside of her. "I was hoping you would tell me that you wanted me to fuck you with my cock. I suppose my fingers will have to do."

"No," she cries, pushing herself back onto my fingers, "please—just!"

"Just? Hm?"

She lets go of her wrists, pushing off the carpet. I pull away from her glistening pussy, sniggering at her groan of frustration as I use both hands to force her back down.

"Tell me what you want." I let her hear the zip of my fly.

"You," she says breathlessly, "please."

One simple word and another weight falls away from my shoulders. I try to reason with my heart, as it pounds in my chest, that she just wants my body, but it refuses to listen.

The fucking heart wants what it wants.

"Voi," she whispers the word in Italian.

I stroke her spine, reveling in the softness of her skin as I close my eyes. My cock at her entrance is impatient, greedily sliding through her wetness as she rocks against me.

"Vous," she repeats the word in French, arching her ass to line my cock where she wants me.

"Anymore?" I tease—my voice tight as she tries to pull me into her. I shred at my shirt until it's in pieces behind me—too impatient to undress like a man who has an inkling of sanity left. I need this.

I watch her knuckles turn white as she grips the carpet, see her strength in holding out.

"Sie," she groans, "it's German for you."

I thrust once, sliding, stretching until I'm buried inside of her. Fuck, her cry of relief echoes into my ears, sending a hot flash into the base of my stomach.

Pulling her up, so her back is flush against my chest, I hiss on a hard thrust. "You've always been a smart ass," trailing my lips across the arch of her neck I breathe her in before sinking my teeth into the one sweet spot she cannot resist.

Olivia moans, digging her nails into my arms around her waist as she meets my thrusts with a frantic roll of her hips.

I feel it as I pull my teeth away, the way her body softens, preparing for the burst of an orgasm. Just knowing she needs me for her release sends me spinning.

She's so reactive. So pliable in her desire.

I arch over her, fingers circling her clit. "Come for me," only ever me.

"Yes!" She cries, as her lips find mine. She rides out her orgasm in fitful waves as I consume her mouth.

She tastes like heaven, and I need more. I don't give her time to come down from her high or to collect herself.

She's facing me in seconds, straddling my hips with my eyes wide with surprise. Her face is flushed beautifully, her nose pink with heat. How could anyone want to hurt her?

"You don't look tired," I tell her with a tsk.

"No," she agrees, against my lips as she rubs her nose against mine. "I think you can do better than this Luca. You know, put in a little more effort."

My laugh catches us both by surprise. Olivia's lips turn up, pleased with her little comment and my reaction.

"You're right," I tell her with my hands tight in the back of her hair. "I need to put in more effort. Enough that you'll ache tomorrow and only think of me."

I don't give her another chance to surprise me with another smart-ass comment. I take her again, over and over until we fall asleep there on her bedroom floor.

CHAPTER THIRTY-ONE

Olivia Heart

Tears pool in my eyes. For God sakes. I promised myself I was done with this exhausting emotion. But here I am, crying in my bed, alone after I realized Luca had left me, probably to sleep in his own room and give me my space.

Space I didn't want anymore, but expected him to know that.

Damn it.

I gulp down my sob, suffocating it before it can swell into a full crying, snot fest.

A warm shower to remove the scent of him and sex off my skin is what I need. And for a few minutes it helps me settle. I relax into the cool tile when my limbs begin to shake from our earlier exertion. Luca hadn't held back, and all effort was applied in insuring nothing but euphoric relief… over and over again.

"I'm a mess," I finally admit to myself, letting my whisper be swallowed by the hiss of the powerful shower. "A damn mess."

Just like Luca and I's relationship. I know in my heart that I should despise him. After all, he is a monster that had several plans to trap me in the web of his complicated life. But he's a monster that I know, that would go to the end of the earth for me without a second's hesitation.

And I still love him in a way that makes it impossible to look at our situation objectively.

I move throughout my morning, going over the last few days with him and relish in memories. Of his arms around me on the beach, his trust in me at the restaurant with his ex-fiancé, and most importantly allowing me freedom without trying to smother it.

"You know you're supposed to eat the cannoli and not just stare at it?" Aida whispered dramatically, nudging my shoulder with hers.

My smile is soft in return. "Sorry. I was miles away."

"Hm. Just like my brother was when I saw him earlier."

A blush creeps up and takes residence on my cheeks. "He's busy catching up on things."

And he was. There were weeks' worth of emails to catch up on, deals to push through, and businesses to run. Aida had done her best to keep things afloat, but his more private, illegal activities had suffered during my disappearance. There was only so much Dante could do to help out, with these particular customers preferring to deal with the boss.

His customers had gotten tetchy at his sudden disappearance, and he needed time to regain their confidence, so I was giving him space to do so. Even though it made me irritable.

"Have you two left this place recently?" she asks me, not so subtly while sipping her coffee.

"Once, to go to the beach. Why do you ask?"

She suddenly looks uncomfortable, like she wished she hadn't opened her mouth. Of course, this piques my interest.

"Oh, no reason. I just thought you two would be going out more now that things were settling down again."

It was a lame excuse, and I didn't buy it, but I wasn't going to pry for information Aida clearly didn't want to share. And sometimes not knowing was a blessing in disguise.

"To be perfectly honest, leaving this place hasn't exactly crossed my mind." I tell her, pushing away my plate of freshly baked cannoli's that had been sent by Dante's mother Fai. "I've been happy spending time around here."

Aida frowns. "Don't get used to it, Olivia. Being a hermit wouldn't suit you that much. You need your freedom."

Her response, although completely innocent, feels like a warning. One that's aimed at her brother I'm suddenly feeling protective over.

"Being out in public feels like a lot right now. I can barely get through the day without some sort of panic attack. I don't fancy doing that in public."

Her smile softens me a touch. "I understand, but just promise me you'll try leaving these grounds—if only for an hour. You'll soon get used to it again."

I agree because she's right and hiding away isn't going to solve anything. But for today I'm happy enough to stay here, close to Luca.

****

"No," he tells me, shaking his head, "there isn't a chance in hell I'm letting them talk to you alone. Forget it, Olivia. It's not an option."

Ugh. This conversation had been put on repeat the moment I told him that the police would be visiting tomorrow.

"I don't want them to focus on you, Luca. Or any of them."
I point to my guards watching us around the kitchen counter,
waiting for someone to make the final decision. "We need to
seem as normal as possible."

"What's not normal about us?" Bones asks with a sly grin.

I roll my eyes. "Four guards for one woman isn't normal.
They'll see me as vulnerable, and they'll question why you're
all required."

"Just tell them it's because Caruso is obsessed with you and
needed to have you watched every minute of every day. I'm
sure they'll understand."

Ignoring Bones' need to get a rise out of Luca, who by the
looks of it is a second away from shooting him, I speak up.

"Look, I need to figure out what they have and why it's so
important they speak to me without having to worry that they
suspect…"

"Suspects what?" Luca looks at me in warning, telling me
to tread carefully.

"You know, that I only ended up here because you had
them take me."

Red chokes back his beer, earning a thump from Rum.

Luca sighs, irritated by them. "Olivia, that's a reach."

"Not if they found some of Adler's files."

"We destroyed them," Chen butted in, coming to his boss'
aide. "We tracked every file, to every hard drive and had Veen
take care of them."

The trainee lawyer still in me cannot let this go. I square my
shoulders, preparing my argument. "And I believe you did, but
there could be a paper trail. A small piece of evidence given to
someone else. All I'm saying is we need to tread carefully, and
me speaking to them alone is our best bet."

Luca walks around the kitchen island and cups my head in his hands, ignoring Bones' glare. His eyes soften on me, shimmering from black to dark chocolate. "No, Olivia. We handle the police together. Wait! I'll hold back and let you take control, but I'm not leaving your side."

And he didn't.

The moment the gates swung open and a Range Rover Defender prowled into the gates, I was suddenly glad for his refusal. The pressure, the possibility that the rug was going to be pulled from under me, hit so quickly that I swayed. Luckily Luca was there to hold my hand.

"Smile," he whispered into my ear. "Take a deep breath for me and squeeze my hand."

I did as he said and sucked in clean air into my lungs, reminding myself with every next breath that I was in control.

The driver's door opened just as I squeezed his hand back. A petite blonde in her early thirties, dressed in a stuffy navy suit stepped out and smiled my way.

Unlike a lot of the detectives I had met, she was confident enough to walk up to me and take my hand in hers without requesting permission.

"Detective Sarah Avena. Thank you for sparing the time to meet with me, Miss Heart." Her handshake was firm if not a touch painful. She meant business and she specifically wanted Luca to know when she shook his hand next "And you too, Mr. Caruso. Thank you for allowing me into your beautiful home."

He was polite enough to shake her hand. "Apologies that you had to fly all the way out here just to ask Olivia a few questions."

Detective Avena waved him off. "No apologies necessary, Mr. Caruso. It's a beautiful country to tidy up some loose ends in, so no complaints from me."

Luca nodded before gesturing for us to take the table outside where Marie had kindly prepared refreshments. As I took my seat by Luca's side, I wondered how my guards were faring locked up in his office, listening in through a mic placed under the table.

I busied my hands, pouring tall glasses of water while Detective Avena took off her jacket.

"I'm sure you're aware from your Aunt Sarah that we've been looking at the death of William Adler."

My mouth dries as she speaks his name. "Yes, she mentioned that you wanted to speak to me, but excuse me for being blunt. I don't understand what I have to do with your investigation into his death or his victims. I was just an old friend."

Luca grabs my hands under the table, stroking his thumb across mine, sensing my need for comfort.

"In normal circumstances we wouldn't need to look this far into a person's background, Miss Heart, but Mr. Adler is an unusual case. We're dealing with several murders and an apparent—" Detective Avena glances at Luca, "suicide and I cannot leave any stones unturned. I want to make sure every crime he committed is pinned to him so that justice is served."

"I understand." I don't. I want her to leave, to take her questions back to England and file them under 'Not required', but instead I focus on Luca's touch. "I'm happy to help in any way I can."

"Thank you. I really appreciate that." She unzips her monolith, revealing a list of questions she's prepared on government paper. "Your Aunt confirmed that you and Mr. Adler were childhood friends."

"We were."

"And that you lost touch just before you went off to university?"

"Yes," my tongue feels heavy in my mouth.

"And why was that?"

Luca, like the fierce protector he was used to being stepped in. "And what does that have to do with anything?"

Detective Avena doesn't miss the cold look across his handsome face, but she's not perturbed by it either. "It's a part of a profile I'm building, Mr. Caruso," she answers him.

Sweat beads at the back of my neck. "We both went to different universities, and it was harder to stay in touch."

She notes my answers down in shorthand. "And not because you didn't want to resume a relationship with him?"

It's me who squeezes Luca's hand as he jolts in his seat, ready to cut this conversation short before it even starts.

"I take it you've been talking to my cousin Alice?" I ask.

"I have. She was worried that Mr. Adler may have hurt you when you were younger."

"He didn't," I bite out, pissed at Alice for being so reckless with my history. "He became a psycho long after me."

The detective agrees with a subtle nod of her head. "Did you have any contact with him after?"

This is the fork in the road where each answer could lead me into a path where it would be impossible to turn back. Luca nods at me, silently telling me that he trusts whichever option I take. God, I could kiss him.

I sigh. "We met briefly at a charity gala a few weeks ago. It was a quick catch up and then he left."

"I have it here that he was escorted out of the property because of an altercation between Adler and—" She glances at Luca, "you, Mr. Caruso. We have a witness here who states that you were extremely angry at Mr. Adler's presence, especially after seeing Miss Heart holding his hand."

Fuck. The shark has smelled blood.

"I was," he agrees, taking us both by surprise. "I've had issues with William Adler and his papers in the past so that was why I was... annoyed at his attendance. I wasn't aware of his past with Olivia until after I saw him bothering her."

She turns to me. "He was bothering you?"

Luca narrows his eyes at the detective, frustrated that she was picking at his words. This was exactly why I wanted to deal with the detective alone, it only takes one slight slip up for them to edge their way in.

"Not so much as bothering me," I smiled at Luca. "You have to ignore him; he can be a little overprotective at times."

If Bones was here now, he would snigger under his breath.

The detective ignores my maneuver to lighten the mood and moves on to her next question. "And that was the last time you spoke?"

"It was."

She pauses, squinting to look at me now the sun is over my shoulder. "I'm going to level with you, Miss Heart, because you know how these things work and I don't want to waste your time. A witness has come forward and stated that Mr. William Adler had an intense fascination with you months before his death."

I swallow past the sickness as she looks at me, waiting to see a crack in my shell. When she doesn't find it, she moves on.

"They also state that he had prepared an elaborate plan to... kidnap you and bring you to the hotel where the rest of his victims were found."

"Who is this witness?" Luca demands.

If it's Emilia... fuck, if she's double crossed me, I swear on Luca's life that it will be the last thing she ever does.

Panic threatens to swallow me up completely until the detective saves me from myself.

"It was his personal assistant. She spotted an email that hadn't been deleted between Mr. Adler and a Stephen Black. She was too frightened about losing her job for snooping that she kept it to herself until she saw the news."

"I-I don't know what to say."

Shit.

Luca reaches for my water and passes it to me. I sip gratefully.

"We think that your chance reunion at the Belmont's gala was a calculated move by Mr. Adler. We suspect if Mr. Caruso hadn't intervened, you would have been taken," she pauses, offering a sympathetic smile. "There was a team of men he had hired in the previous weeks. They were waiting outside of the property in unmarked vehicles."

Horror flashes across Luca's face before he can smother it. I squeeze his hand hard, finding comfort in his touch.

"What happened to these men?" I ask, even though I know the answer.

"They died in the fire." Detective Avena stares at Luca. "Their bodies were littered with bullets and left piled up in the kitchen before the property burned down. We have only identified a few so far using dental records."

The edge of Luca's voice. "Do you know who killed them? I'd like to pay their legal fees."

She sighs softly while pushing a silky tendril away from her eyes. "No but whoever did this has made sure their trail is well and truly covered and even our investigation into this Stephen Black character has dried up," shaking her head she turns back to her notes. "Anyway, the victims we have identified share a likeness to you, Miss Heart. I apologize for putting this on you, but it's of my opinion that you were his intended victim, but because he couldn't get to you, he found... equivalents."

"We need to stop here," Luca stands up abruptly, coiled tight just ready to snap. "You can't just walk in here and put this on her. I won't allow it."

"Luca!" I hiss. I grab his hand and tug at him to sit back down. "Sit down."

Detective Avena isn't fazed. Her eyes simply gloss over his temper as if she expected it. I suddenly feel cold at the thought. Had she been testing his reaction? Sizing him up, trying to find a connection between him and William?

"He's right, Miss Heart. I'm sorry. I shouldn't have been so abrupt."

Luca scoffs down at her. "Abrupt? This is an ambush if I've ever seen one. So, let's get one thing clear, Detective Avena. From what you've told us, Adler and his men so clearly got what they deserved for hurting those women. And under no circumstances will that be put on Olivia. So ask the rest of your questions and leave."

"Luca!" I hiss wanting to kiss the stupid man. "Don't be so rude!"

Detective Avena laughs, waving us both off. "He's just found out you were under the watch of a psychotic man who wanted to kidnap you, Miss Heart. He's allowed to be angry."

"Not at you," I bite before turning to Luca, glaring up at him. "Go take a walk while I finish up here."

He glares right back, challenging me. "I will not."

"Yes. You will."

"Are you two always like this?" she asks.

"Yes," we say in union, not tearing our eyes away from each other.

"Five minutes," he tells me.

"Ten," I fight back, waiting for him to concede.

Luca shakes his head in frustration and then sends a curt nod at the detective before storming off back into the house.

"That man loves you an awful lot," she tells me when I bask in my second win. The freedom he gives me in these small moments mean a lot, if not too much.

"He does," I agree.

"You're lucky to have a man in your corner like that, especially one willing to go to severe lengths to protect you." The corner of her lips turn up into a slight smirk, one of knowing.

"There isn't anything he wouldn't do for me, Detective. Not a single thing."

"Including murdering the man that may or may not have kidnapped you two weeks ago?"

Chapter Thirty-Two

Olivia Heart

My instinct had been right this whole time but yet I wasn't prepared for the words to slip through her lips. She had been careful in her questions, using tact and precise moves to separate Luca and I, and I had been too out of practice to notice is.

She would have known that.

"Are you accusing Luca of murdering William Adler?"

She takes a sip of water, gauging my reaction over the rim of her glass. I'm certain she can hear my heart thud-thudding its way out of my chest.

"Miss Heart, I don't have any proof of what I'm... suggesting, neither am I here to find evidence —"

"Then why are you here?"

She closes her monolith and leans over the table. "My investigation into Mr. Adler is closed. We didn't want to push this anymore as the press are having a field day, which is upsetting to the victims' families. We're satisfied enough to conclude our investigation, labelling the fire an accident."

Her words wash over me in small waves, cooling my heated blood with everyone that passes by. But not enough. I know by the steely look of determination in her eyes that this isn't over yet.

"I've investigated you separately, Miss Heart, when I saw the abrupt move from New York and followed this path to a grisly end. I suspect many bad things have happened to you in recent months, but yet I can't prove them."

"I'm fine. You can see me with your own two eyes, detective."

"I can," she agrees quickly, "but I can also see healing bruises under makeup, a recent break in your fingers," she laughs gently, "your fingers aren't as tan as your body, Miss Heart, and you favor your right ear to listen to me."

"I—"

She holds up her hand. A wedding ring glints in the sunlight—it's simple and elegant like her, "and there's subtle tells in the way you look at Mr. Caruso, like you're not sure if he's going to disappear right before your eyes."

"This," I snap, pointing down at myself, "is not his doing. Luca would never lay a finger on me. He would sooner die than hurt me."

"That's some love."

I hate the insolent tone she effortlessly delivers. It's like she wants to bait me into confessing all—based on the unreliable notion that women need to stick together.

"It is. It always will be, and you're right about one thing. I need Luca. I've always needed him to protect me, to care for me, to make sure people like Adler couldn't... take any more from me."

I shift in my seat, trying to find a better position from the sun's glare. Sweat beads at the back of my neck. I sip my water for relief. I'm too close and she senses it.

"I've not questioned his love for you, Miss Heart. A man can love you and still hurt you."

God, damn it to hell and back. No wonder I wanted out of law. When it became personal, I couldn't separate myself very well.

"I'm only here as a courtesy. Woman to woman. I know that there is more to your story, and I just want you to know that you have someone out there who's willing to listen and protect you."

Protect me? It's almost laughable that a 5ft 4 woman is offering her assistance in securing my future when four guards couldn't.

Leaning back in my chair I cast my eyes over her, checking for any signs of a lie, but the microphone under the table is all I can think about. I picture my guards around Luca's desk panicking, worrying that any moment I'm going to spill all. Had Luca joined them? Was Chen pinning him to a wall, keeping him from leaping out of the house and snatching me up?

We need to leave.

"Would you mind if we walk and talk?" I say. "I'd really like to show you the grounds."

It's a lame excuse but I need her away from my family.

"Sure."

I guide her past the pool, into the rose garden before making our way to the vineyard where workers are scattered, taking care to assess the grapes ready for harvest.

"Stephen Black was a part of your security, was he not?"

"He was," if she wants further details, she's not going to get them. There isn't anything left in me to say about the man who betrayed me.

"Five guards for one woman. Seems excessive don't you think?" she pauses to drink in our beautiful surroundings.

My laugh is tight, barely slipping past my lips. "Everything Luca does is excessive. It's the Italian in him."

"And you're okay with that? With being under surveillance twenty-four seven?"

"It saved my life, didn't it?"

A knowing smile crosses her lips, but I cannot help but notice her eyes gloss with sadness.

"Mr. Caruso took you first, didn't he?" She holds her hand up. "Stole you from your life in New York and brought you here. How do I know? I don't... it's just a guess from the little I know of your relationship and its timeline."

Frustrations boils, tapping at my vocal cords to say something. Anything, but I wait. Sometimes it's smarter to hold back, let other person state their intentions before planning a rebuttal.

"You've been tightly contained since your arrival here. No access to your bank accounts, social media accounts, passport, and sometimes even your phone. It struck me as odd that you could fall off the face of society so quickly."

Her words are true, coated in her soft voice as if talking to a victim.

"I needed... a break from work. It was killing me."

"And then there was a hospital stay in Paris where you sustained several injuries," she continued, making her way down a path of grass, towards the opening. It smells of sweetness and hot earth out here and I sigh with pleasure. It really is one of my favorite places on Luca's land. I feel safe here.

Unguarded, with her back to me, the detective must have felt safe too.

I followed. "You seem to know an awful lot," especially when everything was supposed to have been wiped.

"Your hospital stay was pure luck. Your admission had been wiped off the system, your stay replaced by a Jane Doe, but it was the medication you left with that flagged up. The pharmacy works on a separate billing system."

Of course it did.

"Like I said before, I don't have any evidence for what I'm suggesting. Everything I have is breadcrumbs that are easily swept up and disposed of."

We pause when she spots one of Luca's staff picking off grapes in the distance. I smile his way, letting him know that he doesn't need to leave.

"Miss Heart, what I do have is enough power to take you with me back to England and yes, Mr. Caruso and his hold over these countries' authorities cannot stop me. And if you chose to leave, you don't have to tell me what happened here if you don't want to, nobody will ever make another decision for you. We can just leave in my car."

"You think I'm trapped here?" I ask, pressing my nails into my hand, trying to stop the shake. "That Luca is keeping me against my will?"

She smiles sadly. "I think at one point he did. Do I think so now? No. But I think you've been through a lot and not had the chance to think for yourself or what you need outside of him."

"Woman to woman?"

"Of course," she nods for me to go on. This woman has a heart too big for her chest and I wonder how long she'll survive in this career. I almost feel sorry for her.

"I'm not trapped here anymore. And I don't think I ever was. Look, I know you probably think I'm crazy, but I have another family here... and a man that I love. Albeit this man that

248

can be a complete and utter idiot, who doesn't understand boundaries..."

My chest loosens a little as I think about him, how much he's always trying to adapt to me and my needs. Even when it nearly destroyed him.

"His obsession for me has made him one of the most selfish men I have ever met," a smile tugs at my lips as she glares back at the house, "but he's the opposite in his love for me. There isn't a thing he wouldn't do. Not a single thing, and that includes hurting himself to do it."

"Forgive me, but that sounds toxic."

"It can be," I chuckle, although I find no humor in her comment. "But isn't that love? Shouldn't we be obsessed; completely undone by the person we want? So much so that we realize love isn't all sweetness and rainbows. It's monsters in the dark. It's bloodied hands and corrupt morals." I shake my head, stopping her from speaking. "I swear, Detective Avena, for all the evil in his eyes I can still see the good and that's why I *choose* to love him. I'm not willing to give up that part of him."

Memories of our time together cling to my conscious in agreement. They want me to remember his soft kisses, his declarations of love and protection. They need me to see how I react to them, bend to them, will him to give me more and more every time.

"We aren't perfect, Detective Avena, and we never will be." The confession slips into the warm air, "but he's mine to hurt and love and I'm his. How we got here doesn't matter anymore. It's how we move forward that I'm more interested in."

She sucks in a tight breath between her rosy lips. "You're a strong woman, Miss Heart, stronger than I imagined after all that you've been through. And even though I'm not a hundred percent assured, I will leave you to find your peace here. But

249

I'm leaving you with my details, okay? If all that goodness runs out, you're going to need someone like me."

CHAPTER THIRTY-THREE

Luca Caruso

I had resigned myself to the fact that Olivia was going to leave me. I heard it in her voice the moment she moved the detective away from the table. The detective, of course, had nothing, but Olivia still asked her to walk, to gain a moment of privacy to probably confess all.

Prison didn't matter. I couldn't care less.

But losing her, well it's too much and I wouldn't let anyone witness the final break.

I stood, bone-weary and cold, ignoring the cautious look my dear cousin sent my way, and left the house I had built for her all those years ago. I'd wanted a sanctuary of light and open spaces for her to relax in, hoping that we could fill the property with everything that she loved.

I had even stupidly hoped, after the first night we slept together, that we would marry here and raise many children in this home.

"Where do you think you're going?" her voice, sweet and light sings from the poolside. She had hiked her dress up to dip her legs in the water, softly paddling in the pool. My eyes traced from her legs, over her flat stomach, passed her beautiful breasts until they met her eyes.

251

She gasped, seeing something that I couldn't.

In seconds, she was out of the water, dancing her way over to me.

I stood frozen, unsure of my own limbs. They were heavy, filled with bricks of ice just waiting on my brain to communicate with them to move.

"Luca…" she cupped my cheek, "Look at me."

I did, but only briefly. I didn't trust this would last.

Her soft, lush mouth touched mine gently. "I'm not leaving you."

It was four words that I needed to hear, but that part of me was locked behind a wall.

Olivia pressed her lips to my cheek, her skin warm and smelling of earth and vanilla. "You're exhausted," she whispers. "This has all been too much for you and I'm sorry, I didn't realize you were suffering too. Come with me, let's go to bed."

"I can't fuck you, Olivia," I rasp, feeling intense pain in the middle of my chest.

"I don't want your body, Luca. Not tonight. I just need you to come with me to our bed."

Our bed.

It was there. It was so close to grasp, but the wall was too thick to punch through. Instead, I let her lead me through the house until we were in my room. She was quick to undress me while worrying her lip between her teeth.

When my back hit the sheets and my head was against the pillow, my eyes instantly snapped shut. How long had it been since I had slept? Eaten a full meal? Had non-disturbing thoughts of her dying?

Was this the breakdown Dante and my sister had warned me about? Had God finally delivered enough karma that now that Olivia wasn't leaving my mind was going to snap?

Olivia swept her hands through my hair, lightly dragging her nails across my scalp knowing it helped soothe me. I wanted to demand she stop, to tell her it was me who should look after her but instead my hands clung to her hips under the sheet.

"Rest, Luca. I'll be here when you wake up."

****

And she was there, hovering over me with her hair piled on top of her head holding a cup of espresso like an angel. A sweet, confusing angel.

"How long have I been asleep?" my throat ached. Jesus. I sat up, noting that she had changed. The summer dress that flared at her hips had been replaced with one of my dress shirts. If I had the energy, I'd peel it off her with my teeth just to check what she had underneath.

"A full day," she sighed, placing the small cup in my hands. "Do you feel better?"

"No," I replied honestly. "I feel like I could sleep for another few days."

She bit her lip. "I'm sorry. You were so busy looking after me..." she surprised me by slapping my arm. A surge of lust slammed into my heart at her touch. I always did love her fire. "Damn it, Luca, you're supposed to look after yourself. I had no idea that you were this exhausted... that you weren't eating and —"

I cut her off, throwing my espresso onto the carpet and pulling her mouth to mine. Damn, she tasted like coffee and honey, and I was very much trapped in her kiss.

"Please," she tried to pull away, "don't ever," I bite her bottom lip, sucking it between my teeth, "do that again."

"I won't," my hand traced the thin column of her neck before I gripped her chin, "because I won't have a reason to. You're not leaving and I'm going to spend every day making sure you don't regret that decision. I swear to it"

Slipping my hands under my shirt, she sighs when I find her without underwear. She's already wet, her folds slick with desire no doubt from telling me off. Feisty little thing.

Her lips open, ready to tell me to stop, that I'm supposed to rest when I push two fingers into her pussy, cutting that stupid suggestion away. I'll never tire of her moans or the way she grips on to me as I work her to orgasm. She needs this, she needs me to strip her of her thoughts so I can consume her instead.

"Look at you, so beautiful on my fingers, Bella." I cup her breast, squeezing firmly and she groans into my mouth. "Now, tell me what you said to the detective."

"I can't," she pants. "I can't concentrate when your fingers — oh god!" another finger tips her over the edge and she comes so quickly I have to hold her to me, afraid she'll fall off the bed.

Energized and greedy I push her back onto the bed, lifting my shirt and settling between her legs. I smell her arousal and see the way she glistens, and decide that this is the only breakfast I'll ever need.

"If my fingers are the problem, maybe I should try my mouth, yes? So tell me, Olivia, what did you tell the detective?"

It seems my mouth was an issue too and my cock. Olivia couldn't seem to find the right words. So like the patient man I'm becoming, I decided it was only fair that I wait until after her fourth orgasm to find out how she had chosen me.

CHAPTER THIRTY-FOUR

Olivia Heart

The men around me had all taken a turn for the worse. After explaining what had happened with the detective and looking after Luca, they had all turned secretive... almost going out of their way to avoid me. It went on for five days before I cornered the two men who would answer for this weird behavior.

Dante grinned when I asked if he knew anything and left. Luca also chose that exact moment to excuse himself— apparently, he had to check on an email, but his phone was in his hand the whole damn time.

I resigned myself to the fact that once again the men in my life were keeping secrets. It stung of course, but honestly? I was all out of caring. I had enough secrets to last me a lifetime.

After the detective's visit, I spent a lot of time with Luca, healing and making sure that he was okay. I had never seen him so lost in my life and it wasn't a memory I wanted to relive, but what came after was beautiful.

After telling him about my conversation with Detective Avena, we had spent a day in bed, forgiving each other and finding new ways to please one another.

I can't help but blush at the creative ways Luca had pleased me.

"What are you thinking about?" Luca asked from the doorway in the kitchen. He was mouthwateringly handsome in his black Prada suit that was my favorite. It brought the darkness in his eyes out and fit his broad shoulders to perfection.

If I could, I'd give his tailor a raise.

"Just how strange the men in my life are being." I tell him over my mint tea. I'm still in my reconditioning phase and struggling with anything minty, so every day I fight with myself to consume one cup of mint tea.

Dante thinks it's strange that I'm punishing myself, but he doesn't understand that I'm taking control of the things I fear. Once I do that I can move on.

Luca chuckles as he walks over to me and bends his head to kiss me. I frown, it's too soft and not enough. "So greedy. Come, I want to show you something."

I stand up, enjoying the way he groans under his breath at my outfit choice. It's a black sundress with crisscross straps at the back. It hugs my waist perfectly, showing the dip of my small waist. It's also Luca's favorite dress that he likes to peel me out of.

"And I'm the greedy one," I tease.

We move out of the house and head quickly towards the front gates. I have to keep up with Luca's long strides, which is no feat when you're wearing wedged heels.

"You have every right to be greedy today, Olivia," he tells me as we stop by the fountain.

"I do?"

He raises an eyebrow, unsure of something. "Yes. It's your birthday after all."

"What!?"

He runs a hand over his face, trying to wipe off his amusement. "This is my fault. I shouldn't have distracted you, but I assumed you would see the date on your phone?"

I blush. My phone was rarely a part of my life. I had gotten so used to not having it that most of the time it spent uncharged in our room.

He chuckles, bringing me into his arms. "You're twenty-six, Olivia. Do you feel older, wiser?"

"Yes, I do." I kiss his chin, enjoying the scruff against my skin, "but why are we out here... in the middle of the drive?"

"Ah!" he nips my nose, "Turn around and see."

Luca grabs my shoulders and gently maneuvers me to face the gates. A second later they open, and four SUV's pour into the entrance. I squint, trying to see through the sun's glare.

"Ti voglio bene" *I love you*. He whispers huskily into my ear, sending a ripple of divine shivers down my spine.

I don't get the chance to reply. The first car opens and out spills my cousin Alice, holding onto her sun hat for dear life as she runs across the drive.

"Liv!" she's quickly followed by her sheepish husband, Harry. "Happy birthday!"

They both envelope me in tight hugs as I stand there completely shocked. They move to Luca when I fail to speak, who greets them warmly, showing them to Marie whose waiting with a big smile and enough refreshments for ten people.

My head whips back to the cars. My aunt is helped out of the car by Chen who nods my way, my aunt is too busy talking his ears off, asking about the house and how long it's been here for.

While Chen brings her over, Red, Rum, and Bones help an eager Lilly, Hayley, and Katie out of their vehicles.

"Bloody hell!" Hayley dramatically whispers, looking up at Rum. "How tall are you?"

"Six foot four," he tells her proudly before offering his arm. "Six foot five on a good day," he finishes with a wink.

"Do you have a girlfriend?" Katie asks Bones over her cat eye sunglasses.

"I don't," he takes her bags, fighting his smirk.

"Would you like one?"

"Katie!" My aunt hisses before pulling her away. "Leave the poor man alone."

"Luca," I turn to him, my eyes full of happy tears. "What have you done?"

"I've brought your family and friends to celebrate your birthday. I want you to be surrounded by love today and always."

****

Luca held on to me tightly, my back pressed against his chest as we watched Katie, Hayley, and Lilly try their best to flirt with and taunt my guards. My aunt had long given up trying to save them and had settled on a tour of the grounds with Marie who was eager to learn everything she could about me from my aunt.

Dante and Aida had turned up and joined us for lunch with gifts, and had also enjoyed the show as my friends reduced burly bodyguards into flirts. It was so nice to see everyone together, to feel the happiness in the air, and Luca's reassuring words whenever I fell quiet.

"Are you happy?" he asked me, pressing a kiss to my neck.

"Yes," was all I could manage. My heart was too full. "Relieved actually."

He nodded his understanding. "Would you mind if I spoke to your aunt alone for a few minutes?" I turned to look at him. He was worried that if he disappeared with her, I'd assume he was going to hurt her.

After all it had been a contingency plan of his when his obsession had reached an unbearable peak.

"No, of course not." I lean closer so that only he can hear me. "I never believed you would have gone through with that plan. I trust you, Luca. Go ahead."

His eyes blaze with raw desire as my words settle into his skin. "When you talk like that, Olivia, it feels like my birthday." He presses a chaste kiss against my lips, but I still feel the promise for more later on tonight.

"Getting you a gift should be easy then," I tease, moving off his lap.

"I don't need gifts when I have you," he says. "Now while I'm gone you're in charge of the kids. Make sure they don't do anything we wouldn't."

"That's not a lot then!" I call after him.

Luca and my Aunt Sarah were gone for longer than a few minutes — more like hours. In fact, it was Bones who told me that they were outside, sharing a glass of wine, watching the sunset as they spoke in hushed tones. Before I could question him further, he was being dragged into a games room by Rum who may or may not have whispered about strip poker.

I was out of there.

Alice and Harry had slipped upstairs an hour ago, whispering in hushed tones to each other. No doubt still in the honeymoon stage and wanting to be physically close.

I grinned as I finished my wine, until I realized that nobody had spoken about William Adler. It wasn't like recent events had clouded my day, but it was strange that Alice or my Aunt hadn't brought it up.

Maybe they didn't want to ruin my birthday? I just hoped it could stretch for their entirety of their stay. If I had my way nobody would ever speak his filthy name again.

"Miss Heart?" Chen called from the doorway.

It was the first time I had seen him dress casually. The dark navy jeans and black fitted top suited him, making it easier for me to see the kindness in his face.

"Yes?"

"I've been asked to escort you to your next birthday surprise," a shy grin plays on his thin lips. "And no, I'm not allowed to indulge in any clues. Mr. Caruso has forbidden it."

I grin, "Oh, has he now?"

Chen passes me a sweater and escorts me outside to one of Luca's cars. I almost stop, unsure of whether or not I want to leave the grounds when Chen notices my hesitation.

"Don't worry, Miss Heart. You're safe."

"I know. Thank you, Chen."

We drive into the night for what feels like forever. Even though I know Luca will be at the end of this journey, I start to feel on edge. It's been a few days since I've been anywhere without him.

"Miss Heart, there's a blindfold in the pocket of the seat in front of you. Once you put that on, we only have a thirty second drive."

His precise timing makes it easier for me to accept the blindfold and place it over my eyes.

I trust Chen.

I trust Luca.

I can do this.

One deep breath, I settle back into my seat, listening as the tires switch from smooth road to gravel. Stones ping up against the metal underneath my feet, hitting at my nerves.

"Ten seconds," Chen calls.

"Five."

"Miss Heart. I'm going to come around and help you out of the car." Chen is efficient as he moves and takes me out of the car, cautious of my feet now that I don't have sight of them.

"Watch your step," I step over the threshold into a vat of heat. It clings to me like a second skin.

And I know exactly where I am.

Excitement pops inside of my chest, mirroring the cork of the champagne bottle Luca had opened earlier in the day at lunch.

I'm moved through a second door, helped through a net, and met by the sweet, sweet smell of nectar plants and an even sweeter memory of Luca and I's time here in The Butterfly House.

"Amore mio, togliti la benda" *My love, take off the blindfold.*

My hands shake to complete his request, and when it's off I step back in shock.

Lit up with a thousand fairy lights, The Butterfly House has been transformed into a tranquil space. Thousands of Butterflies flutter and fly high, greeting me with an array of colors. I feel as though I'm floating in a Christmas globe, surrounded by perfection at every turn.

I find Luca standing by the bench we made love on, a small smirk playing on his lips. Earlier he had been dressed casually, in jeans and a t-shirt, but now he was impeccable in a crisp blue suit. A color rarely seen on the man who demanded the dark.

Oh he was very pleased with himself and my instant joy. My cheeks reddened, my pulse hammered as I crossed the space in seconds, throwing myself into his arms and kissing him with abandon.

Chuckling against my lips he pulls away, pushing a strand of hair behind my ear as I pout. "You haven't had your surprise yet and you already want to take my clothes off?"

I blush. "Isn't this my surprise?"

"No," he kisses my lips once before pulling a small black box out of his pocket. Luckily he opens it just before my heart spasms. "This is —"

A silver key glints up at me. A key? Is he asking me to move in with him because I think we've passed that point...? "I don't understand..."

"This key fits that lock over there," he juts his chin towards the door I came in. "And it belongs to you, Olivia. You're now the new owner of La casa delle farfalle."

My heart stops. My throat dries to match the Sahara desert, but god damn the tears didn't get the memo. They refuse to quit.

"I bought this place weeks ago after I saw how much you loved it here," he presses the key into my hand. "You were so open and free here, Olivia. It was a pleasure to see you like that." He presses the box into my hand. "This place was made for you. It was only fair that you own it too."

"But..." I stopped to look around. Jesus Christ. "I don't know anything about running a place like this, Luca. I know about butterflies and —"

He laughs, expecting my panic. "Everyone is staying on including that strange man, Mr. Jeritila, that you like so much." His smile fills me with relief. "You just have to enjoy it, Olivia.

I want you to have this place to be free... even if that's from me."

Spread your wings little one, prepare to fly, for you have become my sweetest baby butterfly, my dad's voice whispered as I looked into Luca's eyes.

I couldn't find the right words to communicate my love. Nothing will ever top this feeling of love and freedom. Swarmed with butterflies and Luca's devotion, I lean up and kiss him.

We melted into each other, our pieces connecting, and sealing shut with finality. It finally felt right. Him and Me. There wasn't anything to hold me back.

Sensing the change, Luca gripped the back of my neck, deepening our kiss until I opened for him. Our tongues danced, tasted each other while my hands worked to remove his jacket. I wanted him. Now and forever.

I needed to press my forgiveness into his skin. It was the only way he would ever believe me.

"Bella, wait," he pulled me, groaning. "I have one more surprise. If you keep touching me like that, I'm going to have to take you right here and I really need to do this."

"That's fine with me," I tried to push myself back into his arms, but he held me back. He huffed a laugh, keeping me at an arm's distance by gripping the top of my arms.

Looking up I saw beneath the darkness of his eyes a flash of worry. Whatever was coming next was worrying him. No doubt he still thought I wanted to leave, and of course he did. I hadn't given him much to believe in.

We hadn't had that conversation. I'd been too busy pursuing my healing in the forms of his body, selfishly forgetting that he had been hurting too. From the outside maybe he hadn't suffered enough but I knew the man before me, better than he did.

Luca's karma, his pain and retribution for loving me so intensely had happened during my disappearance. He nearly didn't survive it and when he had me back in his vicinity, I punished him further. Lashing out. Pushing him away.

"Olivia, I have another surprise, but you may not... want it. I just want you to know there's no pressure. You get to make the decisions now and I don't want to ever take that away from you again—"

I take a step back. "Luca, you're scaring me."

He barked a laugh, running a hand through his hair. This was strange. I'd never seen him so nervous, especially not to ruin his perfectly styled hair.

"I'm sorry. Just remember what I said okay?"

Nodding I looked at him, my eyes raking over his tense body. Luca took a deep breath, pulling himself into the composure I was used to seeing before taking a step forward.

Our eyes connected. Both of us afraid to look away.

"Olivia," he dropped to one knee.

Oh my god.

Shit.

Is this real?

Air was nonexistent already in our warm little globe, but now I was close to passing out.

"Bella, you know that my love is reserved only for you. There isn't a woman that could ever compare, who could make me feel this way," his hands slipped into the side of his suit pocket, producing another black velvet box.

"Oh, god," I whispered as my eyes darted from him to the box.

"And I know that I'll never be worthy of you as a man for all that I've done, but with this I'd like to be worthy of you as a husband. I will spend the rest of my life righting my wrongs, loving you, providing for you if you will take me. Olivia, will you marry me?"

CHAPTER THIRTY-FIVE

Luca Caruso

S hit. Did I butcher it *that* bad?

Olivia hasn't said anything in a minute or is it minutes? I wasn't sure. Down here time had stopped. If only my nerves had.

Shit. The ring, the one that belonged to my Ma shook in my hand. Its platinum band glinted underneath the warm fair lights, making the emerald diamond pop in its princess setting.

Maybe it's the ring. Maybe she hates the color or the setting. When I'd shown her aunt the ring, she had assured me through watery eyes and hiccups that Olivia would love it.

Doubt crept it.

It wasn't the ring she didn't want. It was me.

"Marry you?" she rasped, her hand sliding to her throat.

All I could do was nod. My tongue had turned to lead in my mouth. My chin had barely come back down towards my chest when she dropped to her knees, meeting me eye to eye.

Up close her eyes were the color of wet moss, beautiful and natural just like her. Lost in the depth of her gaze I hadn't noticed her hands around me, clutching my wrists.

A brick dropped into my stomach. It was a no. It would always be a no.

She leaned forward, filling the warm air with vanilla. "You are worthy of me as a man, and you will be as my husband. Of course, I'll marry you, Luca."

Her gently spoken words filled the space around us. Wild possession and desire roared to life. I needed to hear her say it again, to remember her words for the rest of my life.

"Say it again."

A devilish glint played in her eyes. "ti sposerò amore mio" *Of course I'll marry you, my love.*

Sent from the heavens above she answered me in perfect Italian with a smug smile playing on her lips. She giggled as I dragged her to me. Her face wet with tears, I took care kissing her, holding her to me so tightly so that she knew just a fraction of how I felt.

"Mi hai reso l'uomo più felice" *You have made me the happiest man.*

I'd become a king by her side. A man worthy of forgiveness when it would have been easier to discard me like I deserved. But yet, the woman, a queen had been gracious — no, strong enough to accept me for who I am.

Her hands smoothed back my hair lovingly, "I love you," she tells me, tracing her finger across my cheekbone until she reaches my lips. "And I would very much like to see that beautiful ring up close."

I laughed, having forgotten about the ring that had been discarded at our sides. We both looked down to find the box open and the ring protected and snug in its velvet cushion. A gasp from her and rough chuckle from me. A butterfly had taken residence on the diamond, fluttering happily up at us.

Of course, it had.

Wherever they were so was she.

CHAPTER THIRTY-SIX

Olivia Heart

Two years later

A scream pierced its way into the serenity I was trying so hard to keep, followed by two other shrill noises that can only be described as banshees fighting.

Followed by my Aunt Sarah, I had just stepped back into the suite, barely keeping steady in my heels when my bridesmaids swarmed.

"Olivia! You... You look. Oh god, Lily, just look at her." Alice burst into tears, ruining her make up that the artist had painstakingly painted on her face. Alice had been feeding her newborn Carter who chose the most inopportune times to fuss, but thankfully the artist worked around the screaming baby.

"Jesus Christ on his actual bicycle. He's going to have a heart attack when he sees you," Hayley spat, rushing to me to inspect my wedding dress.

Her overzealous inspection made me nervous, so much so that I took a step back suddenly wanting to remove the gown and protect it. It was one of Katrina's creations that she had spent two hundred hours on, perfecting until it was exactly how we both envisioned. Like the wonder woman she was, she made my dress while running a successful empire alongside raising her son.

It was on her description of me that she created an ivory mermaid dress made from pure silk. The off the shoulder sleeves were structured never to fall so that the nip of my waist would be on show, right down to the figure-hugging material that flared elegantly at the bottom. It was dreamy and completely perfect.

I just hoped Luca would love it too.

"Olivia," my aunt placed a warm hand on my shoulder. "Are you okay, love?"

Her eyes scanned my face, looking for signs of nerves and she smiled so softly when she found them.

"I'm a little nervous," I laughed, pressing a hand to my hammering heart.

"You have no reason to be nervous, love."

She was right, I didn't. The man waiting for me at the end of the aisle was a dream come true. We had spent the last two years rebuilding our relationship, ensuring that we catered to what the other needed before we jumped into marriage.

Luca understood my need to trust him, and he did everything possible to deliver it. He relinquished his controlling tendencies to provide me with a normal life and I ensured he had what he needed to never feel out of control. We worked together rather than apart.

"Luca loves you, Olivia," my aunt kissed my cheek. "He has that endless love that you need."

"I know," I whispered, remembering how he snuck into my hotel room last night to show me his 'endless love'. I'm surprised my legs aren't still shaking now.

"Then smile. Today is the day you become a wife."

"To the hottest man on the planet," Katie grinned while fixing her hair for the twentieth time this morning, "you lucky cow!"

"Watch it," I growled, protective over my man. "Bones will get jealous."

Katie's fierce blush made me laugh. Her crush had developed into somewhat of an obsession from the first moment she had met him at my birthday celebration. Bones unfortunately never made his move even though it was obvious he liked her too.

"He doesn't like me like that."

Alice and Hayley scoffed at the same time, and I rolled my eyes.

Hayley had better luck and was currently in a long-distance relationship with Rum which turns out is quite... a freak between the sheets. We're only aware of this information because every time Hayley gets drunk, she likes to share the details.

I could have gone my whole life without seeing my old guard that way, especially knowing how good he was with ropes....

"Are you ready?" it's Aida, dressed in a lilac sheath dress that glitters underneath the warm light of my suite. Another Katrina creation come to life. Her breath catches in her throat when her eyes land on mine and for a second, I think she may cry. But like the Caruso in her, she keeps the tears at bay, too worried about seeming weak.

After smiling at me, her eyes survey the rest of my bridesmaids in matching dresses, and she grins at them, pleased that everyone is ready to go.

Nobody was more excited for this wedding to go ahead than Aida Caruso.

She had practically helped organize the whole thing, even Luca's wedding suit which annoyed him to no end.

"I can pick my own suit, Aida. I don't need your fussing or your incessant emails about the damn thing!"

"You can't wear black on your wedding day, you fool."

"Why? Olivia likes me in black," he winked, earning himself my blush.

"Ugh, typical man. Just no. Olivia, tell him he has to wear a navy suit like Dante!"

My aunt stopped me before I reached his sister. "Wait Olivia, you need your veil."

A flush of grief caught me quickly at the thought of my eight-foot veil, the same one my mum wore when she married my dad. It had luckily been in my aunt's possession, so it wasn't destroyed by the fire.

I had sobbed into Luca's arms when she sent it a few months ago. It was a part of my missing family, my something old and my something new.

I had asked Katrina to create butterflies made out of lace which she so delicately stitched in so that they would float near the ground when I move. Not only would I have my mum, but my dad would be with me too.

My aunt fixed the veil into my updo, carefully spreading it behind me so its weight would be distributed evenly.

"Your mum and dad would have been so proud of you, Olivia… they," she stopped, choking back a sob. "My god, you are so beautiful just like your mother," she whispers before dropping the lace over my face. I could cry at the happiness shining in her eyes.

"She is," Aida agrees behind, holding in a sob.

CHAPTER THIRTY-SEVEN

Luca Caruso

"S he still mad at you?" I mumbled to Dante who stood at my side, pretending not to feel the pressure of Laura's fierce scowl. We were standing on the steps at the back of the church, watching thousands of guests take their seats.

"Furious," he grins. "Wants to cut my balls off and post them to my Ma. Can you believe her? Like anyone sends anything in the post anymore."

My idiot of a cousin had fallen hard for Laura to an extreme that nearly *rivalled* mine. Never one to care for a relationship until he met her, he had pursued her constantly, swarming her with gifts and attention until she caved and agreed to one date.

Then just as he settled into a somewhat normal relationship, he began what can only be described as pestering her for a baby. My lothario cousin wanted to settle down and have a child...

"Hiding her pill was stupid," I told him while nodding at Harry, Alice's husband, as he took a seat at the back with their newborn baby. He was a screamer, so Marie had kindly offered to sit with him in case the baby fussed during the ceremony.

"Let's not throw stones, Luca," he shoves my shoulders just enough that I fall into Chen. Like the perfect guard and friend, he rights me quickly, throwing Dante a cautious look.

"I never went through with my plan," I hiss, "there's a difference."

"Maybe," he says. "But if Olivia asked you for a baby now, you would have no qualms about ripping her dress off and creating one right here in this church."

I grinned. He was right. I wanted nothing more than to have children with Olivia, enough to see her belly swell and to fill our house with little hers and me's. But I wouldn't push the issue. I would wait until she was ready and not a moment before.

"I do not want to see that," Chen joins in, a smile playing at the corner of his lips. "Or have to guard you while you... do it."

Dante throws his head back and laughs, earning him another fierce glare from his possibly pregnant girlfriend.

When I asked Chen to be one of my best men, he almost cried. Well, I say cried, it could have been dust in his eyes, but of course he graciously accepted. And then rushed off to check the perimeter of our house.

"There was one thing I wanted to see and that was you all nervous and sweating, Luca. I feel robbed."

I shrug. "I have no reason to be nervous."

"What if she runs?" Chen flinched. It was a poor joke on Dante's part, he knew it could possibly trigger a knee jerk reaction from me, but instead I laughed.

Olivia would never run. Not now that she knew the real me. She sees that I'm not perfect, forgives me when I mess up, and is still strong enough call me on my shit when I go overboard.

And I still go overboard a lot.

"I'll run with her," I tell him.

He doesn't say another word, just smiles in understanding and takes a step back with Chen when Theo approaches.

"You better have the rings."

He pats his pocket, smirking. "Of course I do. I learned from your mistake Luca and made sure I had them before I left my hotel this morning."

Theo never stopped ripping into me about leaving his and Katrina's rings in my hotel room. I'd been distracted by thoughts of a certain someone who was at the time in a meeting with the New York mobster. Luckily for me, Katrina's parents stepped in and provided their bands temporarily until I could get them after the ceremony.

Katrina thought it was hilarious, unlike her husband who wanted to carve my eyes out with a spoon. Speaking of, I sent a wink to his wife who was sitting on the second row, rocking their son.

"Good."

"You know you're one lucky son of a bitch," he whispered. "I saw Olivia a few moments ago and I wouldn't be a very good best man if I didn't warn you."

"Warn me?" I hissed, suddenly feeling an edge of nerves creeping in.

Theo grins smugly, the bastard's got me on his hook. "You're going to have a heart attack when those doors open. Your bride is beautiful."

Beautiful did not cover how Olivia looked. Under the warm light spilling in from the church windows, she was impossibly gorgeous. Radiant. An angel who graced this church, blessing it with all of her beauty.

My bride was a ray of her own light, shining bright between her Aunt Sarah and Bones who guided her to me in time with the soft violins.

Everyone gasped as they watched her smile at me through her veil.

My heart stuttered and stopped. Stuttered again, and I was certain I'd have a heart attack if she smiled like that at me again.

"Santa merda" *Holy Shit.* Dante whispered.

"Exactly," Theo agreed, placing a hand on my arm.

Bones caught my eye first and nodded, passing on a simple message that for Olivia he could extend his forgiveness, but if I hurt her, he would be ready with that knife of his. It had taken me a while, but I learned to appreciate his protectiveness.

Olivia's aunt, who had been nothing but gracious towards me, smiled her brilliantly white teeth with happiness.

I took my bride's shaking hand. "You are..." the words clogged in my throat.

"Stunning," Theo leaned forward with a wink at Olivia.

"Hot," Dante added, which nearly earned him an elbow to the face.

"Beautiful," Chen joined in, surprising us all.

Olivia laughed, stealing away the little air I had left in my lungs. God, I don't know if it'll ever be possible to be worthy of her. She was a gift sent to me from heaven and such gifts required the right amount of admiration and love.

"Luca..." she stepped up to me. "You need to lift my veil."

Everyone laughed, enjoying my stunned look and Olivia's impatience.

"Sorry," I smiled, lifting the veil over her head. "I got distracted by you in this dress... Jesus, you take my breath away every day, Olivia, but today, now...?"

Our family and friends watch us with rapt attention. Our priest steps up, ready to start the wedding, but Olivia has other ideas. She leans forward, quickly kissing my lips and pulling away before I can deepen it. Tease.

"You're supposed to wait," our priest grins. Everyone laughs except for her Aunt Sarah who's bawling into a tissue.

"I know, but I didn't want to," she tells him while winking at me.

I fight my own grin. Those where my words last night when I snuck into her room like I'd die if I didn't have her before she became Mrs Caruso. Even after all this time, it's impossible to stay away from her, my craving never ceasing even now when I have her completely.

But that's okay. I know there are two things I can't live without in this life, and it's Olivia and her body.

I'm insatiable for her.

Never getting enough. Always wanting more.

Speaking of more, the priest needed to hurry up and do his thing—there's a wedding dress that needs to be taken off with my teeth and a marriage to consummate.

CHAPTER THIRTY-EIGHT

Olivia Caruso

Our wedding was perfect. There wasn't a single part that I would have changed and by looking at Luca, who smiles lovingly over at our family and friends, I know he feels the same way.

Our reception was being held in Aida's house, more specifically the ballroom which Luca had told me was never used when his parents were alive, but it was his mother's favorite room. I could see why. It was grand with marbled floors, high ceilings full of gold chandeliers and tapestries, but it was the painting on the ceiling that stole my breath away.

It was of a ballroom painting in the early 1920's, of couples dancing the night away in their finest with smiles on their faces.

"Was it everything that you wanted?" he asked me while cradling my hands. I watch our rings glint together, a symbol of our continuous union and smiled.

"It was," I lean into him, pressing a soft kiss to his cheek. "Thank you for making everyone's dream come true and mine."

He smirks, knowing that our wedding was very much a team effort. We had been more relaxed in what we wanted but our family and friends had strived for more.

"Well, while our family is distracted, why don't we slip off and get working on consummating this marriage," he raises a suggestive eyebrow.

"As much as I would love to get a head start on that, I have a surprise for you." I press a kiss to his lips, laughing as he groans when I pull away to quickly. "Come with me, husband."

"I'd love to *come* with you, wife." I roll my eyes even though I enjoy his filthy mouth. Taking his hand, I shuffle out of my seat, careful not to snag the train of my dress before making my way over to the dance floor.

Matteo, sweaty with red cheeks, catches my eye mid airplane dive and races over to us. In two years he's grown incredibly fast, but he's yet to fill out. He's a gangly boy with a love for fast cars and his uncles who spoil him rotten.

"You ready?" I ask him, holding out my hand.

"Yes. Hold on," he turns to the crowd and places two fingers in his mouth and whistles. "Come on everyone. I have a surprise!" When the music cuts, he turns back to his uncle and smirks.

God, he's going to break many hearts when he's older. I just hope Aida is prepared for the carnage he's going to bring when girls start to notice him.

"What's going on?" Theo asks Luca, rocking baby Levi in his arms. My heart turns to instant mush as I peer at milk-drunk sleepy face.

"No idea," Luca shrugs, eyeing me suspiciously.

Matteo takes my hand, and we move towards the back gardens, past the pool until we're facing the small forest at the bottom of the estate. It's time to create new positive memories in Luca's childhood home.

Darkness has settled and it makes it hard for some guests to see, but it's all a part of Matteo's great distraction. He said that nobody would know what he was doing until 'it hit the sky'.

We grin at each other before he lets go of my hand and rushes down the garden to the team of men waiting.

"Should I be worried?" Luca whispers, wrapping his arms around my waist. "He looks like he might combust with excitement."

"No," I'm grateful for the dark; worried that he may read too much into my face and start a tirade of questions I wouldn't be able to answer. If he did, there was no way to pull this back and I'd ruin all of Matteo's hard work.

"Everyone!" Matteo yells once he's back, panting and puffing. "Please look up to the sky."

On his final word, a sharp squeal sounds off in the distance. The first of Matteo's fireworks shoots towards the sky until the color blue erupts silently, spelling out:

Luca Caruso

Everyone gasps, and a few aww.

"Olivia..." Luca growls into my ear, gripping my hips. "What is this?"

"Shush," I bite my lip, swallowing down nerves. "Just watch."

The second firework hits the sky, dazzling brightly above us:

Is going to be

My stomach knots and I grip Luca's hands for reassurance. I feel him tense behind me, holding his breath.

"Wait," I hear Alice call in the background. "Oh my god!"

The third firework explodes, racing towards the sky matching the same pace as my heartbeat.

I manage to take a breath before the letters paint the sky:

A daddy

The crowd erupts into cheers and cries. A bottle of champagne pops in the distance as I'm spun so quickly that I almost lose my footing, but Luca would never let me fall. Everyone's eyes are on us, but their shock and happiness cannot rival my husband who is scanning my face so rapidly for the truth.

"Olivia," he rasps, tilting my chin with his finger.

"Surprise," I whisper, biting down on my lip. "You're going to be a daddy."

He looks down at my stomach and backs up, trying desperately to make sense of the bomb Matteo and I have dropped on him. He won't find it on my body, it's early and Katrina worked her magic to ensure nothing would show.

"Dillo di nuovo" *Say it again.*

"Sorpresa, diventerai papà" *Surprise, you're going to be a daddy.*

My aunt sobs in the background, pulling my attention away from Luca for a second. It's enough to pull him from his shock, he sweeps me up carefully with the biggest smile on his face.

It brings fresh tears to my eyes.

"You have made me the happiest man on the planet, Olivia Caruso. I'll forever be indebted to you."

"Remember that when it's time to change diapers and bottle feed in the middle of the night."

He agrees to all of it through a fierce kiss.

CHAPTER THIRTY-NINE

Luca Caruso

7 Months later

Theo warned me that this could happen, that Olivia wouldn't slow down when she needed to and gave me some helpful advice.

"Don't tell her what to do because that really pisses them off. Make her think it's her idea and she'll come willingly."

And that's what I came here to do today.

My wife was heavily pregnant, tending to the plants that required watering in the hot box called The Butterfly House. To this very day, I still don't understand how she can stand to swelter in these conditions for long periods of time. I could handle ten minutes until I needed to feel the cool breeze on my face.

Dressed in a pink sundress, she had kicked off her shoes, favoring bare foot now that her ankles were starting to swell, not that I would ever point it out. My wife would have my head if I so much as peered at them.

She was slightly self-conscious of her changing body, but I spent all of my time assuring her how beautiful she was. I'd kiss her belly, help massage cream across her stomach and spend extra time massaging her back when it hurt. And even scour the internet for hours looking for a pregnancy pillow that would help her sleep while she grew our child.

Apparently, there are twenty-five types of pregnancy pillows, and my wife didn't like any of them. They were too lumpy, didn't fit her bump, or my favorite, they didn't smell like me. So, I became her pregnancy pillow and I didn't mind at all.

Dante was eager to help too, being pulled in when my wife woke up in the middle of the night craving pistachio gelato. We scoured the whole of Italy until we found a small gelato shop willing to open for a hefty price.

"Are you going to stand there and stare all night?" she asked me, spraying me with the hose.

"I've actually come to take you home." I take the hose from her and angle it away into the small pond that she had changed a few months ago. I press a quick kiss to her warm lips. "You haven't eaten Mrs. Caruso."

Her eyes widen, caught. "I lost track of time."

"You always do in here." I turn off the hose with a small smile. This place was Olivia's haven and I'd often have to come get her when time slipped away.

"How did today go?" she asks me, taking a hold of my arm as she slips back into her shoes.

"Good. It's all signed over."

The last piece of my father's legacy was gone and Olivia and I were finally free to live a life without the threat of repercussions from pulling out of the underworld.

My shipping company, along with all forms of other transport, had been sold to a Jack King, the head of the New York Mafia who was pleased to acquire the responsibility and stay the fuck out of my life afterwards.

My focus was on my legitimate businesses and my growing family. Everything else ceased to matter.

"That's good," she smiled. "No more looking over your shoulder or worrying. You must be relieved?"

"I am," I tell her, while locking up the building behind us. "I never wanted to be a part of what he built, and I certainly don't want our little boy growing up in a world under constant fear like I did."

I feel how proud she is just from the way she smiles up at me. "You think it's a boy?"

I nod, pressing my palms to her belly. "I know it's a boy. The way he keeps you up at night tells me as much. He doesn't like to sleep like his Pa."

Olivia rolls her eyes. "A few kicks here and there doesn't mean it's going to be a boy. It could be a girl, stubborn like me and impatient to get out."

I pause. It could be, and if it is, well shit if it's a girl that changes everything. I can already picture Dante and I questioning her boyfriends, running background checks, and chaperoning their dates.

No.

Hell no.

She will never have a boyfriend.

My wife laughs, picking up on the panic on my face. "Oh I hope it's a girl. She'll bring you to your knees, Luca Caruso." She pokes my chest.

I grab her finger and playfully nip at it. "There is only one woman capable of doing that."

She grins, a lustful glint in her eyes. "Damn right and don't you forget it."

THE END

ACKNOWLEDGEMENTS

Firstly, I want to thank all the readers that have followed Olivia and Luca's story from the start. You don't know how much it means to me that you have taken a chance and read a new authors work. Huge hugs and kisses to you all!

I want to thank Kingston Publishing Company for all their support and hard work in making my dream come true.

Brandi, you came to me during the second book and thank heavens for you. You took my manuscript and breathed life back into it and I'll forever be grateful to you.

Drew, thank you for being such a shoulder to lean on when imposter syndrome tried to kick my ass. You are a star, and I cannot wait to watch you shine.

Shani, you are such a love. Thank you from the bottom of my heart for all of your support. You have become a friend for life, and I cannot wait to watch you grow as a writer.

Charli, your hate and love (haha) came to me at a time when I was so full of self-doubt. Your support spurred me on to no end. I am so happy to have found you and all your sass. Keep the GIF's coming, okay?

Hayley, well what can I say about you? Not only did you support a new author/old school friend, but you have been gracious enough to bring me in to your book world. Thank you!

Katie L, we found each other through your mum and thank god for her! Having your support in my corner has been amazing. You're such a sweet, kind person and you really deserve it all

To these girls that I love and adore, you never fail to make me smile and supporting me right from the start- Katie, Mel,

A. L. Hartwell

Sam B, Lynn, Bianca, Ceri, Tina, Leah, Kirsty, Giulia, Jodie—
Love to you all!

ABOUT THE AUTHOR

A. L. Hartwell lives in Nottingham, England with her wonderfully patient husband and sassy dog Lyla. From the age of fifteen, as part of an escape, she spent years writing short stories, accumulating them, and sharing them online. With a vast taste in genres, she found herself drawn to the wonderful twisty world of Dark Romance. When she discovered the freedom in writing within this genre, she delved headfirst into writing her first novel, Bending to Break.

When she's not working or spending her time locked away in her writing cave, she's reading, drinking tea, or obsessing over her niece and nephew.

ALSO BY THE AUTHOR

ABOUT THE PUBLISHER

Kingston Publishing Company, founded in 2018, is dedicated to providing authors an affordable way to turn their dream into a reality. We publish over 100+ titles annually in multiple formats including print and eBook across all major platforms.

We offer every service you will ever need to take an idea and publish a story. We are here to help authors make it in the industry. We want to provide a positive experience that will keep you coming back to us. Whether you want a traditional publisher who offers all the amenities a publishing company should or an author who prefers to self-publish, but needs additional help – we are here for you.

Now Accepting Manuscripts!
Please send query letter and manuscript to:
submissions@kingstonpublishing.com

Visit our website at
www.kingstonpublishing.com

Printed in Great Britain
by Amazon

78699918R00169